Set the City on Fire

SOPHIA PEONY

Dedication

My grandmother, Norma, who will probably be scandalized by this story.

Chapter One

Leo made a mistake. It wasn't the first time it's happened, but it might damn well be the last. He got careless. He got too comfortable. He hadn't been thinking straight when he decided to walk the streets like he was an ordinary man. He wasn't, far from it. He was the son of Giovanni Costa, an heir to the Costa family. And he walked the streets of San Francisco like a fucking dumbass. He was surprised they hadn't just popped him on the street. It would have been a hell of a lot easier than kidnapping him and taking him to the middle of fucking nowhere, just to kill him.

The three fuck heads didn't seem all that bright. Leo had no idea how the assholes managed to knock him out and get him all the way out here without anyone seeing anything. All he could think of was sheer, fucking dumb luck. They were smart enough to kidnap him but too stupid to figure out that the rope they'd used to tie his hands was not secure enough.

There were three of them and two guns as far as he could tell, but he had the element of surprise. They were taunting him, trying to scare him by speaking in Spanish, mostly with the prison slang a lot of people would be familiar with. They didn't realize he understood them. You had to know your enemy if you wanted to beat them. While the families in New York and Florida had issues with the Russian mobs, in California, the families dealt with Mexican gangs and cartels, which meant that learning Spanish was essential for survival.

While the Costa family wiped out most of the gangs in Northern California some thirty-something years ago, there were always little gangs starting up. You take one group out, and another one forms from the scattered remains of the debunked gangs. Most of the gangs fought each other over what little territories they had, and some got hired by people with money to do the dirty work.

These fuckers were hired by someone. He listened to them brag about how much money they could milk his family for, which would be the reason they hadn't killed him in a drive-by. They got greedy. Unfortunately for him, they were smart enough to quickly realize that they had a higher chance of being killed than getting away with the ransom money.

Good for them, bad for him because now they needed to kill him. He has no regrets and no problem dealing with death when it does come for him, but he sure as fuck wasn't going to make it easy for these three fuck heads.

Leo would guess they were somewhere in Mount Diablo, the mountain range on the eastern side of the San Francisco Bay Area, and off the many hiking trails it was known for. Animals lived there; he could feel eyes on him; they were probably being watched by some hungry mountain lion.

He wasn't planning on becoming a lion's meal, not if he could help it at least. He was just waiting for the perfect spot to attack; somewhere where it was harder to keep their balance. Maybe he could even knock one or two, or hell, all three of them off a cliff; that might almost make up for this.

"Tenemos que matara ese hijo de puta ya!" the one behind him complained. Let's kill the motherfucker now.

He's run out of time.

Now or never Leo, he told himself.

He braced himself, angled low for full impact,

and hopefully, if he did get shot, they'd miss anything vital.

"Turn around, *Pendejo*! Get ready to die."

Leo would have rolled his eyes if he wasn't too busy trying to stay alive.

Chapter Two

Freya wasn't made for hiking. Her short legs weren't made for hiking. Her endurance wasn't made for hiking. Her hair wasn't made for hiking. She wasn't made for hiking! Why the hell did she think hiking at the crack of dawn was a good idea? She probably made herself a bigger target by bringing her dog along, looking like a tasty meal for a hungry cougar.

She was going to freak herself out if she didn't stop imagining things that probably wouldn't happen.

She wanted the early morning fog shot and forced herself out of bed, way too early for a Saturday; she better damn well get that shot. Her friend Alice had introduced her to photography in high school. Alice had given Freya her first camera, knowing that Freya couldn't afford one. Alice was the only friend from high school that she still spoke too, but even back then, she hadn't had that many friends. She owed this little hobby to Alice.

Photography was a hobby, something she loved, but not what paid her bills. She probably could have made a hell of a lot more money doing it, but she didn't want it to become a job. She only accepted people she knew or were referred to her by clients. She was good at it because she saw things for more than what they are. She didn't know how to explain it but when she looked at ordinary things like branches, rocks, and windows, her mind pictured them as something else, saw them in angles that no one thought to look at. And then she did exactly what she saw in her mind. It wasn't just things; she was good at capturing people. too She had a waiting list and not because she was famous or charged an obnoxious amount, but because people liked seeing themselves as she saw them through her camera lens.

Freya was practical, and most people who knew her would say she was realistic, but her head was filled with daydreams that translated into her photos. She–

Honey's bark pulled her out of her thoughts.

Honey, her chocolate Labrador, was a runt and only weighed about fifty pounds at most, but she was as protective as the one-hundred-pound Rottweiler one of her mother's ex-boyfriends had around while she was growing up. Freya only meant to foster Honey three years ago, after her beloved Lilly, a twenty-pound mutt, had passed away. She'd missed having a dog around but wasn't sure she was ready to adopt so soon after Lilly had died of old age. Honey had been rescued from an abusive situation and was scared of her own shadow when she'd first come to live with Freya and her cat, Lestat. It didn't take long for Freya and Lestat to bond with Honey; they needed her as much as she seemed to need them. Honey was the sweetest and gentlest dog she had ever met but was fiercely protective of her and Lestat.

Honey was barking frantically, facing to her right. At first glance, Freya didn't see anything out of the ordinary. She looked again to see why Honey was frantic and saw it; a man on the ground. She searched the area, checking to see if anyone else was around, before remembering it was only five in the morning. No sane person hiked on a Saturday, especially not this early.

Please don't be dead. Please don't be dead. Please don't be dead; she chanted in her head as she hurried towards the motionless body. She gasped as she came closer and saw blood all over him. He either fell from somewhere high or he'd taken a serious beating. She knelt next to him and noticed a couple of areas where wounds were still bleeding, one of them on his chest.

She couldn't tell if he'd been stabbed or shot, but she knew she had to stop the bleeding and get help.

He was cool to the touch, but he was alive. She could see him struggling to breathe. She reached for her phone and called 911.

"911, what's your emergency?"

"I found a man, he's injured badly, bleeding heavily," she hastily responded.

"Where are you?"

"Hiking! I mean I was hiking, and I found him." She gave the trail and direction since she'd gone off the path. "Hurry, he's really hurt. He's bleeding a lot."

"You need to stop the bleeding. Do you have anything to use to put pressure on the wound? Put me on speaker and use both of your hands if you need to. I have your GPS location and help is on the way." She quickly tore her sweater off, bunched it together and placed it over the wound on his chest.

"Make sure he's breathing. Is he awake?"

"No, he's not awake," Freya answered.

"Try to wake him up."

His blood soaked through her sweater. The cold

temperature made the blood on her hands feel like needles.

"Honey, lay down next to him," she ordered her dog who was licking the man's face, trying to comfort him. Honey did as requested. They needed to keep him warm, and that was the best she could do. She didn't know how long she stayed frozen, keeping pressure on the wound. She prayed in her head and probably out loud.

Please don't die. Please don't die. Please don't die.

She heard the helicopter before she saw it appear in the sky. It was red with a white cross, indicating that help was here. The rangers and police came running up the hill almost the same time as the helicopter appeared in the sky. A vehicle wouldn't have been able to get anywhere near their location, the path had been up high on the trail, and she'd stepped off the path to get the pictures she'd wanted.

"Help's here," she told the unconscious man as one of the cops came and took over. She held his hand before she was forced out of the way by the rescuers, and for a moment she swore she had felt him squeeze her hand. Or maybe it was all in her head. When help had arrived, Freya ordered Honey to retreat but forgot her phone on the man's bloody stomach and her camera bag. The same bag that was now being trampled on. *Ugh*. A broken camera wasn't okay, but the man being alive, that was okay... more than okay.

Chapter Three

Please don't die. Please don't die. Please don't die...

Leo heard the frantic whisper over and over in his head. He opened his eyes and was immediately greeted by blinding pain.

"About time you woke up, Sleeping Beauty." Leo turned to the voice that was almost as familiar as his own. Although Vito's greeting was said in sarcasm, Leo heard the worry in it.

"How long was I out?" Leo asked Vito as he struggled to sit up. Vito stopped him.

"Stay down; you're not ready for that yet." Vito forced him to stay on his back, not that Leo would have been able to sit up anyway. He was familiar with pain, but everything hurt like a son of a bitch.

"What happened?" Leo demanded.

"What do you remember?" Vito asked.

Leo forced his mind to see past the pain. He was ambushed and kidnapped, then taken to a mountain. Why? He'd fought back, but there were three of them, and someone shot him; several times. Then what? He was left for dead. He'd lain on the ground, staring up at the clear night sky. His attempted murderers weren't smart enough to blow his brains out or shoot him in the heart. He would have laughed at their stupidity if he didn't hurt so bad.

"Someone found me," he blurted out. He wasn't sure why, but the first thing he remembered was her voice. He'd heard her, softly repeating over and over, *please don't die.* He'd been too weak to open his eyes, move or even respond, but he'd heard her. In between the *please don't die's,* she mentioned how it would be very ungrateful of him to die on her. He couldn't very well let her think he was ungrateful.

"A woman hiking found you just in the nick of time. One hour later and you'd probably be dead," Vito explained.

"I was ambushed near Washington Square Park–" Leo started.

"Because you're a dumbass and left alone," Vito

cut in.

"They didn't know I understood them. A Mexican gang hired to kill me. They got greedy and kidnapped me for ransom before realizing that was probably stupider than killing me."

"Who hired them?" Vito asked.

"Don't know. They didn't answer me when I asked," Leo answered sarcastically.

"If you're strong enough for sarcasm, you're strong enough for me to pummel you." Vito was serious.

"I don't think they really knew either," Leo answered truthfully. "They just seemed like hired goons. Is every–"

"Everyone's okay. Drago didn't want Giovanni here too long, but Luciano just left to pick up Valentina."

Luciano had come home from Las Vegas. While Leo took care of the family business in San Francisco and Lake Tahoe, Luciano ran the hotel and its attached nightclub and casino, and another underground casino, in Las Vegas. Hell, he missed his brother, but he hadn't wanted him to come home like this.

"Cops?" Leo knew they had been called by his

rescuer and even if she hadn't, the hospital would have.

"They have nothing. They're waiting for you."

"The woman?" Leo asked.

"Just a bystander. She was out taking pictures when her dog spotted you. We've checked her out. She's clean. Odd, but clean."

"Odd?" Leo questioned.

"She hasn't talked to anyone, but the cops. Said she wanted no rewards or recognition. She just wants to be left alone."

Leo understood why Vito found it odd. Nowadays, everyone wanted their fifteen minutes of fame. It was even odder that she hadn't wanted money.

"Did you recognize the hired help?" Vito asked.

"No." Payback was going to be worse than they could ever imagine. You didn't go after a Costa, and if you did, you made sure they were dead and couldn't talk because you're dead if you didn't.

Chapter Four

That's what happens when you hire greedy mother fuckers. He should have seen it coming. If those stupid sons of bitches had just shot Leo in a drive-by like what he'd paid them to do, Leo would be dead. This was why he hated these gangs. Unlike *La Famiglia*, they had no loyalty, no organization, no other fucking purpose but to make money. *La Famiglia* is about more than money; they're about power, loyalty, respect, and family. Small and fast money didn't distract or control them. This was the problem with hiring an outsider, but he had no choice because the Costa family was royalty and no one in *La Famiglia* would touch them. He'd be dead before he even finished asking.

Chapter Five

5 Months Later

"Happy Birthday, Lena!" The eight women cheered as they clicked their shot glasses before downing the shots. Freya hated shots; she wasn't a fan of drinking in general, but special occasions required sacrifices. Lena was one of her longest friends, even though Lena was four years older, and was the opposite of Freya when it came to their personalities.

Thankfully, she could get away with nursing one drink for the rest of the night. Freya guessed they wouldn't be club hopping since this was one of the best clubs in San Francisco. Elite catered to high profile people and was almost impossible to get into. The only reason they got in was that a friend of a friend had an in with one of the bouncers. Fifty bucks each landed their names on the guest list.

The club was huge with balconies as VIP sitting areas that Freya was sure they couldn't afford, even with eight of them splitting the cost. Just the eight shots of Hennessey cost nearly $150. Knowing Lena, Freya expected several more shots tonight, on top of the drink she was planning to nurse for the rest of the night. She wasn't into mixed drinks, but the Tokyo Tea drink she ordered was one of her favorites. It was like a Long Island but better, with a harder kick to it. As birthday party rules demanded, Freya also bought Lena's first drink, a blue beverage called Adios. A fitting name in Freya's opinion since it always made her want to say bye and go home whenever she had it.

***

"Guess who's here?" Romano asked as he strutted into Leo's office, overlooking the dance floor of Elite. The club, like several others in the city, was owned by the Costa family.

The Costa family owned two high-end hotels in San Francisco, one in Vegas and one in Lake Tahoe. They also owned several nightclubs in all three cities that ranged from typical to high end and exclusive. Their hotels in Las Vegas and Lake Tahoe had casinos in them, where it was legal.

Outside of the legality, the Costa family had underground casinos in all three cities, exclusive and high end, in places no one would ever think to look. Each underground casino provided escorts that were included in the membership fee.

Leo stared at Romano, waiting for an answer but not playing along.

"Oh, come on," Romano egged. Romano was young, only twenty-six, but Leo liked him and had personally chosen Romano to be on Leo's crew. He'd also grown up with Leo, Vito, and Drago; their families were longtime friends and allies.

"I'll bite. Who?" Vito answered from the chair he occupied across from Leo.

"Oh, just Leo's photographer," Romano answered nonchalantly, knowing it would get a reaction from Leo.

Leo was surprised, but he didn't show it.

"She just bought $150 worth of shots, celebrating someone's birthday with a bunch of ladies," Romano added when Leo didn't show any reaction to the news that his savior was in his club.

"Don't charge the party and give them a table," Leo ordered.

Romano had a stupid grin on his face as he left to do Leo's bidding.

Leo headed to the one-way window in his office which overlooked the club. There were too many people to look for her and the lights were too dark, but he followed Romano's progress as he passed on Leo's orders to a waitress. He followed the waitress to a group of women, still watching as she led them to the best VIP table in the club. It cost $800 to book one of their smallest booths in the VIP lounge with the cheapest drink option and Leo had just given them the best one in the club that typically went for $6000 a night.

Leo hadn't been able to pinpoint her until they settled into the balcony lounge. He knew what she looked like. Actually, he knew everything about her on paper; from her no-good mother to how much her 401k was worth. He also knew how much she made at her job, what kind of birth control she was on, and what her college GPA had been.

He hadn't seen her or even talked to her since she'd saved his life. To his relief, she hadn't talked about what happened to anyone outside of the cops. She'd also refused the reward they had offered to her again for saving his life. She wanted to continue living her private, normal life and he respected that. His own kidnapping and rescue hadn't made the news. He hired people to make sure it stayed as quiet as possible.

The cops never found his kidnappers, but that's because Leo found them first. He tortured and tried to coax their employer out of them, but they offered nothing on who hired them. Leo took pleasure in his revenge, making sure they died a slow, painful death before he ensured their bodies would never be found.

While the rest of the group was excited about the VIP upgrade, she was hesitant making him think that she didn't trust easily. She was also a lot smaller than he'd imagined. He knew she was listed as five feet and two inches tall but looking at her now made him realize exactly how tiny that was. She was far from being the shortest in her group of friends, who looked mostly Asian, but to his standard, she was tiny.

"You should go say hi while she's on your turf," Vito teased him.

Leo ignored him and continued watching her and her friends as they made their way back to the dance floor. She seemed to have relaxed enough to enjoy herself. It was probably best that he left her alone; no sense in putting a target on her. He turned to finish working on the books but instead scowled at Vito before heading out the door. He had no idea what he planned to do and almost scolded himself for being foolish. Instead of going to her, he headed to an empty VIP table, reserved just for him.

Vito joined him and handed him a glass of scotch to replace his empty one, while Leo watched her and her friends. She didn't like to be the center of attention; he noticed that she had the same drink for an hour now, drinking it one sip at a time, nursing it.

"You've watched her for almost an hour now, go make friends already," Vito said to him in disgust.

Leo ignored him and watched a man...no, a boy, approach her at the bar. Leo told himself he was only looking out for her and that was why he wanted to bang the boy's head against the bar. Vito laughed at him.

***

Freya knew she'd only had two shots and a drink, but she felt dizzy and sluggish as she made her way to her friends on the dance floor. It had been a surprise to be offered a VIP table free of charge, but the waitress said the club sometimes offered it as a courtesy to customers. Lena had been so happy that she hadn't wanted to question it. Freya didn't have any of the complimentary drinks that came with the VIP service, but instead, nursed the same drink for the last hour. She wasn't much of a drinker, but she could handle her alcohol just fine, yet she felt buzzed, and the annoying man who kept hitting on her wouldn't leave her alone. She felt like she was going to be sick, so she decided it was better to take a break.

Lena was already drunk and probably wouldn't notice if Freya left. Freya let Lena's sister know she wasn't feeling well and was heading out early. She had originally planned to spend the night with Lena, but she really wasn't feeling well and didn't want to be a party pooper. She decided to take an Uber back to her place. She lived forty-five minutes away, and as much as it was going to cost her to take the Uber, she hadn't spent as much as she planned on tonight.

Lena was in good hands with her sister, and Freya knew she wouldn't mind if Freya left early. She hugged her drunken friend, cheek kissed, and hugged the other girls before she forced her legs to take her out of the club.

The bouncer gave her a look as she nearly stumbled out of the club. She used the wall as leverage, knowing she couldn't stand on her own anymore. Her legs, no her whole body, felt heavy and sluggish.

"Hey. You left too soon." She heard the annoying man from the bar before he appeared next to her. He smiled at her as he took her arm and started to lead her into the ally.

"No, I–," she struggled to get him to leave her alone, she didn't want him. She wanted to get away from him and pushed as hard as she could.

She wasn't sure if she did it to herself or if he

pushed her, but all she knew was that she landed on the ground, hard. She felt a stinging pain but couldn't tell where or what happened. Before she could push herself up, he was on her; shoving her onto her back.

She knew what was happening then and she knew she had to fight him. She tried to drag herself away from him by turning on her stomach and inching away, but he kept pushing her. Or was he pulling her? Her hands gripped something hard and cold. She didn't know what it was, but she swiveled around, swinging it as hard as she could. He fell off her. She tried to push herself up but couldn't. She tried again, only to fall back down. Shoes appeared in her fading vision. She looked up at a face she knew she'd never forget, before everything went dark, and she faded into oblivion.

***

Leo had never felt as murderous as he'd felt when the fucker who'd followed Freya out shoved her to the ground. He heard her slurring as he followed her and the boy outside and realized that the asshole had probably drugged her. He reached to pick her up just as she fainted at his feet.

He'd seen their struggle, but she'd taken care of him before they could reach her. The loud clang of the pipe she'd used to hit him with was drowned out by the loud music coming from the clubs.

Vito pulled the body off her. He checked the body for a pulse and shook his head.

"Get rid of him," Leo ordered as he lifted Freya, and carried her towards the back of the building, where Romano waited with the SUV.

She'd killed him, and she didn't even know it.

He left Vito, knowing he'd take care of the body and any evidence that might lead to her. The son of a bitch died too soon.

***

The elevator from his underground parking garage opened directly to his penthouse. The lights in the elevator showed her skinned knees.

He laid her on his bed before grabbing the first aid kit from the bathroom. He checked her for other injuries, finding her elbows and hands scraped, along with the outside of one of her thighs. He cleaned her injuries and covered what needed to be covered for the night, before settling her into his bed. She hadn't even stirred through his cleaning, adding ointment, and covering of her wounds.

He thought about stripping her but decided against it before settling down next to her. He should have put her in one of the guest rooms, but he told himself he needed to check on her throughout the night to make sure she was breathing, and that the drug didn't affect her more than it should. It was going to be a long night.

Chapter Six

"You're alive," Freya said, the first thought she had as she woke up. She had no idea where she was or if he was even really there, but she knew it was him and that he was alive. Freya let the rest of her wake up. She was in a soft bed, softer than hers. She never wanted to leave it. She turned her head and looked around, trying to figure out where she was. The room was dark, but she could tell that the sun was shining brightly behind the window shades.

"I am," a voice had her turning her head to the other side of the room.

The detective and lawyers she had met after the hiking episode, mentioned the name, Leonardo. He was more handsome than she remembered. Then again, he was bloodied, beaten, and dying the last time she had seen him. The detective hadn't been able to tell her much "due to the sensitivity of the case." She hadn't wanted to know what happened; she just wanted to know if he was okay.

She eventually heard from his lawyer, who offered her money for helping him. The second it was mentioned, she rejected the offer without even asking how much. She could have used the money, but she didn't want it... Not for doing something any decent human being would do. She just wanted to make sure he was alright, but all they told her was that he was in recovery.

"What happened?" she asked as she tried to remember how she ended up with him. She looked down and found herself in the same blue dress she'd gone out in for Lena's birthday. She remembered not feeling well, wanting to leave early, stumbling, seeing him and then nothing.

"You were drugged," he answered.

"Oh geez... How? I had my drink with me the whole time. I-" *She turned away.* "That jerk!" she said indignantly. She remembered there was an annoying guy hitting on her at the bar. He wouldn't take the hint when she brushed off his advances. The place had been dark, and she couldn't really see him, but she would never be interested in a guy she'd met at a club. That was just asking for trouble.

"You found me...you saved me?" It wasn't really a question, even if it came out as one. She sat up; it was a struggle. She still felt a little sluggish.

"I kept you safe," he replied.

"I guess we're even." She tried to smile at him, but it bothered her how easily she'd been drugged.

Leo didn't respond. As far as he was concerned, they would never be even. She had saved his life, made it possible for him to be here now. There was no paying her back for that.

"Where am I?" she asked as he watched her struggle with the duvet.

"My house. The bathroom is there." He pointed to the door on the left, which led to a walk-in closet and a master bathroom. "Leave your clothes on the bed, and I'll have them washed while you shower. There's a robe in there. Join me for breakfast when you're done." He left her alone and waited until he heard the shower before returning to retrieve her clothes. He gave them to Paula, his housekeeper, with the order to have them washed as quickly as possible.

It took Freya a half an hour to join him. His robe was too big for her, and her hair had been brushed and dried. She looked around his forty-million-dollar penthouse; the 15,000-square-foot condominium overlooked the Bay Bridge and had a view of the Embarcadero waterfront. She paused to take in the view. He knew she'd never been around such money. He knew her mother was a drunk, who'd ended up pregnant by one of her Johns when she was a prostitute. He knew that the only reason Mariana Santos had Freya was that she'd been locked up until she was eight months pregnant and had no choice but to keep her. Freya had all the cards against her, but she somehow made it out.

"Come and join me for breakfast while we wait for your clothes."

"Do you go by Leonardo?" she asked as she joined him.

"Call me Leo. How are you feeling?" He gestured for her to serve herself. There was a lot of food, way too much food for two people, even if she did have a bottomless stomach.

"Much better after the shower, thank you," she answered truthfully. She felt awkward having breakfast with a virtual stranger in just a robe.

The place oozed money; if the size and furniture didn't tell her that, the view would have. The view told her she probably would never make as much as the whole place was worth, even if she worked her whole life...twice.

"You're not eating. Do you want something else?"

"Oh, no...I'm just not sure if my stomach can handle it. I just feel a little iffy." She was being honest, but it wasn't because of the drug or what was even done to her. It was the man; he made her nervous.

"Would you like me to call a doctor?" he asked. She realized he was serious, like he could just call a doctor up to check on her. Then she realized that with his money, he probably could.

"Oh no, I think it'll pass. I'll just have some orange juice," she answered. Before she could reach for the juice, he picked it up and poured her a glass.

"Thanks," she mumbled. A woman, probably in her late forties, entered the room through a sliding door. She didn't say anything, just bowed her head, and left after Leo gave her a nod. A silent communication Freya was not privy to.

"You were out celebrating a friend's birthday?" Leo inquired.

"Yes, my friend, Lena. Her birthday was actually two weeks ago, but she finally found a way to get on the guest list for that club. It's almost impossible to get in there." Leo liked the way she scrunched her nose as she added, "and ridiculously expensive."

"How did you guys get on the guest list?" He was curious.

"A friend of a friend knew a bouncer, I was told. It cost us fifty bucks each." She sounded disgusted.

It wasn't illegal or unheard of, but it was against his rules. Family rule meant no one took money from *La Famiglia* business without a say from the boss.

Elite was exactly that, a club for the elites. It was the best and most expensive club in San Francisco.

"Which bouncer?" he asked.

"No idea. Why?" She gave him a look that told him it wouldn't be dropped.

"It's against the rules," he explained. He had ways to figure out who was doing side business in his club.

"Rules? Like the law?"

He smirked. The law didn't matter to him.

"My rules."

"Your rules? You own the club?" She was surprised.

"Yes."

"Is that why we got the VIP upgrade?"

He didn't think he needed to answer that. His people were obviously slipping. Not only were bouncers taking side money, someone let the asshole who had drugged her into his club. He'll have Romano check. Shit like that wasn't tolerated in his clubs, even in his underground business endeavors; his customers did not do anything that was not of their own free will.

"Your name will always be on the list from now on, and you may bring guests as long as they are not on our blocked list."

"That's really not necessary. I'm not sure I'll be back anyway. Not that there's anything wrong with your club. It's just hard to enjoy it when you're deciding between your credit card payment and a drink."

He almost smiled. Yeah, he supposed there was that.

"You and your guests will always have a complimentary table as long as you call it in and reserve it, free of charge." He was being generous, but then again, she did save his life. If she had taken the money she had been offered, he wouldn't feel as obligated.

"That's too much. You're only being nice because I found you. Though, honestly, it was my dog who found you. I wouldn't have stepped in your direction if she hadn't alerted me," she confessed.

"You saved my life, if you hadn't found me and slowed the bleeding, I would have died."

"Well, you saved mine last night, so we're even."

"You weren't dying."

"Well, I could have...He could have been a serial killer!" She was being ridiculous, and she knew it.

"Not on my watch."

"What-"

"Your clothes are ready and are in the room," he interrupted her to stop her from questioning him.

"How do you know?" she asked as she pushed her chair back to get up.

"Paula," he answered indicating to the sliding door where his housekeeper had informed him. They didn't say anything, but Paula had been his faithful housekeeper for over ten years. "When you're ready, I'll be in the library on the left, you'll see it."

***

It didn't take her long. Her hair hung loose, and she carried her heels in her hand when she joined him, less than ten minutes later. The dress was a simple blue lace dress; it was modest for clubbing but did show off toned legs. She was short, but the heels made her legs longer last night.

She blushed when she noticed him appreciating her legs.

"Ready?" she asked as if she was the one waiting for him. He almost smiled.

Chapter Seven

Freya couldn't stop thinking about Leo. It had been three days since he'd brought her home, and she knew she might be a little infatuated with him. Who wouldn't be? He was handsome, and there was something about him. Something mysterious and dangerous that called to her. She'd always been attracted to bad boys; it's probably why she had such a bad track record when it came to men.

She pulled into her parking spot. Work had dragged on all day and to make it worse; there were two men at her door. She hoped they were just sales people, rather than those church people. She had no problem saying no to salespeople, but the church people made her feel guilty, especially those little old ladies.

Both men wore button-up shirts with a tie,

slacks, and dark coats. They looked like how detectives looked on TV shows. She should have sat in her car and waited for them to leave.

They turned to face her when they heard her approach, her heels clicking as she walked.

"Can I help you?" she asked as she approached.

"Miss Santos?" The shorter of the two asked.

"Yes."

He reached for his wallet and flashed his badge, introducing himself as Detective Davis and the taller one as Detective Wilson. "We need to ask you a couple of questions about Saturday night-" The short one stopped his explanation as their attention was drawn to something behind her.

Before she could turn to look, she felt an arm slip around her waist. She looked up to see who was touching her.

"Leo," she whispered his name in surprise.

"Hello, Love," he greeted warmly as if he'd done it a million times. She felt a flutter in her stomach at the sound of his voice. He surprised her further when he leaned in and kissed her. The kiss was quick but left her knees feeling a little shaky. For a moment, she felt like she'd stopped breathing. He pulled her against him before facing the detectives.

"Officers," Leo's greeting sounded like a warning. "What can we do for you?" *We.*

"Actually, we're here to question Miss Santos, but we also have questions for you. We were told you weren't available earlier." Detective Davis sneered.

"Well, I am available now," Leo replied.

"Your whereabouts on Saturday night, Miss Santos?" Detective Wilson questioned her, purposely directing the question at her. He stared her down as if daring her to lie.

"I was clubbing with friends," she answered.

"At Elite?"

"Yes."

"A club you own, Mr. Costa," Detective Davis stated.

"You obviously know, get to the point," Leo responded sounding nonchalant, yet the tightening hold on her told her he was anything but.

"Do you recognize this man?" Detective Wilson handed her a photo of a man who looked to be in his early twenties.

"Not that I recall," she answered as she handed the picture back.

"He's the Mayor of Hayward's son, Michael Jones and he's been reported missing. His last sighting was leaving the club with you," Detective Davis said to her in an accusing tone.

She had been drugged and barely recalled what happened between being inside the club and waking up in Leo's house.

"I don't know him," she answered truthfully.

"We have eyewitness saying he walked out of the club with you," Detective Wilson explained.

"But I left the club with Leo," she replied as she turned to look at Leo who still had his arm around her.

"That's not what the eyewitness saw," said Detective Davis almost aggressively.

"Your witness must be confused detectives," Leo countered. "Freya left with me and spent the whole night with me, in my bed." She blushed. "My men drove us to my house. If you'd like to confirm this, they're over there." Freya followed the detectives gaze towards two black SUV's with three men standing guard. They were watching their surroundings, not looking in their direction, but she had a feeling they knew everything that was going on between her, Leo, and the detectives.

"We'll be sure to question them," Detective Davis replied sarcastically.

"Why would the witness believe they saw you leave with Mr. Jones?" Detective Wilson asked her.

"I don't know," she answered.

"Are you sure?" She almost thought Detective Davis asked the question jokingly. She really didn't like him.

"Detective, do you really think she'd leave with him when she has me?" It was a cocky question and completely legitimate. Leo was handsome and oozed money and class. But given a choice, Freya would have probably chosen the man in the picture over Leo; he would have been the safer choice for her sanity. "We'd be happy to answer more of your questions, but you'd have to go through our lawyer." Leo handed Detective Wilson a business card.

"And your lawyer represents both of you?" Detective Davis replied sardonically.

"Yes," Leo answered without hesitation. She didn't understand what was happening, but she stayed quiet. She didn't understand, but she knew Leo was there to protect her. From what, however, she didn't know.

"What's your relationship to Miss Santos?" Detective Wilson asked suspiciously.

She turned to face Leo because she wanted to know too. To her surprise, he looked down to face her before answering.

"She's my fiancé."

Chapter Eight

It was an impulsive decision, but he didn't regret it. His father thought he'd lost his mind. Upset wouldn't even begin to cover his father's reaction to Leo's decision to connect Freya to him, no matter how temporary it was. Leo felt something for Freya because she'd saved his life. He didn't meet decent people like her, not in his world. In his life, everyone wanted something. No one in his world would do something without some ulterior motive behind it. Even his family and closest friends, they all had an agenda behind their actions. Freya didn't, and she proved that by refusing the money. She was just a decent person who didn't deserve the consequences. Even if she did kill the fucker in self-defense, Leo wouldn't let her face that and how she'd feel about herself if she knew.

Leo might kill and hurt people, but everything

he'd dealt out had always been deserved. He felt no regret at making that twenty-eight-year-old punk's body disappear. He deserved it for getting off on drugging women and forcing them to have sex with him. If it hadn't been Freya, it would have been another woman he'd drugged in Leo's club. That shit didn't belong in Leo's territory. You didn't fuck with Costa business. Leo saw things in black and white because seeing shades of gray could get you killed in his world. Michael Jones was in the dark side of Leo's world, he'd done wrong, and Freya was in the light, she'd saved his life.

Leo would put up with Vito's teasing, his father's discontent, the cops' scrutiny, and Freya's arguments to do what needed to be done to save her. Sure, attaching a fiancé to him for the foreseeable future could inconvenience him, but Leo owed it to her.

He had never felt as hopeless as when he was sure he was going to die alone in the middle of nowhere. And then he'd heard a voice saying, *'Please don't die'*. He'd clung to it. She'd given him hope and kept him alive when he was so close to giving up. He'd thought he was ready to die, but she'd touched him and pleaded with him to live. It had given him the strength to keep breathing. Something in that moment had told him he couldn't die, not then and there. His will to survive hadn't been for him, or his family, but for her.

Revenge had kept him going as he'd struggled

through his recovery. The pawns in this little game had been easily dealt with. He'd planned to thank her one day, but he hadn't known how. He tried having his lawyer offer up a reward, but she'd refused the money, and that was all he'd had to give her. Now, she'd fallen into his lap, promptly reminding him of what he owed her, and giving him the perfect opportunity to settle his debt. So, when the cops on his payroll warned him about the detectives' interest in Freya, he wanted to be there. To save her, as she'd saved him.

Granted, getting engaged was more impulse and emotion than protection, but unknowingly he had found a way to keep her near him. She needed his protection, and she was getting it, whether she wanted it or not.

So, there he was, waiting for her to return from walking her damn dog in the fucking dark. He's trying to protect her, and she goes and walks into the dark alone and unprotected. He was itching to teach her a lesson, but he kept reminding himself that she wouldn't understand. She wasn't born in his world. She wouldn't think about dangers that lurked in the dark, waiting to attack when you're unprepared. He'd had someone keeping tabs on her, watching from afar, since he'd taken her home that first morning. Leo had sent Sandro to follow her. When he arrived, he'd been told that she had taken the dog for a walk. Knowing Sandro, it was going to be a short wait.

Leo leaned against the hood of the BMW waiting for her as he watched Freya stomp towards him with her dog. Though he didn't remember the dog, the dog recognized him. The dog had jumped on him the first morning he'd taken her home. It wasn't much of a guard dog especially with a name like Honey. Freya was upset with him, but her dog was ruining her dramatic effect by tugging her towards him.

He absently patted the dog as Freya stood in front of him, arms crossed. It wasn't impressive since he towered over her. She hadn't liked the idea of being engaged to him. He couldn't say he blamed her since his own father and friends thought the same. He could have just said that she was his girlfriend, but Leo wanted everyone to know how important she was to him. He wouldn't put up with anyone messing with *his* Freya. He had sent his lawyers to speak to the cops about what he'd tolerate when it came to their investigation regarding Freya, to reiterate that Freya had nothing to do with the missing man and that she was under the Costa family's protection.

"Why do you have that hulking man ordering me around?" Freya demanded as she came closer, stopping in front of him with a look that was supposed to show her displeasure. Leo thought she was too pretty to pull it off. Her brown eyes were too kind to look irritated, and no amount of frowning would make him change his mind.

"Hello to you too, Love." Leo took her arm and pulled her in for a kiss, surprising her. She tasted as sweet as she looked, like a kitten trying to look fierce.

"Wha-why?" she sputtered as he pulled away. He kissed her again, this time longer. His tongue demanding entrance and swirling with hers as he held her tightly against him. She pulled away when his hand gripped her a little too tight. He needed a moment to get his bearings, keeping a loose hold on her, and ignoring Vito who stood behind her with a stupid grin on his face.

"Let's talk inside." Leo led her to her apartment, taking her key to unlock her door, and frowning when he realized she hadn't even locked the deadbolt. The dog rushed in before them as Leo took a quick look around to make sure it was safe. Out of habit, he always checked to make sure there was no danger lurking. Her black cat stared at him from its perch on the windowsill. He watched her put the dog leash away and then wash her hands before turning to face him.

"He was following orders. Do you have any idea how unsafe it is for a woman to walk alone in the dark?" Leo had ordered Sandro to follow her, and make sure she was safe, but Sandro had obviously bullied her into returning home before she meant to.

"This is my neighborhood, I know most of the

people here, and I have Honey."

"No offense, but she's not much of a guard dog. You might know most of your neighbors, but you don't know them all, and danger can come from anywhere."

"I'm just walking my dog."

"Walk in the daylight."

"You're annoying. Why are you here?" He almost expected her to stomp, but instead, she crossed her arms and leaned against the sink. He shot her a look, but she didn't seem to care nor was she intimidated by his look, the same look he'd given countless men, who'd peed themselves, knowing they were about to die. She didn't know that though, so it did not affect her. He fought a smile at the irony of things.

"We need to talk about our engagement." Leo leaned against the wall facing the door and windows with his arms casually crossed, looking relaxed but if he needed to, his gun was easily within reach, tucked at the back of his pants.

"Easy, we're not engaged."

"Easy, we are."

"This is silly. We don't even know each other. We've barely met!" Freya was frustrated with Leo's nonchalant response. An engagement between them was absurd.

"We met five months ago."

"That doesn't count; you weren't aware."

"I was, and I heard you. *'Please don't die'*. So, I didn't."

"That's not funny." She uncrossed her arms and headed to the only chair in the studio, a wingback chair next to a bookcase that looked ready to collapse from all the books stuffed in it. "I'm serious, Leo. This engagement thing is too...too...too much!"

"It's protecting you from being accused of murder."

"I didn't kill anyone. I don't know the guy they're looking for." Something in her face told him she was trying to force her memory.

"Our lawyer talked to the detectives, and they're pretty convinced you were last seen with him." And Leo made sure that his lawyer convinced the detectives that she wasn't and that if they tried to approach her again without her lawyer present, he'd pull every connection he had to make sure they lost their badge.

"I don't understand why." Freya seemed to

deflate in front of him, and he hated it.

"Because they're grasping." Because the cops were always looking for reasons to catch the big guys. Their target wasn't really Freya; their target was Leo. She'd been seen with Leo; he'd come to her rescue, she'd saved Leo's life. Cops were always trying to make a name for themselves and catching someone like Leo would make them legends. "A mayor's son is a noteworthy person. They don't want to look bad."

"I really don't know why me though. I had nothing to do with it. Right?" She was asking him for the truth.

"You were stumbling when I found you outside. I recognized you, and I took you to my home where you spent the night sleeping off the drug. You have nothing to do with his disappearance." She looked relieved, and his lie didn't feel like a lie. What he told her technically wasn't. She had been stumbling around, he did recognize her, he did take her home, and she technically didn't have anything to do with why the man was missing. Leo's men had taken care of it. If Freya hadn't killed the man by accident, Leo would have killed him for daring to touch her.

"That's it?" She stared at him in the eyes. It didn't happen often. Most men couldn't look him straight in the face, but this little woman could.

"That's it." It was the hardest and easiest lie he'd ever told. He struggled with the need to tell her the truth and not lie to her, but his desire to protect her made the decision easy.

***

She thought it was a joke when he said it. She thought it was a joke when Leo had excused them from the detectives the day before and promptly left her after telling her not to talk to the detectives without him or the lawyer present. She still didn't understand why he'd want to be engaged to her. She argued with him for almost an hour about it. In the end, they were still engaged but only temporarily; at least until the investigation about the mayor's son was over.

Leo told her that he had a reputation and a family name to protect. She hadn't wanted to go on with their fake engagement for the sake of reputation; she didn't take that issue all that serious; she was nobody. Leo then pointed out how often innocent people ended up in jail for crimes they didn't commit. He also pointed out that their fake engagement benefitted them both; she would have his protection and lawyer, and his family would get off his back about settling down. She doubted that his "benefit" was worth all that much; she couldn't imagine anyone telling Leo what to do. Their engagement was going to be real but temporary; they're going to pretend to be happily engaged in public. It was going to be real; he was firm about that; it would just have an expiration date.

Chapter Nine

"Do I really have to meet your family?" Leo tried not to grin at the aggravation in her voice. It had been three days since their impetuous engagement. As far as relationships go, theirs was speeding along. He saved her on Saturday, became engaged to her on Tuesday, had their first argument on Wednesday, and was now at the meet the parents stage, all in a week. He could have thrown money at the situation or let the lawyers handle Freya's situation, but Leo had purposely inserted himself into her life. He didn't want to look too much into it with everyone already telling him he's crazy.

"Yes, you do. Just like I will meet your mother," he answered her.

"That's not necessary," she replied quickly.

"It's necessary. You're my fiancé-"

"Temporarily," she cut in.

"For as long as we need to be. We're going to do what engaged people do."

"You mean-like-I mean." He kept his smile in check. She was scowling at him and blushing at the same time. He was attracted to her, and he had decided that their engagement was going to be real enough. Only his father, Drago, Vito, and Romano knew that their engagement was temporary, and they all thought he'd lost his mind. His excuse, that he wanted no doubt of her alibi, was flimsy at best. He didn't care. He'd told them he wanted them to pretend that his engagement was anything but fake. His mother was happy, thinking that this engagement would be real and that he'd finally settle down, especially with the woman who saved his life and asked for nothing in return. His father, on the other hand, had grumbled about the idiocy of this engagement and the fact that she wasn't Italian or one of "theirs", meaning part of *La Famiglia*.

As the San Francisco syndicate of New York's Vetrano Family, the biggest crime family of New York, there was plenty of "theirs" for Leo to pick from when it comes to choosing his wife. He would eventually pick from them; he had to. The life of *La Famiglia* wasn't something just anyone becomes a part of *or left by choice.*

"The engagement will be as real as it gets. No one but you and I know that it's temporary."

"You mean your family really thinks–"

"Yes."

"What if they don't like me?" she asked in distress.

"They'll like you."

"You don't know that," she argued.

"You saved my life; they like you already."

"Saving your life and marrying you are two completely different things."

"To them, it's not." At least in his mother's opinion, they were both just as good.

"I don't even know you. I don't know your birthday, favorite color, favorite food or even your age!" she raged.

"September twenty-two; I'm thirty-four; Italian, and black."

"Black is not a color, it's a shade," she said with

contrite and a pout.

"She'll love the flowers," he decided to change the topic. He had an expensive wine with him, but he was surprised to see that she'd gotten his mother flowers. He had handed the flowers to Romano to hold, but he liked that she thought about it and made an effort. His mother loved flowers, had a garden full and the bundle of summer flowers that Freya had brought was something his mother would love.

"Are you sure? I wasn't sure about the sunflower, but the colors looked good together and-Oh my God! I forgot about your dad-" Before she could freak out, he stopped her.

"I brought wine. Stop worrying."

"I know nothing about wine. I don't even drink it."

"We need to meet your mother after this."

"No." He waited for her to explain and when he realized she wasn't going to expand on her answer, he asked for a reason.

"My mother and I don't really have a relationship."

"You're all the family each other has."

"Well, we don't talk. She hasn't talked to me in, like a year."

"Why?"

"Because she wanted money, every time we talked and I–" she stopped.

"You what?" he pushed on.

"I didn't want to give her any more money because she uses it for alcohol."

He had already known her mother's status as a drunk and a bit of a menace, but he wanted her to tell him about it.

"I understand. Enablers never do their loved ones any good."

"I don't want to see her."

"We still need to. I need to make sure she's not a danger to us."

"Well, don't say I didn't warn you," she mumbled, crossing her arm over her chest.

If the fancy car, the breathtaking penthouse, expensive clothes, and bodyguards hadn't clued her in on how rich he was, then his parents' Piedmont mansion would have. Freya had never even seen a mansion up close. She had a feeling that she was meeting royalty when the gate opened for their limo. The long driveway led to a Venetian style mansion. She was so taken by the architecture that she stopped and just stood staring up at the mansion.

The double doors were opened by a housemaid, complete with the conservative black and white outfit, without Leo knocking on the door. They were greeted by a butler and were led to a grand living room. Did they even call it a living room? Two men, one older, she assumed Leo's father, one younger than Leo and a woman who she presumed was Leo's mother, greeted them.

She was so nervous; she couldn't say anything but a strangled "Hi" during the introduction. A short awkward silence followed, and she realized they were staring at her.

"Freya got these flowers for you, mother," Leo explained, and she realized she was about to squeeze the flowers to death.

"Oh, I'm sor–these are for you." Freya stopped talking as she almost shoved the flowers at Valentina. At least she remembered their names. Giovanni was his father and Luciano was his brother. "I'm–well–I'm sorry, I've never done this before, meet you, I mean meet people. Well not meet people, but meet you know...parents." She stopped and knew her tan skin couldn't hide her embarrassment.

Luciano laughed.

"Luciano, you stop it," Valentina scolded her son, but she smiled and accepted the flowers from Freya. "They're beautiful my dear and we're happy to finally meet you." Valentina pulled her into a hug and just as quickly pulled away and started to lead her to the dining room.

Freya almost sighed in relief when she saw that dinner wasn't going to be a fancy one that required six or eight utensils. She was surprised to see that it looked like an ordinary family dinner. The plates were set with bowls for soup on top, a napkin on the side and three simple utensils; a spoon, fork, and knife. Though the dining room itself screamed money with its marble floor, expensive China on display, a gorgeous Persian rug, and one large chandelier over the 12-seat table, the atmosphere was casual. She was even more relieved when Drago, Vito, and Romano joined them for dinner. Everyone seemed to know where they belonged.

Giovanni sat at the head of the table with Valentina on his right side. Leo sat on his left side. Romano, Vito, and Drago sat on Valentina's side, leaving Freya sitting between Leo and Luciano.

"So, Freya. Tell me something about you. Like

you know, when you'll be dumping my brother, so I can ask you out." Freya nearly spit out the water she'd just drank.

"Luciano, give it a break. Everyone knows I'm the better-looking brother." There was a bite in Leo's tone.

"You wish, big brother. Freya, he's too old for you. Look at him. Old man." Luciano was handsome, a total pretty boy, but Freya liked Leo's grittier look. Leo looked more mature, manlier. She didn't know how to explain it. But if she had to choose between them, she'd choose Leo.

"She's older than you." Leo shot back.

"Perfect. I've always wanted to date a cougar." Luciano gave her the most mischievous look she had ever seen. She couldn't help but giggle, and she wasn't the only one. Romano and Vito weren't even hiding their amusement.

"Leave your brother alone, Luciano," Giovanni's tone was somber, but Freya saw a glint in his eyes that told her he was amused.

"I'm just saying, Freya has more options. She doesn't have to settle for Leo."

"Luciano–" Leo was cut off by their mother.

"That's enough. Start eating, your food will get cold." Valentina knew how to handle boys.

Leo glared at Luciano, not looking like he was ready to let it go. Freya placed her hand on his leg, trying to take his attention away from his brother. She was already a nervous wreck as is; she didn't want to make it worse by being the reason Leo and his brother fought. Leo noticed her touch right away, his attention turning to her. He gave her a brief nod before focusing on his food. The curt nod had her thinking she'd overstepped her place and was about to remove her hand from his leg when he placed a hand on top of hers. He patted her hand, giving it a brief squeeze, making her realize that they were on the same side. She relaxed knowing they were on the same team and focused on the beckoning food.

***

"She doesn't seem all that bright. Does he really have to do this?" Giovanni Costa wasn't a man to deny or argue with. Forty years ago, Giovanni and his father, Giuseppe Costa, had ruthlessly taken over San Francisco, claiming the Bay Area as Costa Territory.

As the head of the Costa family, he'd killed more men than he could remember, and Leonardo Costa was his heir. Giuseppe hadn't given Giovanni a choice. Giovanni had married the daughter of a Chicago Outfit boss at his father's order to seal the alliance between both families. Though Valentina and Giovanni hadn't known each other and only met on the day of their engagement, they eventually learned to love each other and raise two sons. Valentina had been soft, had no part in the mafia life and was much too kind for this life, but she'd been smart.

Giovanni had respected his father, but he resented him as well. He'd promised himself that his own children would not resent him and that he'd let them have a choice when the time came. He'd even worked to legitimize many of his businesses so that his children would have options. He hadn't wanted a life filled with blood for his family, and he had Valentina to thank for that.

After meeting who Leo had chosen to marry, Giovanni doubted his choice. He knew his son, and Giovanni had a feeling that this temporary engagement would only end in marriage. He'd seen the way his son looked at her. Giovanni was grateful for her; if she hadn't been there, his son would have died. When she hadn't wanted the money and fame for saving his son's life, she'd earned his respect. But now, he wondered if she was an air head. She had seemed unusually shy, and he had a feeling that a full family party would have overwhelmed her. He wondered if she had a personality at all. He seemed to scare her.

"I like her," Valentina said as she joined him in bed.

"She's soft," he said, the nicest word he could find for weak.

"She's sweet and smart. Much smarter than she lets on."

Giovanni didn't see it. He knew she graduated college with a 3.8 GPA and her job involved medical devices. There were plenty of book smart people, and he figured that was her.

"She was mute. How would you know?"

Valentina gave him a look he'd seen hundreds of time in their thirty-five-year marriage. The look that told him she thought he was being stupid.

"You scared the poor girl," she replied.

"I did nothing of the sort" he argued.

"You did. You kept glaring at her, every time she answered my questions. I thought Leonardo might stab you with his steak knife," she responded with a smile

***

"Your dad hated me." Freya knew it, and it didn't help that she acted like a blabbering idiot.

She had been nervous, and Giovanni was also scary. There was something about him that screamed danger. He'd made her nervous and twitchy throughout dinner.

"He didn't hate you." Leo's answer was firm and without hesitation.

She gave him a doubtful look, but it didn't matter, he was focused on the road. They'd arrived in the limo, but he'd decided to take a two-seat sports car back to her side of the bay. The drive usually took forty-five minutes without traffic, but this was California, traffic was part of life. Thankfully, they were making a good time. She knew that his bodyguards were following in a black BMW. Why they had to take two cars was beyond her.

"He didn't like me," she insisted. She didn't know why it mattered so much to her.

"He was probably trying to figure out why you were so nervous," he replied with a smile that had her forgetting her concerns. She decided to accept his explanation for now and leaned back in her seat, glad to finally be able to relax and close her eyes.

Her eyes shot open when she remembered where they were going.

"Do we really need to see my mother?" Besides

meeting his family for their fake, no, *temporary* engagement, they were also meeting with her mother.

"Yes," he answered.

"We really don't. She really won't care."

"But I do."

"I don't. She may not even be home. She's unpredictable." The truth was, she hadn't seen her mother or even spoken to her in seven months since she'd last asked Freya for money. Her mother was a drunk. Freya had learned to raise herself at a young age. She understood that her mother couldn't be depended on. As an adult, she supported her mother until she finally got it through her head that she needed to stop being an enabler.

"She'll be home," he simply answered.

***

The cars stood out. The small mobile home community was poor, and the sports car and BMW stood out. They parked in front of an old RV trailer. Barely big enough for a person to live in, let alone two people. She'd grown up in it, living in one trailer park, only to move to another when they'd get kicked out for not paying rent. It looked worse than she remembered, even in the dark. She didn't bother to ask how Leo knew where her mother lived. He seemed just to know everything about her.

Leo got out, walked around to her side, and helped her out. The three bodyguards were already standing outside, guarding both vehicles as the trailer door swung open.

Her mother was five feet and five inches tall, just three inches taller than Freya and looked a lot older than her fifty years of age. Years of alcohol and cigarettes made her that way.

"What do you want?" her mother's raspy voice called out.

"Mariana, it's me," Freya called out. Her mother hadn't wanted to be called 'mom' because she said it made her feel old. Freya had grown up calling her by her name like they were friends or sisters.

"Freya? What's with all of the fancy cars and people?" Mariana Santos demanded.

"Nothing, I just wanted you to meet someone."

"Why?" she asked in a hostile tone.

"Because I do." Freya tried not to show her frustration.

"Who is it then?" Mariana demanded as she came closer.

"His name is Leo," Freya simply answered.

"Leo, you take care of your mother?" her mother demanded.

"Yes."

"Well then maybe you can teach that ungrateful child of mine how to."

"You've been drinking again," Freya accused when she smelled her mother. She reeked of alcohol and cigarettes. Freya hated the smell of cigarettes.

"You don't give me money, so you shut your mouth! You don't tell me what to do!" Mariana stormed in her direction, they had had fights before, and Freya was used to it. She was shorter than her mother, but Mariana was weak from her addiction. Leo hadn't known that and surprised both Freya and Mariana when he stepped in between them.

"That's enough," Leo's voice was calm but filled with warning, something even her drunken mother seemed to understand. "We're leaving." Leo had Freya back in the car in seconds. She watched Leo exchange words with her mother before he got into the car. They left the trailer park faster than she could ask him what he said to her.

"I'm sorry. Mariana can get-" she didn't finish her statement. Her mother had embarrassed her. Compared to Valentina, she could only imagine what Leo was thinking.

"Mariana?" he asked as he drove to her apartment.

"Growing up she wanted me to call her Mariana because mom made her feel old. Sometimes she'd introduce me as her sister." And Freya had loved it. Those days, it was like their little secret. Her mother had been young, wild, and fun and all she wanted was for her mother to love her and include her.

"I'm-I'm sorry. She's been getting worse."

"You have nothing to apologize for," he simply told her. Nothing else was said the rest of the drive. He parked his car, illegally, and Vito exited the BMW to take control of the sports car while Leo walked her to her door.

Honey excitedly waited for her on the other side of the door, and she hesitated. "I should say 'bye' now. Honey will be jumping all over you if you come in."

"I'll be fine. I want to check your apartment before I leave."

She almost rolled her eyes. Since the first day, when he'd dropped her off, he'd always insisted on checking her apartment first. Taking her keys from her and entering first to make sure it was safe. She lived in a studio where the only place someone could hide was the bathroom. She always liked the open space because she hated sleeping by herself in the dark and not knowing what's in the other room. Call her paranoid, but she hated hearing sounds that she couldn't see.

He unlocked the door and was ready for Honey when she jumped up to greet him. Honey wasn't normally so welcoming of strangers, but Freya thought that Honey recognized him after saving his life. It didn't take Leo long to make sure no one was in her apartment, and Freya didn't bother to remind him that Honey was a great guard dog.

She dropped her purse on her lone wingback chair before facing Leo. He surprised her when he pulled her against his body and kissed her. It was a real kiss. A hot, wet kiss that had her melting against him. When she thought she was going to drown in him, he pulled away.

"Good night," he whispered against her lips before placing a soft kiss on her forehead and detangling from her. He pulled her to the door. "Lock it," he ordered as he stepped out. She knew he'd probably stand on the other side of the door until he heard the lock. She locked the door and leaned against it. The kiss had shaken her and left her wanting more, much more.

***

Leo waited until he heard the door lock into place. He ambled slowly towards the waiting cars. The cold air helped control his need for more, more of Freya. Today had gone as he'd expected. He expected his mother to like her, his brother to flirt with her, and his father to put her under a microscope. He even expected what happened at her mother's place. He'd insisted on meeting Mariana Santos to ensure that there would be no threat to *La Famiglia* and to Freya.

What he hadn't expected was his attraction to her getting stronger. He'd almost fucked her in her tiny studio with her dog probably howling. Damn, she tasted good. Their engagement might be temporary but he sure as fuck isn't going to pretend it's fake.

Chapter Ten

"Are you okay? You've been acting funny," Lena asked, surprising Freya out of her thoughts. They were on their lunch break, and she'd been looking at the menu but wasn't really seeing it. She was thinking about Leo, the police, the missing man, and everything else. Sometimes she wondered if she was dreaming, it seemed surreal.

"No, I-I just have a lot on my mind," she answered.

"Hopefully me." The deep voice behind her raised the hair on her arms.

Lena's reaction was just as telling.

Too bad he's mine. *Kind of.*

Freya looked up as Leo appeared beside the table.

"Leo," she greeted in a husky voice. The man looked good, really good. He leaned down and gave her a quick kiss before turning to face Lena. He gave Freya a look, waiting for her to introduce them.

"Leo, Lena. Lena, Leo. Leo is my...Leo is my fiancé."

Lena couldn't hide her surprise.

"Fiancé? What? Since when?"

Freya wasn't surprised. It wasn't like she had ever mentioned she was seeing anyone or even hinted about anyone. She felt like shit about it too because Lena was the closest friend she had. Freya had even spent the last four Christmas Eve's with Lena's family.

"And I'm his best man." Vito surprised Freya and Lena as he appeared on the other side of the table. Vito was Leo's bodyguard, but Freya suspected there was more to their relationship than boss and employee. She hardly ever saw Leo without Vito nearby. Vito had even joined dinner with Leo's parents, as well as the other two men that were attached to Leo's hips, Drago, and Romano. Today seemed to be just Vito.

Vito sat next to Lena, crowding her, distracting

her from Freya's sudden engagement. Even if Lena forgot about it now, it was definitely going to come up later when they were back at work. They worked together; Freya had gotten Lena the job when she had been promoted to her current position, a little over three years ago.

Lena shook both of their hands but gave Freya a look.

"What are you doing here?" Freya chose to deal with Leo first, as he settled himself on the chair next to her.

"Was in the area doing business." He leaned in and stole another kiss from her.

"When did this happen? When did you guys meet? Engaged?" Lena wasn't going to wait as she ignored Vito's attempt to distract her.

"We met about six months ago while I was...hiking," Freya answered truthfully, omitting the rest of how they met.

"Six months? And you're engaged? Must have been something special!" Lena replied excitedly.

"The moment I saw her I just knew she was going to save my life." Leo grinned at her and Freya barely stopped herself from rolling her eyes.

"That's so freaking romantic! Where's the ring?" Lena was a romantic, the kind who falls in love with all of her heart, every single time.

"Oh umm, you know how I am about jewelry...and I wanted to keep it quiet for now, until I get a chance to tell everyone first... That's why I asked you to come to lunch with me."

The waiter came, saving her from explaining her sudden engagement. The café was a regular for her and Lena; the outside sitting area had a perfect view of the plaza. The sky was clear and sunny, a rare break from the April showers, so they'd chosen to enjoy the nice weather and sit outside. She and Lena ordered their usual, but Leo and Vito declined to order which meant they weren't staying, a relief of sorts.

"She's the only woman I know who doesn't like jewelry," Lena explained. It wasn't that she didn't like jewelry, she just preferred not to wear it. Jewelry always felt odd to her, almost a bother.

"Well, I just came by to say 'hello.' I have other business to deal with. I'll pick you up after work,"

"After work?" she asked Leo in surprise.

"Yes, after work," he simply answered. He turned to Lena. "It was a pleasure to meet you, Miss Cruz." Leo kissed Freya again before leaving with Vito trailing after him...well after Vito gave Lena a flirty smile.

"Oh my God, you're engaged! And to that fine ass man!" Lena nearly shouted after they watched Leo and Vito walk out of sight.

"We've kept the relationship quiet." She tried to think of an excuse for why they would. "He's a little rich, and well, we decided that it would be best to...you know," she explained lamely.

"What does he do?" Lena asked.

"He owns clubs."

"Clubs?"

"Clubs."

"Clubs?"

"Yes Lena, Clubs. Specifically, Elite. It's how we got the VIP upgrade."

"Oh my God! Are you serious?" Lena was a lot more excited about this engagement than Freya was.

"Yes, now calm down. This is why we didn't tell anyone..."

"Wait, if he owned it why didn't we just get on the list rather than try and beg the bouncer to get in?"

Of course, Lena would be thinking about that.

"I hadn't realized it was one of his clubs. I told you I'd never been to Elite, and you know I don't really like clubbing...so I never really asked him about it. When he saw us in the club, he set us up..." Freya hoped that was enough for Lena. Lena seemed to think it over before deciding it was an acceptable explanation.

"When did he propose? How did he propose?" Freya knew she needed to answer Lena's question or she'll just badger Freya until she did.

"He proposed about...two weeks ago...while he was over. We just kind of talked about it...and...yeah." *God, she sucked at this.*

"Two weeks and I'm only just finding out now?"

"Well, we were keeping it quiet and then we had to meet each other's families."

"You mean he met your mother?" Lena was shocked. Lena knew how volatile Freya's relationship with her mother was and how terrible Mariana could get when drunk. "How'd she take it?"

"Awful and I was mortified. She was her usual self."

"How'd he take it?"

"Perfectly," Freya answered honestly. He'd been caring and hadn't treated Freya any different after meeting Mariana.

"Perfectly?" Lena questioned, doubtful.

"Perfectly."

"Oh my God! That is so sweet! Was it love at first sight?" Lena asked excitedly.

"Maybe for him," Freya joked. *No, it was far from it.*

"I can't believe you're engaged! When's the wedding?"

"No date yet. We decided on a long engagement."

"A long engagement? Why?"

"Well, to make up for the short time we've been...dating." Freya hated lying to her friends, and she knew she'd have to lie some more to all of them. She wondered if Leo was overreacting in believing the cops would arrest her for the mayor's son's disappearance. But then again, she did think that the cops were unnecessarily aggressive towards her. She couldn't remember anything beyond leaving the club. Leo had told her he'd found her after she fell and didn't notice anyone. She couldn't have done anything to that man...could she?

***

Freya handed her keys to Romano. Leo mentioned Romano would take her car home while they went to an appointment. She hoped not more people to meet. Lena had talked about her engagement for the rest of the afternoon. It concerned Freya how easily she could lie to her friends. She'd had to exaggerate her time with Leo in order to answer Lena's questions.

"Where are we going?" she asked Leo as she joined him in the back seat of the slick, black BMW with tinted windows she knew was too dark to be legal.

"Dress shopping."

Her stomach dropped. *Dress shopping*?

"Dress shopping? What for?" she asked suspiciously. She couldn't imagine any reason she would need a dress unless he was expecting her to buy a wedding dress, which was taking this a little too far.

"Dress shopping," he clarified.

"What kind of dress?" she demanded.

"Formal gown," he simply answered, not

bothering to look at her as he continued to type on his phone.

"A formal gown?"

"Yes."

She became irritated and reached to pull his phone away so that he'd pay attention to her. Her boldness surprised her, but his quick reaction surprised her even more. His hand shot out and gripped her wrist tightly, almost painfully. They stared at each other in surprise. He seemed to realize what he was doing at the same time his grip began to hurt. He quickly let go, and she cradled her wrist to her chest.

"I apologize. Reflexes," he quickly explained. "Let me see–"

"No, it's fine. I surprised you." She was hesitant to let him touch her. He almost scared her.

"Let me see. I want to make sure I didn't hurt you."

"It's nothing. You just surprised me."

"Let me see," he insisted.

She figured it was easier to let him see and get it over with, than argue. She didn't think he'd really hurt her. She showed him her wrist, and he held it close to him, inspecting it. His hold on her arm was gentle, nothing at all like the strong grip he had reacted with.

"I don't think it will bruise," he said as he gently touched her wrist. He let go, and she pulled her hand back to her lap, unsure of what to do or say. "We need to get you a formal gown for a fundraiser we will be attending."

"What fundraiser? Why?" she asked confused.

"Now that we're engaged," he gave her a look that told her not to interrupt him when she wanted to remind him that their engagement was temporary. "We will need to act engaged, and that means being seen in public as a couple."

"Couldn't we just go to dinner or something, like normal people?" she asked.

"I'm not normal, and our engagement isn't either," he answered.

"I haven't gone to anything formal since prom."

"Prom will probably be a lot more exciting than this."

"What kind of fundraiser is it?" she asked.

"Political campaign."

"Political? Like government?" she asked stupidly.

"Yes," he answered patiently.

"I-I'm not sure I can do that," she replied honestly.

"You can, and you will. All you have to do is smile, look pretty and make googly eyes at me," he replied lightly.

She paused at his use of 'googly eyes'. It almost made her smile. He *almost* seemed like he was being playful with her. She wasn't sure how to handle *this* Leo.

"I'm serious," she insisted.

"It'll be okay. We'll just talk, eat, and dance-"

"I doubt I'll have anything in common with anyone there to talk about."

"They're just normal people."

"You said you weren't normal."

"I'm not. But they are."

"I-"

He cut her off. "It'll be okay. You'll enjoy it. We're here."

She looked out to see where *here* was. They were at a ridiculously expensive boutique. It was popular for formal gowns and wedding dresses, and she knew it was by appointment only.

"Are you going to make me model for you?" she asked jokingly.

"I should, but I won't make you. I'll wait in the lounge."

"How fancy is the fundraising?"

"Think of it as a fancy dinner."

"Fancy like meeting your parents?"

"No, a little fancier."

Before she could reply, the store associate joined them, and before she knew it, she was being led away and towards the racks of dresses. She had no idea where to start, but the sales associate was kind enough to ask her what she liked.

Freya liked to be comfortable. She wanted a dress that was comfortable and made her look taller since her short height always made her look frumpy.

The store associate was quick to point her to several dresses. The first dress was red and fit her just right; it was beautiful and elegant. Freya would have said yes to the dress right away, but Lindsey had insisted she try other dresses too.

She fell in love with the second dress the moment she saw it. It was somewhat conservative and probably was not fancy enough, but she *really, really, really liked it*. She decided to try it on. The blue Escada ruffle pleated gown fit her perfectly and made her feel tall and sophisticated. She loved it, but as she looked at herself in the mirror, she knew it wasn't formal enough.

"You look beautiful in that." Leo suddenly appeared behind her, and they both looked at her reflection in the mirror.

"I don't think it really screams fancy dinner," she replied critically.

"I would have to agree," he replied.

"That's okay. I think the other dress will work." She looked at herself in the gown one last time before turning to face him. She showed him the red, fitted, Dolce & Gabbana, lace gown. It was the first dress she had tried on and would have said it was good, but the blue dress had caught her eyes.

"What do you think?" she asked him, holding up

the dress against her. It was a $6000.00 dress, but she didn't think the price mattered to Leo considering nothing in the store cost less than $1000.

"I think you will look just as beautiful in it," he answered.

"I've already tried it on, so I guess I'm done," she explained.

"What about shoes?" the store associate asked.

"I'm not sure," Freya answered. "Maybe nude heels?"

"We have a large selection of them," she replied as she started walking towards the shoe displays. Leo gave her a nod, telling Freya to go. She settled on a pair of thin strapped, light beige heels. The heels were about four inches tall, but they were surprisingly comfortable and probably cost a lot more than all of her shoes combined.

She looked at herself in the Escada gown one last time before heading back to the fitting room. She would have bought the gown herself if it didn't cost nearly $4000! She handed the dress back to Lindsey and quickly changed back into her own clothes.

By the time she made it out, Leo had already purchased the items, and Vito was heading out to the car, carrying large shopping bags. Overall, she would guess that Leo had spent close to $8000 just for the dress and shoes.

"Ready?" she asked him as she met him at the door.

For some reason, he smiled but held the door open for her as they exited the obnoxiously expensive boutique. She thanked Lindsey as she headed out. Leo held the car door open for her as well, like a gentleman, and she suddenly wondered if she was going to be the next Pretty Woman.

"We're having dinner with Steven Lawrence," Leo told her as they settled in the back of the car.

"Who?" Freya asked, confused.

"Our lawyer." The lawyer who was handling the detectives.

"Why?"

"So, you know what you need to do in case the detectives come around."

They arrived at an Italian restaurant, a little-hidden gem in Walnut Creek. The place wasn't fancy, but it was crowded and boisterous. The lawyer was already there and greeted Leo like a friend.

"Steven, meet Freya, my fiancé." Steven Lawrence was tall and younger than she had expected. His friendly greeting put her at ease. She listened to Leo and Steven discuss business she didn't quite understand, and then went over what was happening with the detectives. Steven had assured her that she had nothing to worry about and that the detectives were simply targeting her to pull something out of a hat since their investigation was going nowhere. He handed her several business cards and instructed her to hand them to anyone who wished to question her. He prepared her with what she needed to say and assured her that she was under no obligation to speak to anyone without him there.

***

Leo checked her tiny apartment like usual before he let her in. He did have business on this side of the bay, and him stumbling onto her, and her friend really was coincidental since he himself had just finished a lunch meeting. He had planned to call her to tell her about the dress appointment once he returned to the car, but he'd forgotten about it once he saw her. She had distracted him.

He knew she usually went straight home after work; a routine she'd perfected. The person he'd sent to keep tabs on her reported back to him. He knew she wouldn't like the idea of having a bodyguard. Freya was independent, and she would hate the idea that she couldn't take care of herself. Leo didn't think there was a threat to Freya, which was why he'd only had someone watching her at her place in case she decided to walk her dog at night, or cops come sniffing around her. He was fairly confident that no one would approach her when she's in public or at work. Her routine made it easier to keep tabs on her whereabouts. As long as she stayed with her work and home routine, she was safe.

Seeing her at lunch had been a pleasant surprise for Leo and provided a perfect opportunity to tell her about their plans to buy a dress. Except he didn't actually tell her they were buying a dress, he just told her he'd pick her up. He didn't give her much of an option. Leo knew who her friend was when he stumbled on them. He had Freya, and any close association of hers thoroughly checked, in the beginning, to make sure she wasn't just another pawn. He quickly recognized her friend as the same one who had been celebrating her birthday the night Freya waltzed back into his life, a reminder telling him he owed her.

He'd been distracted when he'd picked her up after work, and his knee-jerk reaction to her reaching for his phone was unfortunate. He didn't like frightening her, and he didn't like her distrust because of his actions. He had to remind himself that she didn't know him, and he had to expect the unexpected from her because of it.

Knowing it was a bad idea, Leo closed the door and pulled her into his arms. What she wore wasn't sexy, it was professional and right for the season. The light gray pencil skirt ended at her knees, and a tiny slit on the side wasn't even enough to show off her thigh, but he had fantasized about it since seeing her at lunch. She looked feminine without trying. She didn't have money, but she looked classy. She didn't wear designer clothes, but she always seemed well put together. He cradled her body with his as he leaned down to kiss her. Her heels gave her needed height, making it easier for him to claim her mouth as his hands explored her body. He'd kept himself from really touching her before, but not tonight. His hands cupped her ass, squeezing the soft rounded cheeks, he loved her curves. He pressed her against the door, grinding himself against her as he devoured her mouth.

***

The feel of hands squeezing her bare behind had Freya gasping and pulling away from Leo. It took her a moment to realize that her skirt was bunched up, nearly to her waist and that Leo's hands were touching her bare skin and holding her body tightly against his. She could feel his bulge against her stomach, and her own hands were pulling at his tucked shirt.

"Leo," she whispered, pulling them both out of this seductive daze they'd entered.

"Ah, hell." He sounded harsh next to her ear as he pressed her between him and the door. It was so easy to drown in their attraction to each other. They both simply stood there for a moment, catching their breath, trying to right their minds.

She missed the feel of his touch when he slowly let go of her and stepped back. She straightened her skirt back down to have something to do.

"Not tonight." She wasn't sure if he meant that for himself or her. He came closer again, his hand going to her head to pull her in, but this time, he simply placed a kiss on her forehead. "Goodnight. Lock the door." Then he was gone. She locked the door. She wanted to look out of her window to watch him leave but controlled herself. Instead, she leaned against the door.

Chapter Eleven

Leo had asked her to get ready at his place, so Romano had picked her up early. He'd taken her to Leo's penthouse, and Paula had shown her to a room with an attached bathroom. Leo wasn't home but had told her when she needed to be ready by.

She took her time getting ready. She had gone to get her nails done that morning and even got everything waxed, and by everything, she meant *everything*. She had always hated anyone else doing her makeup, so she chose to do it herself. While she normally kept her makeup more natural, she loved lipsticks and had a lot of them. For the fundraiser, she'd chose a matte, dark red shade. She'd kept her hair down and simple. She was ready an hour before she needed to be.

She hadn't seen Leo once she was ready, so she decided to explore his home. The penthouse was breathtaking, and she loved seeing the city lights. The first time she had been there, well at least aware of being there, it was daylight. At night, there was nothing like the city lights.

She found a white grand piano and couldn't resist. In school, she had joined the band as a piano player after an old neighbor had given her their old keyboard. She loved playing the piano and had bonded with her high school band teacher. Piano became her escape from her reality. The only real piano she had ever played on was the upright piano at school; even now she only had an electric keyboard piano that she hadn't played in a while. She couldn't resist and decided to play after looking around and finding no one. She decided to play her favorite piano piece, Primavera by Ludovico Einaudi.

***

Leo leaned against the column and watched her play a hypnotic song that almost sounded like a repetitive pattern. He'd known she'd taken the band in school but nowhere in his background check did it say that she was talented. Very talented. The piano was there for decoration; it had hardly ever been played.

He'd seen her looking at the view of the city,

looking striking in the beautifully fitted red gown. He was about to announce his presence but was distracted by her lovely back. The dress revealed a large portion of it with the point of the diamond shape opening ending just above her shapely ass. He had never thought much about backs before, but he'd suddenly found hers so damn seductive.

When she sat down on the piano bench, he decided to come closer so he could get a full view of her. When she started playing, he just wanted to listen to her. He didn't know how long he stood there listening, it seemed to go on and on, but he didn't want it to end. The song seemed to go from hopeful to haunting to almost like a sweet lullaby.

A door shut somewhere behind him, and she stopped playing. Looking behind her as if guilty, she jumped a little when she saw him. She blushed.

"That was beautiful," he told her. He wanted her to keep playing. "Who taught you how to play?"

"An old neighbor at first and then school."

"You are very talented." He didn't play, knew no one who played and had never been interested in piano before, but he knew she was good.

"I'm just okay. That was a piece that a lot of pianists probably know or can easily play." She was uncomfortable with compliments.

"It was beautiful, and you are free to use the piano any time you like. No one has played that piano in years. It was just for decoration," he explained.

"What a shame. The piano is gorgeous and finely tuned."

She was embarrassed to be caught by Leo. He looked handsome. He was in a suit, but she didn't think this was his outfit for the night. The creases told her he'd been wearing it all day and though he still looked remarkably neat, he was mussed enough to make her think that he'd spent the majority of the day working. But he still looked devastatingly handsome.

And he was staring at her.

The Dolce & Gabbana gown was surprisingly very comfortable. She liked that it didn't feel fragile, like how she often felt whenever she wore lace. It was a gorgeous dress. She didn't usually like such bold colors that stood out either, but she loved the dress more and more every time she looked at it. The dress was conservative with its high neckline, but it was fitted and molded to her curves, the back opening also made her feel sexy.

"So, what do you think?" she asked as she playfully spun for him to show off the dress.

"I think that I will have a hard time keeping men away from you." She blushed even though she knew he was joking.

"You look beautiful," he added seriously.

"Thank you. The gown is amazing, and I still can't believe you bought both dresses and the shoes!"

He'd spent almost thirteen-grand on both dresses and the shoes. When he took her back to her place, he surprised her with both dresses. He had a hard time convincing her to keep them. Both dresses looked perfect on her, and he'd seen how much she liked the blue dress. Thirteen-grand was how much just one of his mother's dresses cost. He had the money to spend, and if anyone deserved spoiling, it was her. Aside from that, he wanted to spend his money on her. There was probably nothing she could ask for that he wouldn't give her.

"I'm almost afraid to give you what I have in my pocket," he half-joked. Her friend had unwittingly reminded him that his fiancé didn't have an engagement ring. He hadn't known what she liked, but the ring had caught his eye. It had a vintage design that brought her to mind, classy, sensual, and beautiful. The five-carat diamond would look large on her, but he instinctively knew it was meant to be hers.

"What do you have in your pocket?" she asked

suspiciously.

"Your engagement ring."

"What? No way! I don't need one. I don't even like rings."

"You're engaged to me, Freya, of course, you need a ring," he replied as he pulled out the small black box. She looked at the case like it would bite her. He sighed knowing she wouldn't reach for it herself. He opened the case and pulled the ring out himself before taking her hand. They both watched as he slid the ring on her.

"Oh my...that's...it's gorgeous," she breathed out. "But you're insane!" she insisted. "I'm going to get robbed wearing this! Is it real...of course, it is! Oh my God! I can't even...How much did it cost? Never mind! I don't want to know." She was tongue tied as she stared at the ring in awe. "This is too much," she finally said, looking up at him.

"Hardly. You're engaged to me," he replied.

"Temporarily," she added.

"Just enjoy it, Freya. Enjoy all of it while we're together. There's no point arguing with me about how I want to spend my money," he told her as he took her arms and gently pulled her close to him. "Just enjoy all of it," he added softly and then did what he'd wanted to do since the moment he'd laid eyes on her in that dress.

The kiss dazed Freya more than the ring. She knew it was coming when he'd leaned down, and she would not lie and say she didn't want it. She angled her head and sighed as his lips touched hers. She lost herself in the kiss. It was a demanding kiss, but she was more than willing. A deep, wet kiss that left her hot and nearly panting.

"Are you still heading out?" a voice had her jumping away from Leo. Leo looked annoyed as he glared at Vito, who smirked at them.

"I'm tempted to say no," Leo replied looking at her. "But she looks too beautiful not to show off." She blushed. He took her hand and led her back to the piano. "I'll be ready in a half an hour. The piano is yours." He gave her a quick peck, making her lips tingle before he and Vito left her alone.

She didn't know much about Leo, except that he was determined to protect her, and that for some reason, she trusted him. He'd insisted from the beginning that their engagement will be as real as it gets, just with a deadline. Did that mean that they would have sex? He'd kissed her more times in the last few weeks than she had been kissed in the last three years! And she liked it. She liked him.

Being with Leo made her feel safe and protected. He also made her feel like a woman. He looked at her in a way that made her feel sensually feminine. Maybe it was because he just seemed all man, like he didn't have a soft side, yet he was a gentleman. He was hard, protective, and unpredictable. When he talked to her, he made her feel like she had his undivided attention; as if there was no one else around, and he devoted his whole attention to her. That was probably what she loved so much about him.

***

"Relax," Leo whispered to her as the valet opened the limo door. Leo stepped out and held out a hand to her. She took his hand, gathered up her courage and exited the vehicle. The San Francisco Mozzafiato Hotel was bursting with lights and money. Leo tucked her hand into the crook of his arm and led her to the entrance. She was surprised to find a few journalists and cameras flashing.

"I wonder what *Mozzafiato* means," she whispered to him.

"It's Italian for breathtaking," Leo answered.

"Really? It's a beautiful word," she responded as he led her up the steps. "It's a beautiful hotel," she added.

"Thank you," Leo replied.

"What?"

"It is a Costa hotel."

"You own a hotel too?" she asked in surprise.

"Yes, we own a couple of them here, in Lake Tahoe and Las Vegas."

"Wow," she sounded lame, but she had no other words to describe her surprise.

"We could have stayed here tonight, but I like being in the comfort of my own bed."

"Whose political campaign is it for?" she asked, trying to distract herself from the knowledge that Leonardo Costa was a wealthy man.

"The Governor."

"What?!" she whispered frantically. She wasn't ready for this. He gave her a small smile and led her towards the ballroom entrance.

"Smile," he whispered.

They were often stopped, people wanted to speak to Leo, and everyone seemed to know him. She hadn't said much, she kept a frozen smile on her face, nodded and shook some hands as Leo introduced her as his fiancé. Everyone seemed shocked, and she wanted to tell them that she was just as shocked as they were.

When they finally made it into the ballroom, she was blown away by the luxurious decoration. It was a lot fancier than any party or wedding she had ever been to. They were led to a large round table near the front by a waiter, and she was surprised to find her fake-future-in-laws at the table next to theirs.

Giovanni and Valentina were well situated but rose to greet Leo and Freya as they neared. She was even more surprised when Valentina *and* Giovanni greeted her like she'd been part of their family for years. They both hugged her enthusiastically. She almost felt overwhelmed when Giovanni turned to introduce her to the other guests at their table as his daughter. Not daughter in law or even Leo's fiancé. *His daughter.* It wasn't that big of a deal, she knew families that considered their in-laws to be one of their own children or parents, but no one had really ever called her their daughter. Her mother certainly never had.

Leo was as popular inside the ballroom as he was in the lobby of the five-star hotel. She was introduced to so many people, but she couldn't remember a single name. She sighed in relief when they finally settled down at their table. Someone went

101

up onto the podium and spoke, but she was too busy trying not to move and draw attention to herself that she zoned out.

She recognized the Governor of California talking on stage and everyone clapping. She had no idea what he was saying, but people were laughing. Did he make a joke? She turned to Leo and found him watching her.

"What?" she whispered when she realized he was smiling at her. It took her a moment to ask her question because his smile blindsided her. It was a roguish and playful smile like he knew something she didn't.

"You look beautiful. Bored but beautiful," he replied.

"No, just nervous."

"Really?" he asked playfully.

"Yea-" she stopped when she realized he was kidding. He leaned close to her.

"Relax. They're normal people too," he half-joked in a whisper in her ear.

"I just don't want to embarrass you," she whispered into his ear. He pulled back and looked at her a little surprised by her confession. She blushed. He reached for her hand as they both faced the stage again and held it on her lap. She didn't know why but it was the most comforting thing she'd ever felt and somehow, she was able to relax. There was just something about Leo that made her worries go away with just a simple touch, a look, or a smile.

***

"Dance with me," he said to her as she finally gave up on her dessert. The six-course meal was ridiculously rich and probably as ridiculously expensive, but delicious. However, after six of them, she wasn't sure she could walk out of there or if the seams of her dress would split.

"Dance how?" she asked.

"Dance as in me holding you close while I think about taking that dress off of you," he replied bluntly. Her surprise showed, and he laughed, a small one, before pulling her up on to her feet.

He held her close to him as the band played a slow song she didn't recognize.

"Your parents introduced me as their daughter," she told him as she looked up at him. Her four-inch heels gave her much needed height, but Leo was over six feet tall. She loved the feel of his arms holding her.

"We're Italian. Family is family," he merely explained.

"You might think it's weird, but that's the first time someone has ever called me their daughter," she confessed.

"Your mother didn't?" he asked.

"Nope. She hated being called mom. Like I told you, she introduced me as her sister sometimes and sometimes, very rarely, she'd say I was her kid. But mostly, she didn't bother to tell people who I was unless they asked," she answered.

He didn't say anything, and she didn't blame him. What do you say to someone who confesses something like that anyway? Instead, he surprised her when he twirled her and then pulled her back to him. She couldn't help but laugh as she fell back against his body.

"Your mother is selfish and filled with regrets, but you are something special. If you don't believe anything else I ever tell you, believe that you are special, special to me." He made her melt against him. She was afraid he'd make her fall in love with him.

"Do they teach you how to charm girls in rich people school?" she joked with a smile.

SET THE CITY ON FIRE

"We're not allowed to divulge rich people teachings," he replied with a wink. He twirled her again, this time she returned to him more gracefully.

"Stay with me tonight."

It was a request. Was she ready for that? Did she want to? She did. It has been nearly three years since someone had attracted her. It wasn't just because he was so alluring and handsome, there was something about Leo that called to her. There was just something about Leo.

"Okay," she replied.

***

She'd been silent on their way back to his penthouse. He'd had to keep his hands off of her since she'd agreed two hours ago. He would have dragged her out, then and there, but he had obligations to meet, and he wanted to show her off.

Freya in that red dress could bring him to his knees with little to no effort on her part. And he wasn't the only one. By tomorrow morning, she'd be on everyone's radar, which was the whole point, but he hated sharing her. He hadn't wanted to let anyone else dance with her, let alone touch her. He granted his father permission *only* because it was expected.

She'd seemed to have enjoyed herself after her initial shyness; his mother had forced her to talk with the other women. But they were the first to leave the event. As soon as his obligations were met, he took her hand and headed home.

They rode the elevator up in silence, but he'd kept his hold on her hand. She was nervous but excited. She blushed when she realized Vito left them alone. The elevator filled with unspoken desire, and when it dinged she nearly jumped out of her skin.

He led her to the same room she'd woken up on that first day, his room. He closed the door before turning to face her. She could hear her heartbeats as he pulled her close to him, before taking her mouth in a kiss that left her knees weak. He pulled her close to him, held her tighter and deepened their kiss.

Freya felt like she was drowning in him. All she knew was Leo, the taste of him, the smell of him and the feel of him. Her arms held on to him as he practically lifted her against him. Their kiss was hot and wet. Definitely something she'd never forget. She wanted to lose herself in him. Wanted every part of her body to touch his. She felt like she was drowning in him.

His hand found the zipper situated on her lower back and lowered it. He unbuttoned the top and slid the gown off her shoulders before she stopped him.

"It's umm," she couldn't seem to look at him. "It's been a while," she explained as she turned to look out the window, into the beautiful night sky of San Francisco.

"Then we better make it worth your while," he said into her neck as his arms wrapped around her. Her neck tilted to the side, giving him access to her precious skin. She was shy and inexperienced but willing and responsive. He carefully slipped the dress off her, revealing her curvy body. It had driven him mad thinking about what she had on under her gown. The opened back showed no bra straps, and he almost swallowed his tongue at the thought of her bare breasts, and he was damn right. She stood in front of him in nothing but a black lacy thong and nude heels.

Her breasts were large, larger than he'd expect, and oh so fucking perfect. Her nipples begged for him, and he couldn't help but answer their call. He pulled her close against him, kissed her, wanting to take everything she had to offer. He cupped her breasts, pushing them together before trailing kisses down her neck and to the delicious offering in front of him. He'd always been an ass man, but her cleavage could convince him to change his mind. His fingers pinched one nipple as his mouth took the other, savoring the taste of her skin, the feel of her. Her moan begged him for more.

His hand left her nipple and reached down, grazed her thigh before cupping her mound and rubbing her, almost petting her. His fingers slid inside of her flimsy underwear, finding her wet and ready for him. He worked his fingers up and down her slit, flicking her clit with his thumb, before entering her. She shivered as he added a second finger. Her hands gripped his arms.

"On the bed," he commanded as he abruptly pulled out and away from her. She was all woman, ample curves displayed in black lace, wild, dark hair enticing him and lips begging to be kissed. He didn't give her a chance to be shy; he picked her up and laid her in the center of the bed, kneeling between her legs. He slipped her heels off, discarding them somewhere behind him and nearly ripped her thong off her. One day he'll fuck her with heels on but tonight he wanted her completely naked and so wrapped up in him, she'd lose herself. He took her leg and laid a gentle kiss on her ankle. She had beautiful skin, soft and smooth. Even her feet felt soft. He kissed his way down to her calf.

"Everything. About. You. Is. Perfect," he whispered each word in between kisses, down her leg. He kissed, licked, and nipped; each kiss and each touch sent tingles through every nerve in her body.

A soft cry escaped her lips as he touched her center. He placed a gentle kiss on her mound then made his way up to her stomach, breasts, and neck until finally meeting her lips. It was a hungry kiss, filled with promise. Her arms wrapped around his neck as she held him as close to her body as she could. One hand gripped her hair, pulling her head back, exposing her neck to his lips, while his other hand pinched her nipple.

Her hands found the buttons of his shirt, but he stopped her as she reached to undo them. He pulled away and quickly undid his buttons. His shirt was discarded as swiftly as her clothes had been. She sat up to touch the hard ridges of his muscles. He was hard everywhere. His muscles rippled under her touch. The hair disappearing into his pants made her mouth water.

She tried to help him take the rest of his clothes off, but she seemed to get in the way. He quickly took over, taking control of his clothes and swiftly undressed. He then stood before her, naked and hard, his hand fisting his penis. All she could do was watch him as his hand worked his length. He was big in every way physically. Everything about him was meant to intimidate. His penis stood erect facing her, looking scarier than when she'd lost her virginity. He was massive, but she wanted to touch him, to taste him, to have him. She crawled closer to the edge of the bed to .

explore him, but he stopped her just short of touching him by capturing her wrists.

He surprised her when he suddenly turned her, flipping her to her stomach. One hand pulled her back against his. Her breasts felt heavy and swollen. He reached around her and grasped her breasts in each hand. Then squeezed them, kneaded them, and pushed them together. He rolled her nipples between his fingers and pinched them almost painfully as his mouth found her neck once again. Her arms held on to his neck.

She let out a gasp as he suddenly positioned her down on her hands and knees on the bed, propping her up. She was embarrassed at the thought of him seeing all of her. His hand pushed down on her shoulders, pressing her head and chest to the bed, her center completely exposed.

Any thought of shyness was dispelled by the touch of his tongue where she ached the most. She moaned loudly as she felt his tongue circle her clit. His fingers slowly entered her as he sucked on her. She didn't care how loud she was, nor did she care that she was pushing back against his fingers. She was lost in the pleasure. She almost lost her mind when he pulled away on the brink of her orgasm.

His sudden entrance quickly cut any thought of

displeasure from the empty feelings she had. She lost her breath at his forceful entry. He pulled back and pushed back in, just as suddenly as his intrusion. She'd never felt anything like this.

Leo hadn't meant to claim her so fast. He'd wanted to draw out their foreplay, but his dick wasn't interested in waiting. He gripped her hips as he pushed deeper. She was tight. Too damn tight. He only had half of his dick in her, and it was almost a struggle.

"You're so fucking tight," he groaned. The muscles of her pussy were fighting his intrusion. Her small cries fueled his blood. He worked himself into her inch by inch until he buried his whole dick so deep in her. They moaned together as if they were meant to do this. Meant to be this close and to fit so damn perfect together.

He pulled out and thrust in, hard. Repeated. Again. She let out a cry with each thrust, encouraging him to fuck her harder. She tried meeting his thrusts, but he quickly took control. He owned her body as he fucked her. He pushed her flat onto the bed with her ass in the air. One hand resting on her shoulder for leverage and his other gripping her waist as he angled her hips for better access. He never wanted to leave her pussy. He wanted to stay buried so deep in her that she'd never forget him. He wanted Freya to feel him in every inch of her body. He wanted to brand her, mark her as his.

She felt every inch, every ridge, every sensation he sent through her body. Her orgasm sent her spiraling. She moaned, in her ears, she sounded like she was screaming and maybe she was. Her orgasm ripped out of her, sending stars behind her eyes. She cried his name. His thrusts faster and harder, his grip tightened. Then he cried out as his thrusts became erratic. He continued plunging deep until he emptied himself into her. He laid on top of her, breathing hard, still buried in her.

His arms came around, pulled her to her side, and held her close to him.

Chapter Twelve

The cold in the empty room woke her up. The delicious ache in her body stirred memories from the night before, and she could still feel him inside her. He was insatiable, but then again, so was she.

She sat up and stretched. The sun was shining brightly behind the shades, and the clock on the nightstand registered 10:00AM. She covered her face with her hand and rested her elbows on her lap, regretting not taking her makeup off last night. She probably looked horrible this morning and was harboring a serious set of raccoon eyes right now...and all night. *Gross.*

"I hope you're not regretting the night before," Leo drawled. She looked up to find him looking too attractive, leaning against the doorway.

"No, I–I was thinking I probably look pretty hideous right about now," she confessed. He wore jeans, unbuttoned, the happy trail teasing her.

"You do look a mess, but I like it. Get in the shower. I'll ask Paula to make breakfast and then join you." He didn't wait for a response. She was about to wrap a sheet around her before she got up, but then she realized it would be silly since he was well acquainted with her naked body. She let the sheet drop and strolled to the bathroom, her muscles lusciously loose from their night play.

His bathroom was gorgeous. A large bathtub rest at the end, against the window in the walk-in shower; there were no doors or steps, you simply just walked to the shower. It was a large open space, and she liked it. She liked the water warm, rather than hot, and stood under the spray while she waited for him. It wasn't long before she felt his arms wrap around her, surrounding her body.

Her body responded to his touch, nipples hard, breasts swollen, and her center craving him, heavy with arousal. She turned to face him; she wanted to touch him. He'd done most of the touching last night, and today she wanted to touch him and taste him. He let her hands explore his body, scrutinizing every ridge of muscle and hair. She leaned in and kissed his chest, nipping and licking his skin the way he did to her last night. His groan told her he liked it and his hands gripped her waist tighter as her hands touched his length. Her mouth watered at the thought of tasting him.

She didn't hesitate, knowing she'd lose her nerve. She knelt and brought her mouth to his penis. Her tongue darted out, licking the head, causing it to jerk. When he didn't stop her, she took him into her mouth, swirling her tongue around the head. She loved the taste of his skin. She took as much as she could of him in her mouth and sucked, inciting a moan from him. His hands gathered her wet hair in a firm grip as he guided her up and down his length. She'd only done it twice and hadn't cared much before, it was just something they had wanted, but this time she wanted it too. She wanted to pleasure him. The slightly salty taste of his semen excited her, and she sucked harder, wanting more.

She growled her displeasure when he pulled out of her mouth, his grip on her hair stopping her from following. He didn't give her time to argue because he picked her up and pressed her back against the wall, her legs wrapping around his waist. One hand supported her back while the other cupped her breast before adding pressure to her nipple. She moaned as his mouth came down, drawing a nipple into his mouth. He bit her nipple, making her moan from pain and pleasure. While keeping her back against the wall, the hand that supported her back moved down and found her aching center from behind. She cried out as his fingers entered her. She wanted more.

"Please," she cried out, unable to say more. His head lifted from her chest, and he positioned her, holding her up, before guiding himself into her. She moaned as his thick length slid into her. He held her against the wall as he pumped in and out of her, his hips controlling his thrusts. Her legs wrapped tightly around his waist, wanting to keep him in her. He continued a slow and steady rhythm that had her begging for more.

"Harder," she cried. His mouth absorbed her cry as he slammed into her, answering her demand. She buried her head against his shoulder as she fought her release, wanting it to last longer. Her orgasm peaked, and all she could do was ride the waves. Her release was followed by his. His pelvis grinding hard against hers as he emptied himself into her, both of them moaning, crying out with their release.

***

She'd never felt so satiated in her life. She and Leo had practically spent the whole time in his bedroom, naked. Who would have thought you could spend all night and all day having sex and still want more? Even now, as Romano drove her home after Leo had taken her out to dinner, she wanted Leo again.

She had her doubts about what they'd done, but he'd convinced her to just enjoy it. Growing up, her life had been so out of control, thanks to her mother. As an adult, she craved the solitary and routine. She spent ten years perfecting that control and routine, and in just one night, he'd destroyed all of it. And she liked it. Not once had she mentioned the fact that they hadn't used protection. Maybe he knew she was on birth control, maybe he expected her to stop him if she hadn't been, or maybe he didn't care, but she should have. She should have insisted on it but either she didn't care, or she trusted him.

He'd wanted her to stay another night but the commute in the morning would have been nearly an hour, and she needed to get home to take care of her pets. He'd offered to have someone take care of them, but she owed it to Honey and Lestat to come home.

In the end, he'd taken her to dinner with plans to go home with her but received an emergency call near the end of their dinner, and he had to leave. He left Romano in charge of her safety as if she couldn't make it home on her own.

Romano kept up small talk with her on the drive home. Out of all of Leo's men, he seemed to be the youngest, most outgoing, and personable. He had an easy smile and was a stickler for rules. Romano had watched her, making sure her seatbelt was securely strapped before he even started the car and was the safest driver she had ever met. He made a complete stop at every stop sign they'd encountered, *no rolling stop for him*, and he never failed to use his blinkers. He drove like he was delivering someone precious and Marco, the other bodyguard, had rolled his eyes the entire time. Marco was older than Romano, but she didn't think it was by much. He was quiet, only really talked to complain about Romano's careful driving.

It didn't surprise her that Romano had insisted on walking her to the door and it also didn't surprise her when he insisted on checking her studio first. She thanked him, and he gave her such a boyish grin that she couldn't help but like him.

She waited until she was sure they were gone before she took Honey for a walk. It was later than usual, but Honey really needed a walk. She normally left a large training pad in the bathroom when she knew she'd be gone longer than usual and Honey had used it in emergency situations. The pad had been soaked, and she didn't blame Honey since Freya had planned to be home last night or at the very latest, this morning. Though it was a little late, she took Honey on a long walk to make up for leaving her inside all day. Leo would probably have a heart attack if he knew she was out alone this late.

***

Leo had handed them the perfect weapon against him. It was like Leo handing the gun that they'll use to shoot him with. He was tempted to kill her now, but the boss wasn't ready, and he'd have to explain himself. It wasn't the right time, but he was tempted just to end it. This bitch was the reason Leo was still alive. He didn't even try to hide. He stood there in the dark for her to see, but she was too stupid to notice him, too distracted by her useless dog. Her cat was a better guard than the dog, it had hissed at him through the window, and tried to attack him through the glass that separated them when he'd peaked in one night. He'd wanted to kill her then too; it would have been easy to make it look like a break-in. He hadn't because the boss said it wasn't time. He didn't get why they had to wait. Leo had taken what was supposed to be his. He hated Leo more than anything, and the sick thing was Leo called him a friend. Ha! Every time he'd spoken to Leo, he had to control the urge to shoot the *stronzo una merda*.

Chapter Thirteen

Killa and his boys had held up and robbed people in the past. What they were about to do wasn't new to him. They'd done it enough times. They go in and wave the gun around to get everyone to give up their shit. By the time they reach the next stop, they're out of there. No biggie. Except for this time, it wouldn't be the same. Today, he was going to kill someone and make it look like an accident. It wasn't the first time he'd kill a mother fucker, but it was the first time he'd be killing a woman. It didn't matter to him though, as long as he got his money.

Though he didn't like not knowing who he was doing a job for, it wasn't a big deal as long as they paid. He'd been given the first half of the payment, five grand. He'd get the other half once the bitch was dead. She was probably some dude's mistress. His boys didn't know this part of the plan, and he wasn't planning on telling them because he wasn't giving 'em his money. He was the one doin' the killin', that's why they call him Killa.

He knew what she looked like, a pretty lil bitch. Too bad he's going to fuck up her pretty face with a bullet. He received a call to let him know where she was, and he told his boys he needed extra cash. They were down; they're always down for him.

He pulled the bandana over his nose. The train would be approaching soon. He knew which train she was in, whoever hired him had someone watching the bitch. He could see the headlights approaching. He stepped onto the platform for car number eight. He nodded to his boys. "You good?"

"I'm good."

"You?"

"I'm good, man."

"Let's do this."

***

Freya couldn't hide the smile or her engagement ring on Monday morning. Lena's eyes nearly bulged out of her head when she saw the ring. Four hours later, Freya took off her engagement ring and pushed it deep into her pocket where she knew it would bother her, but at least it would be safe. Freya needed to go to the city to have some documents legalized at a consulate for work. She would normally have driven, but she'd been to this consulate before, and parking was a nightmare, but at least the BART station was only three blocks away. She knew the ring would catch a lot of attention. Though the city was generally safe, she didn't want to take chances and decided to hide the ring that probably cost more than all of her possessions combined.

The trip to the city was uneventful. The trip back, however, was at the beginning of rush hour. The train was crowded, and she had no choice but to stand by the doorway. Trouble started when she was six stops away from her work, at the edge of East Oakland.

"Alright nobody moves! I want wallets!" A guy covered with a hood and half his face concealed with a bandana yelled as he raised a gun in the air. Two other men dressed similarly spread around him. While the two other men roughed up other passengers demanding their wallets, the man with a gun turned to her.

"Let start with you, sweetheart. Why don't you show me what you've got?" he said mockingly while pointing the gun in her direction.

She didn't know if it was her original paranoia or stress, but she swore he was talking about the ring. The ring. The one, deep in her pocket, that's poking her. She struggled with her purse reaching for her wallet as he came closer.

She was looking down in her bag and didn't know what happened, but the gun went off, people screamed, and she was knocked off her feet. Another shot went off; more people screamed as the train stopped. The crowd seemed to surge, rushing to get out while people struggled with the would-be robbers. She felt a stinging pain on the side of her head when she fell and hit the corner of the seats. She lost consciousness for a moment, but when she came to, people were still rushing in and out, struggling with each other.

***

Leo had a long night. An empty warehouse by the docks that he'd planned on turning into a casino and club had caught on fire. Whether it was an accident or arson was still unknown. After spending half of the night dealing with that mess and spending all day fucking Freya into oblivion, he felt exhausted.

"Leo," Vito called him as he headed to his room.

"Freya's fine, but something happened," Vito

rushed. Leo schooled himself to hide his reaction, but he knew he let his worry slip and Vito understood. "Freya's fine," Vito repeated knowing that it was important to Leo.

"What happened?" Leo asked as they turned and headed back to the elevator.

"Not much detail but an incident happened on BART, and she was there. Contact from police recognized her."

***

"Do you feel dizzy, nauseated or have a headache?" the paramedic asked her again as he cleaned the wound on her temple.

"That's my friend, get out of my way!" Freya heard Lena's voice before she could answer. She expected Lena to come. Freya knew that Lena spent all day checking the local news to make sure that her world was safe. Lena who became a mother in her early teens and now has two children had become the mother hen of their group of friends. Lena checked the news to make sure that everyone was okay. It had taken nearly forty-five minutes to get the scene sorted out. Police had briefly spoken to her before taking her to the paramedic to be treated.

"I'm okay. It just stings," Freya answered the

paramedic.

"You said you lost consciousness?"

"It was only for a second. I probably had the breath knocked out of me," she answered just as Lena appeared at her side. Lena nearly knocked the paramedic away when she engulfed her in a hug.

"Are you okay? I saw the news, and I was worried! And you stopped responding! And-"

"Ma'am, please step back. We're treating her right now," the young paramedic interrupted Lena. Lena moved next to her like a worried mother even though she was only five years older than Freya. The paramedic finished cleaning the blood from her face and wound before partially closing it with small bandages.

"You need stitches on that, and the hospital needs to make sure you don't have a concussion," the paramedics told her. "Let's get you loaded in-"

"No, I'm okay. I-"

"We'll take her to the hospital," a familiar voice interrupted. She turned to find Leo and Vito.

"It would be best if-"

"I'm her fiancé. I'll take her there right now. Just let the hospital know we're on our way. For safety reasons we prefer to take her unless you can fit us both in there too," Leo replied. The paramedic wanted to argue but could tell Leo wasn't going to budge. In the end, he had her sign papers stating she was going against their order and was cleared to be taken to the hospital.

She assured Lena that she would be okay before giving her the Consulate documents. Leo ordered Vito to take Lena back to work before leading Freya to the SUV where Drago awaited. Until now, Leo hadn't directly addressed her but instead gave orders to everyone until he had her in the back seat, next to him.

"What happened?" he asked her as his hand and eyes roamed all over her, making sure she was alright. She told him everything, even her paranoia about the ring.

"Where's your ring?" he asked. She took the ring out of her pocket. He took it and slid it back on her finger, where it felt right. "I don't ever want you to worry about the ring's cost. Its cost means nothing to me. Are you hurt anywhere else?" he asked as he checked the wound on her temple closer.

"No, just my face," she answered truthfully. She didn't understand it, but Leo made her feel safe. She'd felt relieved the moment she saw him.

***

The cops came and questioned her again after she'd gotten her stitches done. Leo had stayed quiet, for the most part, but stayed at her side while Drago stood guard outside of the room she was being treated in.

"I want you to move in with me," Leo told her as soon as the doctor left to get her discharge papers.

"What? No, that's crazy," she replied in surprise. She'd been prescribed pain meds for the stitches and the bruising on her cheek and was given a shot of antibiotics to help prevent infection. She was given some pain meds, but she knew it wasn't enough to make her high. She must have heard him right.

"I need to know that you're safe," Leo replied.

"I'll be fine. This isn't really something you can control," she answered. "Next time, I'll drive," she reassured him.

"Why didn't you tell the cops about the ring?" he asked her. She hadn't mentioned anything about her paranoia over her ring. Instead, she told them that she assumed he'd targeted her since she was closest to him.

Two men had been captured, and one

escaped. The one with the gun had gotten away, and the shots that were fired were from his struggle against passengers who tried to be heroes. The bullets hadn't hit anyone but caused a panic which was when most of the injuries occurred.

"I didn't think they needed to know I was paranoid."

"They could have targeted you for your ring."

"But they didn't know I had the ring."

"So why were you paranoid that he knew about the ring?" he asked.

"Because I had a feeling that he knew me even though I didn't recognize him," she answered honestly. It could have been her paranoia, but she did feel like he'd targeted her.

Leo hadn't wanted to make her more paranoid, but he knew he couldn't bully her into moving in with him. He didn't believe in coincidence. Someone was gunning for him. The warehouse fire and the attack on Freya were too close. Someone wanted him distracted by the fire while they went after her. Taking her from her apartment, especially when he had the place watched would have been too obvious, so they staged an attacked that could have been pure coincidence. Leo knew it had to be connected. He was the heir of the

Costa family; it's why he'd been targeted before when Freya had saved him. Their engagement had put a target on her back, something he hadn't considered.

"For your safety and my peace of mind, I need you to move in with me. Our engagement was announced to the world on Saturday, and the moment you're alone, you were attacked." He wanted to scare her so that she'd agree.

"You really think I was being targeted?" she asked.

"I don't believe in coincidence, and you said it yourself. You thought you were singled out."

"I thought I was paranoid. I can't...I mean, I have pets, and work is out here. The commute would be ridiculous, and I have a lease on my studio."

"I'll buy you a house when you decide to move out of my place. You'll have a driver to take you anywhere you want. I just need to be sure you're safe. At least, until our engagement is over."

"A house? No. And my pets–"

"Can move in too," he answered begrudgingly.

"This is crazy. I–"

"Just temporarily, Freya. Just until I know you're safe."

***

He'd taken her back to her place from the hospital to get what she needed for the night and pick up her pets. She enjoyed watching Vito struggle with Honey and Lestat while loading them into her car. She hadn't wanted to ruin Leo's car and had Vito tow them in her car, which he drove back to the penthouse. She'd gotten an overnight bag, and Leo assured her not to worry about the rest of her things, someone would deal with them tomorrow. She'd called work who understood that she needed to take a couple of days off while they sat in traffic during peak rush hour. Leo hadn't said much to her; he was busy on his own phone, giving orders.

The penthouse was a welcome sight. She was exhausted. Though she and Leo hadn't talked much on their way to his home, he'd kept a hold on her throughout the drive, either by holding her hand or pulling her close to him or simply just touching her. It helped reassure her that she was fine and that she was safe.

"You can use the same bedroom to store your things or if you need space," Leo told her as they stepped into the hallway that led to the bedrooms. "But

I would like you to stay with me, in my bed, if that's what you want."

She hadn't even thought about where she'd stay until he'd mentioned it. She simply nodded and went to his room.

"What would you like for dinner?" he asked as he deposited her overnight bag on the chair.

"I'm not hungry. I want a bath though," she answered, unsure of what to do.

"You have to eat to take your meds," he replied as he walked towards her. Oh yes, the pain meds and antibiotics for her stitches and bruised face. "Tell you what, you take a bath, I'll get the food, we'll eat and then head to bed."

She didn't know if it was welcomed, but she hugged him. His arms wrapped around her and they stood there holding each other for a moment. "Go," he told her, untangling from her. "Take a bath, and I'll be there in a moment." He turned her towards the bathroom before giving her a little push to get her moving.

Affection wasn't new to him, after all, he was Italian, and his family liked hugging each other, in his opinion, more than necessary. He'd been with other women before, and he'd held them, kissed them, and fucked them, but Freya was different. Sure, they had slept together, he'd explored every inch of her body with his eyes, hands, and mouth. He knew more about her than anyone probably ever did. He'd had her most intimately, but the affection was different. A simple touch from her had the ability to cool his temper like she had the night he'd introduced her to his family, and he was ready to beat his brother to a pulp. A hug from her? He'd felt like she was breaking down walls he didn't know he had.

***

Leo looked over at Freya. In the dark, you couldn't see the bruises, but he saw them in his head. They were imprinted in his mind. He got up, already dressed, knowing he'd be leaving tonight. He'd waited for Drago to find the fucker and got dressed when he got the text. Romano would be taking over guard duty while Freya slept. As for Leo? Well, ...he's going to make people pay.

***

He was fucked. He'd fucked up cause some fucking asshole tried to be a hero. He kicked a bottle on the ground. God damn mother fucker! The bitch wasn't dead, he'd checked the news, and his boys got caught. He could still fix this. God damn son of a bitch! He wanted to scream. It should have been easy. He punched a newspaper box, hard enough to crack the plastic cover. Son of a bitch! His hand hurt like a mother fucker. He wanted to kick it, to take his anger out on it, but the metal box would hurt him more than he could damage it. He'd shoot it, but he'd lost the gun during the fight.

He was so busy fuming he didn't notice the black car following him until the lights were suddenly turned on. The car pulled up next to him and slowed. The black heavily tinted window lowered. A good-looking mother fucker stared at him. He wondered if this guy was here cause of the fuck up. Well, they ain't getting the five-grand back.

"The fuck you looking at?" he demanded as he came closer to the car.

"A dead man."

"Fuck you mean–" Something hit him hard on his back, sending him to the ground. Fuck his back hurt. Did he break bones? He tried to get up but only managed to roll to his back. A big ass dude stood over him holding a fucking pipe.

"Fuck you man," Killa yelled. He tried to stop the pipe he saw coming towards his face, but he was too slow. A blinding pain on the side of his head was quickly and blissfully followed by unconsciousness.

Chapter Fourteen

The arm wrapped around her was heavy but comfortable. This was the first time she'd woken up with him next to her. She didn't want to move and just lay there absorbing his warmth and how right it felt. She turned to face him and cuddled closer to his body and to her delight, his arm tightened around her. She decided then and there that she never wanted to leave his arms as she drifted back to sleep.

***

The next time she woke up, she was alone again, and the clock on the nightstand told her it was nearly noon. She stretched before leaving the comfort of the bed. She'd worn her underwear and his shirt to bed when she'd realized she'd forgotten to bring her pajamas. But then again, her pajamas were far from sexy, just old t-shirts and old pajama pants. She liked his shirt better. She wasn't sure what she was supposed to do so she decided to start with bathroom necessities. She took his robe, the same one she'd used the first time she'd been there and wore it for modesty as she stepped out of the room. Her bruised faced looked awful in the morning light. The dark blue and black mark on her cheek made the rest of her face look pale. It hurt too; it was sensitive as she brushed her teeth and washed her face.

She headed towards the dining room and was happy to find Paula setting up a plate.

"Good morning," she greeted Paula who smiled in return.

"Mr. Costa had to leave for work, but Romano is at your service today," Paula explained. "Marco is walking your dog at the moment, and your cat is in your room. Mr. Costa didn't want him to get lost in the house."

"Thank you," she replied as she took her seat. "How long have you been with Leo?" she asked Paula.

"Over ten years now ma'am."

"Oh please, don't call me that. It makes me feel old," she joked. "Freya is fine."

Paula nodded her acknowledgment before leaving her to eat alone.

She and Leo had talked about what she could do with her things. He horrified her when he told her that he wanted to pay for her apartment while she stayed with him. She told him that was a waste of money. In the end, she decided that she'd let her apartment go, put most of her things into storage and the things she wanted, like her books, she'd take here. She'd been ordered not to do any lifting and told her he'd make sure the people he'd send to help her would make sure of it. She wanted to roll her eyes, but she'd admit that her face did hurt a bit.

By the time she'd finished eating, Marco and Honey had returned from their walk, and her dog happily greeted her.

"How was the walk?" Freya asked him.

"Best behaved dog," Marco almost growled.

"Breakfast?" she asked him, there was plenty of food left on the table.

"Already had it. Romano is the one with the bottomless stomach," Marco replied just as Romano joined them.

"I smell bacon," was Romano's way of greeting.

"There's plenty," Freya replied.

Romano didn't need an invite. He plopped himself across from her as he took a piece of bacon from the serving plate. Paula returned and frowned at Romano before handing him a plate.

"That's her food," Paula scolded Romano who didn't seem affected.

"That's alright; there's no way I can eat all of that," Freya replied.

"You don't eat enough. Mr. Costa said you have to eat more before you take your medicines."

Freya could only smile. A couple of days with Paula and she was more of a mother to Freya than her own mother had been.

"It was delicious, but I am full."

"I'll get your medicine, and you need to drink your juice," Paula replied before heading back to the kitchen.

"I need a little bit of time to get ready, but I'd like to get going with my apartment as soon as possible. When can we go?" she asked Romano.

"Whenever you're ready, a crew is already there

to pack up your apartment. They will do all the packing for you, and Leo said no lifting for you, period. They are vouched for, don't worry." Romano's answer puzzled her. Vouched for? She didn't think people said that kind of thing nowadays. She didn't mind having someone pack her things like her kitchen and furniture, but she had a thing about other people touching her clothes and books.

It didn't take her long to get ready; she figured she'd shower after she got done packing and unpacking. The drive to her studio was quick, probably because she'd been lost in her head. She didn't like the idea of not having her own place and depending on Leo. She spent her whole life trying to build security and stability, but Leo had a way of making her feel complete while he simultaneously wreaked havoc on her life. He gets what he wants, but he doesn't control her, or at least she didn't feel controlled even if he was essentially taking over her life.

***

Junior 'Killa' Goldberg was stinking up the warehouse with his piss. He was nothing but a thug trying to make quick money, but he'd made the wrong choice. He'd tried to kill Freya and would have succeeded if it wasn't for a passenger trying to be a hero. Hell, he was a hero, he'd saved Freya from death. Leo will have to make sure the man got something. It didn't take long for Junior to start spilling his guts. By the time Drago was finished breaking his arms, he was telling them everything he ever knew. He'd been hired to eliminate Freya, but he didn't know who hired him. Leo guessed he was employed by the same rat hiding in the shadow who had tried to kill Leo.

It wasn't the first time Junior had robbed and killed people, but it would be the last time because he'd made the mistake of targeting Freya. Junior was crying, begging for his life, and pissing all over himself; he wasn't much of a 'killa' now. He'd pointed the gun at Freya and had every intention of killing her, and for that, Leo was the one who got to kill him. You could tell a lot about a man when he's staring down the barrel of a gun. He felt no remorse for pulling the trigger. He handed the gun to Vito who removed the attached silencer and would be in charge of making sure it was untraceable to them. The cleanup crew was already there. The body would be sent to the crematorium to be turned to ashes and then dumped into the bay. He'd let the others live since the cops had them and he believed Junior when he told them they knew nothing. Lucky for them.

***

She hadn't needed to lift a hand, in fact, she wasn't allowed to. She was glad that Paula had come with them to help her pack her clothes and personal items. Her clothes and her books were the only things she really needed to take. The rest of her things were packed by the "crew" which consisted of two men and two women, excessive in her opinion but they were out of there within a couple of hours. All of her possessions were loaded into a van. It wasn't until she saw the boxes being loaded into the cargo van that she realized she had a lot of things. Not knowing what she'd need, she took her whole closet with her, her two bookcases and the books that occupied them, and personal items like hygiene and electronics. They were nearly done packing when she noticed Romano speaking to two men. She decided to see who they were and recognized the detectives that started her and Leo's engagement.

"Officers..." she greeted hesitantly. Romano stood between her and the cops.

"Miss Santos, we'd like to ask you a few more questions," Detective Wilson told her as he tried to get around Romano. Romano stopped him with an arm out, acting like a wall between them.

"I've already told you what I know, which is nothing," Freya replied. She didn't understand why the detectives were so keen on her being involved with the missing man.

"We'd still like to talk to you without your bulldog here," Detective Davis insisted.

"Mr. Costa has already informed you that any questions you have for his fiancé need to go through their attorney. If you persist on harassing my employers, a complaint will be filed against you and your department," Romano explained.

"I'd like to hear it directly from Miss Santos," Detective Wilson insisted.

"Please speak to our lawyer. It is for the best," Freya replied. She was glad that Leo had talked to her about this. About how she needed to respond to the police, should they come sniffing again?

"You going somewhere, Miss Santos?" Detective Davis asked as he looked at the moving truck. The three men who were packing her small studio were suddenly behind her, arms crossed over their chests, glaring at the detectives.

"I'm moving in with my fiancé," she replied. "We're busy right now detectives. If you have any more questions, please confer with my lawyer." She wasn't surprised when Romano handed them a business card that they probably already had. The detectives left knowing they weren't going to get passed her guards and she was glad for that.

***

She was jolted awake when the car door opened,

and she found herself staring at Leo. She felt an immediate sense of relief when she saw him. She didn't bother to think why but she was just glad for it. She had rarely ever felt that relief her whole life. She spent her life worrying and planning to get the stability she craved, but one look at Leo and she just knew that everything would be okay, no matter what the problem was. She didn't like her dependency on him, but she liked the way he made her feel like everything would be okay.

"You up for going out to dinner?" Leo asked her as he helped her out of the car.

"After a shower and nothing fancy," she answered as they headed for the elevator.

"I have to stop at a couple of clubs tonight and then we'll go wherever you want."

"Clubs? In the city? Where?" Clubs in the city were often surrounded by pizza bars and other late-night food joints. Many of the pizza bars had to die for pizza, with slices that were the size of her face.

"Yes, a couple on Broadway and Polk."

***

"People go clubbing on weekdays?" she asked, amazed. She followed Leo as he checked on businesses before the clubs opened for business.

"The San Francisco nightlife is a six-billion-dollar industry. My clubs are open every night, except for a few holidays. Have you decided what you'd like for dinner?"

"Yes, there," she answered pointing at the pizza bar across the street. She loved mom and pop shops and had spent enough nights out in the city to know several that catered to the drunks and night crawlers. Leo frowned at her, and for a moment she thought he'd tell her to pick something else, but he eventually nodded in agreement.

"Can we eat there?" she knew she was pushing it. Again, he surprised her when he agreed. She thought it was excessive for Drago, Vito, and Romano to join her and Leo across the street at the tiny pizzeria. There were only three small tables that sat two people each, leaning against the wall since most people just picked up pizza slices at these kinds of places.

The smell of freshly baked pizza greeted her. At 7PM it was still early for the night crawlers, but the restaurants around were already bursting with the dinner crowd.

"*Buona sera*!" Romano greeted the older man behind the counter in a friendly manner that indicated they knew each other.

"*Ciao*," Vito and Leo greeted. Drago merely nodded as he turned his back to them and watched the street.

The older man behind the counter happily greeted them in return, and more Italian flew over her head. She knew she became the topic of their discussion when they all turned to look at her.

Leo introduced her, first in Italian before switching to English. "Alfonso, Freya, my fiancé. Freya, Alfonso."

The old man said something in Italian and Leo replied before they seemed to shake hands affectionately.

"What would you like? Alfonso says it is on the house," Leo explained to her.

"Are you sure?" she asked Leo but really meant to ask Alfonso.

"Yes, and you will offend him if you don't accept," Leo replied with a rare smile.

"Cheese and lots of it," she replied. "And Alfonso's invited to the wedding too," she added mostly as a joke, but if she actually got married, she didn't have a family to sit at her side.

"Of course," Leo replied in a nonchalant tone.

They were quickly served their pizza on paper plates. She thanked Alfonso as she was handed her slice and Leo led her to the far table while Vito and Romano sat on the two other tables in front of them. She hadn't realized how hungry she was until she realized she was halfway done with her slice and Leo had just taken one bite. She noticed that Drago didn't move from his casual lean against the entryway.

"What about Drago? He's not eating?" she asked Leo.

"He is on guard. He doesn't like distraction," Leo answered.

A sudden thought made her smile as she took another bite of her folded pizza. Leo inquired with a raised eyebrow.

"I was just thinking, this is our first date," she joked. He seemed surprised.

"What about the fundraiser?" he asked.

"Doesn't count. We weren't actually alone," she replied. He seemed to think it over before he nodded.

"I suppose you're right. I guess I owe you a real date."

"This is good for me. Formal stuff makes me feel out of place," she replied honestly.

"How does your face feel?" he suddenly asked.

She'd forgotten about her bruised face and stitches, and they began to ache the moment she was reminded of them.

"It's okay. The bruise probably hurts more, like it's really sensitive."

"Have you taken your meds?" he asked.

"Yeah, Paula has been reminding me."

"Good."

"Want Romano to take you home?" Leo asked her as soon as she finished her pizza.

"No, I want Marco to take me back," she replied as a joke. He frowned. "I'm kidding," she clarified. "I don't mind following you around if you don't mind."

"I don't and excuse me for saying this, but you look tired."

She could have joked that he thought she looked less than her best, but she wasn't sure he'd take it as a joke. He didn't seem to joke much.

Leo tossed their garbage before saying goodbye to Alfonso. Though the food made her feel better, she felt tired which was weird considering she hadn't done all that much today. She barely lifted a finger when they'd packed up her apartment.

She was happy that Leo took her hand as they left the pizza bar. They had to cross the street and walk to the back of the club to get to the cars. They had barely stepped onto the curb when Drago grunted. She turned to look at him, but he was looking somewhere behind her. She turned to see the rest of them looking in the same direction.

"Leo," came a jolly greeting. She looked past Leo to see a man approaching them. Leo and the others, with the exception of Drago, returned his greeting. He approached them, and Leo, Vito, and Romano accepted his friendly handshake. Italian was spoken, and it sounded friendly. The man looked to be in his forties, but he was good looking and behind him stood a hulking giant.

Freya thought Drago's six and a half foot frame was big, but the hulking giant was bigger. Though he probably had an inch or two over Drago, he was built like a bull on steroids. He was also ugly. Freya wasn't one to judge people's appearance, but this man just had a face on him that didn't invite any sort of warmth, and it made him look ugly to her.

"Freya, this is Bartolo, he's a family friend." Leo introduced her. "Bartolo, this is Freya, my fiancé."

"Please to meet yo–" Bartolo was pulling her into a hug before she could finish her sentence. It was an awkward hug because Leo hadn't let go of her hand. She almost felt like she was in a tug-of-war between the men. Leo's hold tightened, and she sensed his tension. Bartolo seemed oblivious to it.

"*Che cosabella.*" Bartolo said to her. He turned to Leo and added, "*Ella é molto bella Leo. Avete scelto bene.*" He wasn't hugging her anymore, but his hands were on her biceps, and he looked her over.

"Yes, very beautiful indeed," Leo responded in English for her benefit as he tugged her away from Bartolo and back to his side. "This is Filipe, Bartolo's second," Leo introduced the ugly giant. Freya tried her best not to stare. She offered a smile and a nod. She didn't offer a hand because Leo had a firm hold on her.

"We'll need to be going. It's dinner time. I need to be at the restaurant," Bartolo explained. Goodbyes were exchanged and then Bartolo and Filipe were walking past them.

"Let's get you in the car." Leo tugged her across the street and down the alley to the garage behind Leo's nightclub.

"I'll be home around eleven," he explained as he helped her into the SUV. "Get some rest," he added.

"Okay, I'll see you later," she replied. She leaned in to kiss him without pondering if she should have. They both seemed to freeze for a moment, surprised at her action but Leo took control of the situation. He leaned in as he pulled her closer to him and kissed her. The kiss held a promise, and she sighed into the kiss knowing that there would be more later, much more.

***

Freya woke to the feel of stroking fingers. She was wet and naked. Ready and willing. She stared up into Leo's blue eyes.

"You sleep like the dead," he joked as he leaned over her, drawing her into a kiss.

Freya decided that she loved the feel of his body against her. He kissed her, hot and long, leaving them both breathing hard. She opened for him, her legs cradling his hips. He moved down and took a breast into his mouth and sucked. The jolting sensation had her hips rising, begging for him. His fingers found her, tested her, and she moaned as his fingers penetrated her. Her hands gripped him by the shoulder and neck. He pulled back, and she looked down to watch him guide his cock into her. Thick and hard, her mouth watered.

Leo guided himself to her opening. As the top of his dick touched her wet folds, he strained for control. Inch by inch, he claimed her. His teeth clenched as he worked himself inside her. She moaned and arched against him, forcing him deeper. She thrust against him, urging him into her, burying his dick so deep in her.

He pulled back and thrust, burying his full length in her, emitting a loud moan from both of them. He withdrew and thrust again, harder, burying himself deep, never wanting to leave her tight, silky, hot flesh. She tried to meet his rhythm, but he quickly took over, pounding into her. Her body tightened around him, and her release came with a whimper. Her orgasm spurred his own. His balls tightened, and his dick spasmed with his release.

Chapter Fifteen

Freya took the rest of the week off from work. She didn't have any project that needed her immediate attention, and her work was trying to be supportive due to her incident. Considering she was on a work errand when she was attacked, her employer was probably scared she would sue.

By Sunday, her bruised face was no longer an angry black and purple. It now had a yellow and green tint to it. She'd be returning to work on Monday and beginning the long commute, but tonight, she and Leo would be having dinner at his parents' house. She wasn't sure how she felt about her engagement now. It was temporary, but Leo reminded her that it needed to be believable. If anyone saw the amount of sex they had, they'd believe it.

He drove them in the black BMW with Vito, Drago, and Romano following in the black SUV.

"Why do you take two cars?" she asked Leo.

"For protection. There is strength in numbers They're less likely to attack if there is back up."

"They? Who would attack you?" She had a feeling she didn't really want to know.

"Enemies. We didn't get to where we are without them," he explained.

Valentina greeted them enthusiastically with cheek kisses and hugs.

"Your father invited Bertie too. They are in his office. I will take Freya to meet Anna and Bianca." Leo gave Freya a reassuring pat on her back before Valentina led her into the other room.

Valentina introduced her to two beautiful women, Anna who looked to be in her thirties and Bianca, Anna's daughter. Bianca seemed to be in her late teens if not early twenties. Freya would guess Bianca was still in school but dressed like a college student on spring break because Anna looked too young to have a college-age child.

Though Bianca was a bit sulky, Anna was

friendly. Valentina and Anna talked about parties and Freya had a feeling the parties were the rich society ones that she'd only ever seen in movies. Freya felt so out of place. Why wouldn't she? Bianca had grown up in it, Valentina and Anna probably had too.

"We'll be planning Freya and Leo's engagement party soon," Valentina announced just as Freya took a sip of her drink. The juice and the announcement were her enemies. She nearly choked and had a coughing fit that left her embarrassed and somewhat astounded.

"Engagement party?" she asked in between coughs.

"Yes dear, it's traditional for us. Here, have some water. This has been a stressful week for you, with the mugging and all. Don't worry dear; I'll help you plan the party. It will be fairly small, just close family and friends, probably about a hundred people." Freya tried not to choke on the water too.

Before Freya could respond, the men joined them. To Freya's surprise, Giovanni greeted her just as enthusiastically as Valentina had. He engulfed her into a hug before introducing her to "Bertie," whom she recognized as Bartolo, owner of one of the best Italian restaurants in the city and the man she'd met near the pizza bar. She was relieved to see that his hulking giant was not with them.

They headed to the dining room, something she was getting familiar with. Giovanni sat at the head of the table, and Valentina sat on his right. To her surprise, Leo lead them to the other end of the table, where he sat her on his right and he took the head, opposite of Giovanni. Bartolo and his family sat on Giovanni's left side, Bartolo being next to Giovanni, followed by his wife and then a daughter, leaving a gap between Freya and Bianca. Vito took the spot at Leo's left, across from Freya, followed by Drago.

Romano and Luciano were the last to enter the room, talking excitedly. They paused at the doorway, looking at where to seat. They both seemed to look at her before looking at each other. In a sudden rush, like little boys, the two fought over the spot next to Freya, pulling laughter from everyone, and a frown from Giovanni. Luciano beat Romano to the seat by pulling it away from the table.

"Romano, dear, you can sit next to me. You already see Freya more than we do," Valentina called out.

"I wanted to sit next to aunty anyway. Your mom likes me better." Luciano tried to hit Romano with a playful punch, but Romano dodged it and quickly sat next to Valentina, leaving an empty chair between him and Drago. The food which had been brought out by the maids before they sat were passed around the table as everyone served themselves. Among the happy chatter and banter, Freya's taste buds were ignited by the delicious smell of the food.

"Freya, try this. Artichoke *Gratinata*, Mom's specialty." Luciano didn't give her a choice; he held the dish out for her to serve herself. She hated artichokes, but he was staring at her expectantly. She was about to suck it up and put some on her plate when Leo reached for the dish.

"She's allergic to artichokes." She gave Leo a grateful look, and he winked at her. The wink went straight to her core, and she tried to control the blush making its way to her face.

"That's an interesting allergy. Can't say I've heard of it." Vito gave her a knowing look. She resisted the urge to kick him under the table and at that instant, she felt like she was a part of their family. Instead of kicking him, she smiled at him.

"So, Freya, is it too late to steal you away from Leo? I mean, I am the better looking one between us."

"I'm afraid so," Freya responded, unsure how to handle Luciano's flirty tone.

"That's too bad. If you ever change your mind, I'm available, babe. I'm not only better looking; I'm sweeter too." He gave her a conspicuous eyebrow wiggle that had her giggling.

"Thanks for the offer. I'll keep it in mind."

"She's just being nice to you, she likes your brother's face better," Romano called from across the table.

"All of you boys are handsome equally," Valentina inserted as only a parent would.

"Valentina, you are going to make these boys even more big headed than they already are." Bartolo laughed like his comment was the funniest thing in the world.

"I agree with Romano. Leo is very handsome." Bianca gave Leo a look that had Freya feeling uncomfortable. The ugly head of jealousy was creeping up on her, and she couldn't believe she had the urge to pull a teenager's hair out because she was flirting with Freya's fiancé...fake fiancé. Freya quickly looked down at her food and got busy putting it in her mouth before she said something that was guaranteed to embarrass her.

"Thank you, Bianca, and I'm sure Freya agrees with you." The mention of her name had Freya looking up, meeting Leo's eyes as he added, "She absolutely could not want for anyone else when she's with me, and I don't want anyone else but her." He reached over to take her hand and gave it a kiss. It was sappy and absolutely corny, but Freya was sure she was going to melt from the look in his eyes.

***

She was glad they left before the Lombardi family. She hadn't wanted to stay longer, especially when the topic of conversation at dinner was Leo's romanticized rescue, and the engagement party Valentina was determined to have. Leo had excused them before nine which was a feat considering Bertie and Giovanni were far from ending their boisterous chat. Leo had explained that they both had an early day tomorrow, but she had a feeling he wanted to leave for other reasons. Leo was insatiable, and Freya found out that she was too. She and Leo spent a lot of time having sex, day and night, the whole week. She didn't remember having or craving this much sex in her past relationships.

"Your mother wants that engagement party. You have to tell her–"

"Plan one. That's the only way she'll let it go."

"No! That's too much. What happens when we break up? It would be such a waste of money."

"Does it look like we care about the cost?" Leo asked with a hint of a smile.

"That's not the point."

"What did I say about enjoying this?" He took her hand, brought it to his lips and kissed the back of her hand, momentarily distracting her with such a sweet gesture.

"Yes, but that's different. This is an actual party-"

"What better way to convince everyone we're engaged than an engagement party?"

Before she could respond, the car indicated that Vito was calling. Leo answered his call.

"You're on speaker," Leo announced as a way of greeting. There was a pause before Vito's voice came on.

"We have friendlies," Vito replied in a tone filled with sarcasm. She could almost picture him rolling his eyes.

"Lose them," Leo replied before hanging up. Leo sped up, fast and Freya realized that he was speeding away from the SUV. Leo zigzagged in and out of traffic, the all black car probably looked like a mere shadow to other drivers.

"What's going on?" Freya asked.

"We're being followed." *Followed? Like in the movies? When bad guys are chasing the good guys?*

"What do you mean followed?" she clarified.

"Someone is following us."

"Why would anyone want to follow us? Who would follow us?"

"People always follow the money. Don't worry about it. You're safe. I won't let anything happen to you." And she believed him. Being with Leo took away her fears, even if it's the unknown. Somehow, she always knew that he'd make everything alright.

"Are you sure they're following us? What if the person is just going in the same direction?" she suggested.

"You'll insult Vito if you ask him that," Leo replied.

"Leo, please tell me the truth." She wasn't stupid, and she hoped he'd be honest.

He didn't respond right away. In fact, she thought he stayed silent long enough to make her think he wouldn't answer her.

"I'll tell you what I can," he started. "The police

haven't found the people who tried to kill me, and that means we are taking any and all precaution when it comes to *our* safety."

She didn't know if that was all he knew, but she believed what he'd told her.

"Do you think the train attack is connected to your...kidnapping?"

"At this point, I don't know, but I am not taking any chances."

His phone rang before she could respond.

"Yes?" Leo answered.

"Our friends left when backup came. Slow down; we'll catch up and escort you."

Leo hung up. The news made her feel a little better. It didn't take long for them to catch up to Leo and Freya. The two SUVs sandwiched the BMW as they exited the Bay Bridge.

"All I want to do is keep you safe, Freya," Leo said as they took their exit ramp. "If you ever doubt me, remember that." She had a feeling that Leo meant every word and she wondered if she would ever regret the day she saved his life. She couldn't, but she wondered if she would.

***

"I had hopes for Leo and my Bianca," Bartolo said in a somber tone after taking a drink of Giovanni's most expensive scotch.

"She is too young for him." Giovanni had hoped that Leo would one day marry one of theirs, but he wasn't going to force him.

"Perhaps she and Luciano will get on."

Perhaps. Giovanni would never suggest it though. Knowing his son, Luciano would do the exact opposite. A knock on his office door saved him from replying. Not that he needed to, he was the boss, he didn't need to answer anyone, even Bartolo, one of his longest friends.

"Yes," he called for whoever was knocking to enter. The door opened, and his wife entered. His beautiful wife. He still felt a little weak in the knees every time she smiled at him.

"Yes, dear?"

"I am going to bed. I just wanted to check if you will be long?" She framed it as a question, but he had no doubt she was telling him it was time to go to bed. His wife was probably the only person in the world who could get away with ordering him around. *To tell him that it was time for bed.*

"Yes, darling, I will be joining you soon."

"Alright. Goodnight, Bartolo."

"Good night, Valentina."

"I can see who the boss is in this marriage," Bartolo joked. Giovanni did not like his joke but did not respond. "You should be the one telling her when to sleep, my friend...ahhh...those were the days. Remember them? We used to run this city like our own little playground." Giovanni would excuse his drunk talk.

"I think it is time for you to join your family." Giovanni did not like that Bartolo sent his women home so that he could drink his scotch. "You seem like you could use a good nap. Your wife ought to be telling you when to sleep since you are not sleeping enough."

"You know my friend; there is no rest for the wicked." Bartolo stood, and Giovanni walked him to the door where his butler would then lead him out of his home.

"There is rest for the wicked when you have the right woman."

"I suppose you are right. It seems Leonardo has found his, yes?"

"Yes, I do believe so." Bartolo shook his head as if it was a shame. Giovanni couldn't say he didn't agree with Bartolo. "Alright, goodnight my friend."

Chapter Sixteen

The first two weeks of commuting was brutal, not only would she spend nine hours at work, she spent another two or so hours commuting. She couldn't complain though, she wasn't the one driving, and she was able to get some rest on the drive since she had a bodyguard/chauffeur, usually Romano or Sandro. Having a bodyguard didn't disrupt her as much as she thought it would, and her job didn't mind it, or at least they didn't say anything about having an extra guy always just there. The first couple of days were awkward, but it eventually returned to normal where she could chat and enjoy lunch with her coworkers. She preferred when Romano was her bodyguard for the day because he was happy to keep her company whenever she asked or just because he's bored. With Sandro, he usually was stoic and refused to join her for meals, and his favorite form of response was a grunt.

Freya and Leo had settled into a sort of routine. Freya being a day worker often woke up before Leo. She did her best not to disturb him while she got ready for work, knowing he worked nights. Most of the time, Leo will join her for breakfast and walk her to the car. Leo worked different hours, but managing hotels and nightclubs kept him busy throughout the day and many times, at night. He was often home by seven at night, just in time to join her for dinner. Sometimes they'd settle into a quiet night, many times; he would do some work in his office after dinner. Most of the time he was there to join her for bed but there were times when he'd leave in the middle of the night when he'd have to do club related work. Weekends were her favorite; they usually spent a good amount of time in the mornings just lying in bed, keeping each other company. Sometimes, she'd join him while he did errands or went to work. She noticed that he had a lot of people who followed orders from him, making it easier for him to manage *La Famiglia* businesses. The long commutes and odd working hours cut the hours they get to spend together. So, she was happy to just lay next to him in the mornings she didn't have to get up for work.

Even in sleep, he looked fierce. The hard lines of his jaw were prominent making him look serious. She loved waking up next to him, and she often woke up wrapped up in his arms. She had never been a cuddler until now, the warmth of his body beckoning her closer. Even in his sleep, he responded by pulling her closer and tucking her into his chest, resting her in the crook of his neck. Though they spent nights together and often made love, she missed him these last two weeks.

"You are thinking too hard," he whispered above her. The rumble of his voice was comforting.

"I was thinking I missed you."

"Did you now?" She felt a kiss on top of her head before he pulled back.

"Just a little," she replied as she looked up to face him. He kissed her on her forehead this time.

"A little huh? How little?" He kissed the tip of her nose. "This little?" he asked as he ground his hardening length against her.

"A little more," she half said, and half moaned. Her hand went to his naked torso as she angled her body closer, lifting one leg over his thigh, trying to pull him closer. His hand lowered, cupped her rear, and ground her body against his. She was practically riding his thigh as he lowered his head to kiss her neck. She pulled back wanting him to go lower. He obligated and trailed kisses down to her chest. His mouth latched onto her breast and sucked, sending an electric pulse through her body. Her hand delved into his hair, holding his head against her, not wanting him to stop.

He laid her on her back, lying on top of her as he switched to the other breast. His teeth scraped against her sensitive skin, and his tongue swiped over the offended skin. He moved lower, kissing the triangle just between her rib cage, before going lower, trailing kisses to her navel until he reached the top of her pelvis. She kept herself bare down there knowing he loved to touch and taste her skin, and she loved having him there. He positioned her legs over his shoulders before delving into her center. He didn't tease, he claimed. He latched onto her clit and sucked the swollen bud while his fingers spread her lower lips. His mouth feasted on her, his tongue gliding through her slit as his teeth nipped her. Her back arched, her hand gripped his hair, trying to force him to do more and to give her what her body needed, wanting him to go deeper. He answered with his fingers thrusting into her, keeping her on edge.

Leo pulled away just as she felt her orgasm peaking, frustrating her, causing her to cry out. "You'll cum on my dick. I want to feel that pussy squeezing me." His voice was hoarse as he moved to take her. He spread her legs wider, held her with one hand, and guided his cock into her heat with the other. There was no working into her. He buried himself deep into her in one thrust pulling a gasp from her. He covered her with his body as he continued to thrust into her, setting a brutal pace that had her crying out with each plunge. Her orgasm washed over her, a punishing reward that had her clinging to him and her sanity.

He didn't stop, Leo continued to pound into her through her orgasm, setting off the second release unexpectedly. "Fuck yeah, that's it, baby." Her muscles clasped him tightly, sucking him in, keeping him rooted. He followed her second orgasm, emptying himself into her. It drained him in ways he couldn't explain. It felt like he was emptying his soul, as if he'd given everything in him to her. And for a moment he thought he'd blacked out.

It took some time for them to recover. They lay there, holding each other, sticky with sweat and need. This was different, and he was smart enough to know it wasn't something he should ignore or let go. Whatever they had between them...he wasn't going to fight it. He had to convince her she shouldn't either. That probably meant taking her on a real date.

"I owe you a date." She sighed as she cuddled closer to him.

"You do." She sounded sleepy.

"Let's go tonight. I'll take you on a real date."

"It doesn't count if you own the property though." He heard the smile in a sleepy voice.

"I can afford to take you out on a real date you

know." She smiled at the sarcasm in his tone.

"Oh, good, cause I thought I'd have to split the bill with you."

"You ever offer that to me; I'll spank you." Just to prove his point, he gave her ass a light spanking.

"Okay Mr. Rich Man, when are we going on this date?"

"Tonight. Be ready by 6:30."

"You're serious?"

Rather than answer he gave her a look that said something like, *are you fucking kidding me*? Instead of being offended, she was excited. Being with him at the fundraiser wasn't what she considered a date. A quickie-food-grab at pizza bars and taquerias weren't either. They've been 'together' for a couple of months, but they haven't gone on an actual date, where it was just the two of them, having dinner or even doing something normal couples do, like bowling.

***

Freya was ready by six with a half hour to spare, and Leo wasn't even home yet. Knowing him, he'd want to shower and change. He was always quick with getting ready, but now she was worried that they were going to be late. She didn't even know what they were going to be late to. Every minute after six was like a slow trickle. She didn't understand why she was so nervous. It wasn't like she hadn't been on a date, or that she and Leo haven't been together. She was living with him for crying out loud, slept with him every night. But she had butterflies in her stomach. She was nervous about going on a date and worrying that he's going to miss their date at the same time.

Leo arrived at fifteen minutes after six. She tried not to show her worry, but it didn't work.

"It's just a date Freya; there's no need to worry," Leo told her as he walked up to her. He kissed her before turning to head to the master bathroom.

"It's almost six thirty. We're going to be late. Where are we going anyway?" Freya followed him into the bathroom. Leo stripped his day suit on his way into the shower, and Freya picked up each piece of clothing he dropped on his way in. Leo was too used to having someone pick up after him.

"I'll be ready by then...unless you want to come join me in here?" He gave her such a boyish grin that she paused, very tempted. He stood under the shower, pure muscle, and looking like a wet dream. She was very tempted.

"No, I'm not letting you ruin my hair and

makeup. It took forever to do them." Instead of answering he washed the soap off his body. She leaned against the door frame just enjoying the magnificent view in front of her. God, she was horny already. Very, very tempted. But no. She wanted this date, and she was going to get her date. She couldn't be engaged to him, regardless of what kind of engagement it was, without going on a real date.

"You're making me horny just staring at me, Freya." She loved how he said her name. He always seemed to drag the 'E' in "Fre" and pause between the syllables. Like he's saying Frey-ya. She liked it.

"Well, I'm pretty horny watching you be horny."

"If you want to leave on time, I suggest leaving me alone, or we'll never leave." She wanted that date more than she wanted to get laid right now. She decided to leave him alone and headed for the living room. The piano greeted her as soon as she entered the room and she knew that was exactly what she needed to settle her nerves.

She loved Leo's piano. She played piano more often now than she's done in the past couple of years. She let the music flow as her fingers played on their own, playing a song from memory. She forgot about watching the time and waiting on Leo as she focused on playing the piano. A soft kiss on her neck pulled her out of her haze. The touch of Leo's lips made her shiver.

"That's beautiful, like you, and as much as I'd love to sit here watching you play, I think you want that date more." Freya turned to face him and smiled.

"Ready?" Freya asked. He smiled, leaning down to kiss her lips this time.

"Babe, I've been ready. You didn't hear me calling you. I've been watching you for about five minutes." Leo helped her up as he handed her the clutch she placed on the side table earlier.

"Really?" Freya checked the time on her phone. 6:32 PM. *She'd made them late.*

***

Leo drove them right to the entrance of the restaurant. The valet opened Freya's door, but Leo had already made his way around and was the one to help Freya out of the car. The restaurant was a swanky place and was recently designated as the most expensive restaurant in San Francisco. Freya had heard of the place, everyone had, but she never thought she'd actually ever go there. To begin with, a simple menu was almost $400 a person. Depending on how many courses you ordered and there was an endless amount of food to choose from. It was also a reservation-only restaurant, and it was usually booked at least a month in advance.

"Mr. Costa, we're delighted to see you again. Please follow me. Your instructions have been followed as expected." Freya wasn't surprised that Leo was known. She, however, did not like how friendly the hostess was towards Leo. It made Freya wonder how many women Leo had taken here on a date. She wondered if she was just another one of a long parade of them. She could see it. Her excitement over their date suddenly dimmed.

Leo placed a hand on her lower back, somewhat patronizing her thoughts. He kept his hand on her as they followed the hostess. People seemed to watch them as they walked by. Maybe it was because Vito, Drago, and Romano trailed them. Or maybe it was because she was with four handsome men. Or perhaps it was Leo; he was an enigma that made you look and keep looking.

Leo was used to being watched. People watched him all the time; whether they were enemies, his people, or people who just saw what he wanted them to see, he was used to it. Freya wasn't. He could sense her hesitance at being the leader of their group. He normally wouldn't let her lead them and would have at least one guard in front of her, but this was his territory, a restaurant owned by one of his most trusted Capo. If he couldn't trust them with this, then he didn't need them. Besides that, he wanted to show Freya off. This date was for her. He didn't need a date to tell him what he already knew, but he was doing it for her.

He had no problem showing her off; she deserved to be shown off. She'd made an effort, and she looked good. He didn't blame them for watching her. She moved with grace and femininity without effort. She was cool, sophisticated, and so fucking sexy. Yeah, he'd let them look, let them see what they couldn't have. She was his.

They were seated in a private booth as instructed. They had a gorgeous view of the water on one side, and a view of the entire restaurant on the other, but they were barely visible to the rest of the world. It was a booth intended for people like him; his Capo knew that. The two closest tables were occupied, one by Drago, and the other by Vito and Romano. This date took some planning considering there was a threat to him, his family, and now, Freya.

As expected, Lorenzo Esposito, the first Capo he'd chosen, came to greet them. He briefly introduced the two, not wanting to make it a big deal, simply mentioning that Lorenzo was a friend. Lorenzo understanding that Freya was not *La Famiglia,* played his part. Lorenzo was an earner for *La Famiglia,* a member who generates income. This restaurant was income for *La Famiglia.* Champagne was brought to the table, the best in the house, worth almost five figures.

Freya wasn't a wine drinker, but he noticed she enjoyed champagne.

"I have no idea what to order," Freya whispered next to him, leaning in close, giving him a whiff of her perfume. She smelled good enough to eat.

"Why don't we get a little bit of everything? There's the twenty-two-course–"

"Twenty-two?"

"Yes, Freya. Twenty-two."

"That's a lot. That has to be ridiculously expensive too–"

"It's good, and it's not too much."

"Twenty-two is a lot."

"Fine, how about fifteen?"

"You really think we'll eat that much? I'm not sure my dress can stretch that much." Instead of being upset, Leo smiled. He pulled her towards him by the strap of her dress, kissed her to shut her up, and ordered the twenty-two-course meal.

Leo flirted, and she touched him, doing things she didn't normally do. Sometime between course eight and twelve, she'd reached over and placed her hand on his thigh. Her fingers drew swirls on his leg, getting dangerously close to what she wanted. Leo stopped her hand from moving closer, but he leaned closer to whisper, "If you keep going, I'm going to pick you up, put you on my lap, and fuck you right here. I have no problem bringing you to orgasm in front of all of these people."

"Would you enjoy it?" she asked, the champagne making her bold.

"I would enjoy sliding into your tight pussy. I would enjoy the way your body clenches around me when you're about to cum. I would enjoy filling my hands with your beautiful breasts. And I would definitely enjoy cumming in your pretty little pussy."

She nearly moaned. She loved when he talked dirty. She took another sip of her champagne.

"Are you wet?" he said in her ear.

"How could I not be?" she whispered in return.

"Wet enough to let me take you to the restroom?"

"Right now?"

"Unless you'd prefer to get on my lap right now."

She took another drink of her champagne before saying, "Lead the way."

Leo stood and held a hand out to her. She took it and forced herself to get up slowly. Leo didn't waste a second, and he led her to pass Drago's table. He shook his head at Drago who started to get up to follow them. Freya barely heard Vito and Romano's laugh, no doubt knowing what they were about to do. She didn't care.

Leo led her to a door that was barely noticeable. He closed the door, and she heard a lock as she looked around. They were in a single fancy restroom. It was clean and elegant, a vintage designed restroom. As soon as he turned to face her, she was on him. Her arms went around his neck as she pulled him into a kiss. He was intoxicating, and she couldn't get enough of him.

He picked her up and placed her on the counter, her dress bunched up, as she spread her legs wide to fit him in between them. His fingers were plunging into her in seconds, deftly pushing her thong aside and sliding deep inside. She moaned into his mouth as he worked her into a frenzy. His mouth left hers and kissed its way down to her neck. His other hand pushed her dress straps aside, quickly pulled the dress down to reveal her braless breasts. His mouth was on her as his fingers fucked her faster.

Her hands reached for him, for his belt, wanting to have him in her. His hands left her body as he pulled away. He put her back on her heeled feet, turned her around to face the mirror, and pushed her dress up as he bent her over the counter. Her thong was pulled aside, and she felt his heavy length against her. He entered her in one thrust. She moaned, loving the feel of him filling her so completely. He slid out and plunged back in hard, making her breasts bounce.

"I want them all to know what we're doing in here. I want them to know that you're mine," he told her as he fucked her hard. She tried to keep quiet, but the moans escaped. It was hard not to make a noise when he was giving her what she wanted. He reached around her, and his fingers found her clit. "Cum, Freya. Let me feel that pussy grip my cock so tight that it almost hurts." It didn't take much coaxing before she came, giving him exactly what he wanted. His release joined hers; she could feel him filling her. It took a moment for her to recover. It wasn't until he pulled out of her that she felt the need to move. She could barely hold herself up.

Leo put himself back together before reaching for a hand towel. He enjoyed that. He loved seeing Freya barely recovered from his fucking. He used the hand towel to clean Freya, between her legs where their fluids filled her and spread all over her, and then her thighs where their arousal had trailed down. He loved that she let him clean her, let him take care of her. He fixed her thong before pulling her dress back down. The little black dress would probably be his favorite dress from now on. She stood up, and he helped her fix the top of her dress, barely refraining from taking her tits back into his mouth, as he placed them back in her dress and pulled her straps up. She turned to the sink, tried to fix herself, as he went to wash his hands.

"How do I look?" she asked as they headed to the door.

"Like you've just been thoroughly fucked."

"Leo!" Rather than let her worry, he kissed her.

"You look beautiful. Perfect. Now let's go, our next round is waiting." He was famished. After what they'd just done, he needed to eat.

***

"I'm not sure I can get up." The food was delicious, and she ate way too much.

"Want me to have Romano and Vito roll you out of here?" Leo took her hand and helped her up from the seat Freya was sure she wasn't going to be able to leave.

"I don't think I can walk either. I really think you could throw me off the pier right now and I'd just sink straight down."

"But it was worth it."

"Oh, yeah." Freya's answer had Leo grinning. He helped her into her coat before placing a hand on her back to lead her out. As they did when they arrived, people watched them as they left. This time, Vito and Romano led the way, and Drago followed behind Leo. She and Leo had enjoyed their meal, while Drago ate by himself, and Vito and Romano argued at their table. It was an unconventional date, having bodyguards and all, but it was still a date, and she thoroughly enjoyed it. Not only was the food delicious, but Leo was relaxed, the most relaxed she'd ever seen him in public. He also flirted with her, every quip feeling like foreplay. She had his complete attention, and he and the waiters catered to her every need throughout dinner. It was one of the most satisfying meals she had ever had, and Leo had kept her champagne glass full.

She'd been embarrassed when they came out of the restroom to find Drago standing guard. She was more embarrassed when people turned to look at her as they made their way back to their table. It didn't faze Leo. He returned to their meal as if he hadn't a care in the world. He filled her with more champagne and told her to relax and enjoy the rest of their meal.

"You want to go for a walk?" Leo surprised her

by asking as they neared the exit. It would be romantic. The pier was lit by streetlights, lights from the restaurants, and lights from cars driving by. The weather was great, not too cold for a walk. Other people from all walks of life were on the street, from joggers to restaurant goers, bicyclists ferrying tourists, and even homeless people getting ready to settle for the night. She loved this city, the good and the bad. It was diverse, not just in race, but in culture, class, and everything in between.

"I would love a short walk."

"We'll go to the port."

Though the area was known for Pier 39, there were many piers and ports with their own attraction. There was a pier on every block surrounding the bay. Leo led her to one of the many ports; this one was just for tourists, to get a closer look at the water. She turned to find Drago, Vito, and Romano stopping at the end of the port so that she and Leo could be alone. She was happy to see that they were the only ones there as they walked to the end. The wind was stronger there due to the proximity to the water, but the sound of the waves was calming. It was a perfect ending to their date.

"Thank you for the date." Freya leaned against the protective rail as she turned to face Leo. His hands went around her waist as hers went around his neck.

He kissed her forehead before pulling her into his body, protecting her from the cold wind. She huddled closer to his warm body, and they stayed there, just being in each other's presence. She loved this city alright but not as much as she loved Leo.

Chapter Seventeen

A month of long commutes made her dread work. She knew she couldn't really complain because she really didn't have to do anything but sit in the car. Having a bodyguard and chauffeur had its benefits. They were always available when she needed to go out, and Lena enjoyed being chauffeured around when they went out for lunch. But it also had its cons like never having complete privacy. She couldn't have her normal boy talks with Lena because the bodyguard, usually Romano, was within hearing distance, and in most cases joining them for lunch. Though Romano was her bodyguard most often, she sometimes had Sandro, Marco, and the other bodyguards with her. Drago and Vito rarely went with her; they seemed to be attached to Leo's hip. Romano was the only one who was allowed to guard her alone. Whenever the other bodyguards went with her to work, there were always two of them, which told her how highly Leo must think of Romano.

Freya was glad it was usually Romano because he was the friendliest of them all. She needed his outgoing attitude after a long day of work. She didn't know if it was the long commute that made her grumpy, but she was starting to hate work. The workdays felt like it dragged on. All she knew was she couldn't wait for the clock to hit five, so she could go home... *Or maybe it was Leo.* Being with Leo was unlike anything she'd ever imagined. He was like a fire that seduced her closer, and she knew that if she touched it, it would burn her, yet she couldn't resist. Every time she touched the fire, it didn't just singe her, it torched her resolve. She knew she cared about Leo beyond friendship, fake engagement, and great sex. She was beginning to love him. She was so afraid to get burned but she couldn't help it.

"Evening, Paula," Freya greeted the housekeeper who'd become a mother figure and friend to Freya in the last two months. She couldn't believe how much life had changed.

"Good evening, Freya," Paula returned as Honey came running to greet her. She gave Honey some love before Romano, who'd been her guard and driver today, called Honey into the elevator.

"I'll have Marco walk him," Romano told her as

Honey excitedly joined him in the elevator.

Freya found Leo asleep on the couch with her traitorous cat on his lap. Lestat normally greeted her when she came home; now she understood why he hadn't today. She couldn't blame him. If she were him, she wouldn't want to leave Leo's lap either.

Unlike Freya, Leo worked odd hours. His schedule was unpredictable. Leo woke as she entered the room. A light sleeper, unlike her.

"Hey," he said as he got up to greet her. She burrowed into his arms and embraced him back. She looked up to meet the kiss he always had waiting to greet her. Kissing Leo and being in his arms were as natural as breathing to her nowadays.

"How was your day?" she asked.

"Busy with the new club. Let's have dinner. Paula has it ready. We were waiting for you; then we'll talk."

The table was set for just the two of them tonight. Vito, Drago, and Romano often joined them for meals.

"We're expanding a casino in Vegas," Leo began. "I have to head over there to oversee construction."

"When are you leaving?" she asked.

"Tomorrow morning. The project manager had an accident, and I need to be there to take over. Luciano is in Tahoe overseeing a new project, so he can't leave."

"How long will you be gone?"

"About a week," he answered before taking a sip of his wine. She fought her instinct to pout. She didn't really know what their relationship was; she figured she'd deal with it when it came to the end of their engagement. But she couldn't lie to herself. She'd miss him. It would be the first time they would really be apart. She already missed him just thinking about it. Had she really come to depend on him that much? No, she didn't depend on him, but he'd become a part of her in more ways than she'd like to admit.

"It's only a week," he added as if to reassure her.

"I'll miss you," she admitted. He grinned, picked up her hand and placed a kiss on it.

"I'll miss you too. I'll come back as soon as I can. You can always join me if you want," he explained as he kissed the tip of each finger, distracting her. His lips were warm and soft and promised seduction.

She wished she could just say 'to hell with work.' But she had bills to pay. Living rent free didn't stop her student loan payment and other bills.

"Maybe if you're not back by Friday," she replied hopefully.

"Just let me know, I'll have the plane ready for you-" Leo was cut off by Paula's entrance.

"Yes?" Leo inquired.

"Miss Valentina wishes to speak with Miss Freya," Paula explained holding up a house phone that Freya had no idea they had. Leo gave a curt nod, and Paula gave the phone to Freya.

"Hello?"

"Freya dear, it's Valentina. Are you free this Saturday?" Valentina replied enthusiastically.

"Umm, possibly. Leo-"

"Great! Let's get together. We need to plan your engagement party. I will be there around; well let's see...I'll let you sleep in. I will be there by ten."

"Well, I-"

"Wonderful. I will see you then. Good night, dear. Do give my handsome son a kiss for me." Valentina hadn't given Freya an option. She stared at the phone for a moment trying to wrap her mind around the call.

"What has she done?" Leo asked, amused.

Freya sighed. "Come back as soon as you can because Valentina is coming on Saturday morning to plan the engagement party," Freya explained with a pout.

Leo grinned. "I'll do my best to be back by then."

***

Freya woke as Leo moved to leave the bed. The sky was still dark, and a glance at the clock told her it was only 4:30 in the morning.

"You have to leave now?" she asked as she cuddled closer to his back. He turned to face her from his sitting position.

"I have to get there to meet with the crew." He lightly stroked her face.

"I'm going to miss you," she replied sleepily.

"And I, you." He leaned down to kiss her. His kiss awoke her senses.

Their lovemaking last night had been soft and slow. A long night of giving, receiving and satisfaction. She deepened the kiss, wrapping her arms around his neck to pull him closer to her. He accepted her challenge, met her demands, and gave her more.

The sheets were pushed aside as he climbed atop of her, their bodies naked and molded together. She craved his hardness, the warmth of his skin, the ridges of his muscles, and the contentment and rightness of him against her.

It never took much for her to be panting and ready for him. She was wet, and her body welcomed his thick, hard length. Her legs wrapped around him as he slid deeper. She moaned as his pubic hair met her bare skin. She met him thrust for thrust and moan for moan until they both cried their release. He fell on top of her, as spent as she felt. He held her close to him, and she clung to him, just savoring the moment. His heat wrapped around her and it felt so damn good that she wanted to keep him there forever.

"I love you," she whispered. She froze, unsure if she'd said that out loud or in her mind.

She knew she'd said it out loud when he pulled away and stared down at her. She couldn't read his face.

"I know," he replied after a moment. "And I want you to know that nothing between you and I has ever been fake." He leaned down and kissed her brow before taking her mouth into a deep kiss filled with promises he hadn't voiced. "We'll talk when I come back, I promise."

Freya watched him get ready to leave. He didn't say he loved her back, but she wasn't worried. Leo wouldn't lie to her, and she knew what she felt between them wasn't just sex. Leo cared for her, physically and emotionally, in ways no one had ever done. He didn't say it now. But he would. She knew it deep down in her soul.

Chapter Eighteen

The first night without Leo was lonely. The bed had felt cold and large. But he called her, and it was enough for her to know that there was something more between them. She looked forward to him coming home.

"If you walk into a pole from daydreaming, I won't even warn you," Drago told her in a serious tone.

Vito and Romano had gone to Las Vegas with Leo. Paula, Drago, and a few other bodyguards have been her constant company in the past three days. She was happy that Drago had his dinner with her and accompanied her on her walks with Honey afterward. Though Drago and the others shared several apartments in the same building, Drago had been staying in one of the guest rooms in their penthouse; she assumed because Leo ordered him too. She felt better having him in the penthouse with her. She would hate being alone in such a big place.

"I can't believe how easily she walks for you. It took me almost a year to get her to walk with me without pulling," Freya commented to Drago who held Honey's leash.

Drago grunted as a reply. While Romano was friendly and loved to talk, Drago was the opposite. He rarely spoke, only when necessary. She noticed that Vito liked to hassle Leo like a brother would and while Vito wasn't as outgoing as Romano, he was a lot warmer towards her than Drago. She didn't take offense since she knew Drago was like that to everyone else.

"You have to show her who the boss is," Marco quipped behind her. She almost forgot he was there. Marco was quiet. It was a different silence from Drago though. Drago was silent in a "get out of my face" way. Marco, however, was a silent watcher. He was always watching and spoke when spoken to, more so than Drago, but there was something about him that nagged at her.

She didn't know if it was because Drago, Vito, and Romano were part of Leo's circle, but she felt secure and safe with them, more so than any of the other bodyguards. She was never without one of the three because Leo trusted them the most. She knew that the four of them had mostly grown up together and that their families were friends. Even though Romano was younger than Leo, Drago, and Vito, who were all in their thirties, he was very much a part of their group.

Before she could respond, the chorus of a Pitbull song buzzed from her pocket. She'd chosen that particular tune as her ringtone one drunken night and decided she liked it. Leo's face flashed on her screen.

"Leo," she answered.

"Are you behaving?" Leo asked in a playful tone.

"Of course, I am. Ask Drago," she replied with a smile. Drago grunted again.

"What is this about girls' night?" Leo asked.

She'd told Drago that her friends were coming tomorrow night and that they would be going out for a Friday Girls' Night Out.

"Just Lena and a few other girls...we're going clubbing, but we're getting ready at home."

"Set it up with Drago, go to one of my clubs, or hell, all of them. Just stay at my club."

"I know. I was planning on it. We're going to Atmosphere," she explained. Atmosphere was a club owned by Leo's family, which she hadn't known until she asked Drago; it was known for playing early 2000 hits and on some occasion, all the way back to the 80s and 90s. What she loved about the city was that there was always a place you can go for any type of music you're looking for.

"Good. Drago will set up a table for you girls."

"I miss you," she added in a husky tone.

"I miss you too. I'll try to be back by tomorrow night. If not, then by Saturday night for sure."

"Okay, I can't wait to see you."

"You have no idea. Call me before you head to bed."

"Okay."

***

Leo sat in the penthouse suite of the Figurati hotel. The hotel the Costa family owned and the hotel he was in Las Vegas to oversee the expansion of. The hotel was named by his mother nearly twenty-five years ago, 'Figurati' meaning 'imagine' in Italian. It was his second favorite hotel, the first being the San Francisco Mozzafiato. Though his brother generally handled Las Vegas business, Leo took this trip to check on Vetrano business as well. Though the Costa was their own family, they were part of the Vetrano Famiglia. As Giovanni Costa's heir, Leo represented the Costa family. He'd told Freya the truth, he was here to oversee some expansion of Figurati, but the real reason was Famiglia business, and to tell Dante Vetrano that Leo was going to marry Freya Santos, an outsider.

When had their relationship turned real? He wasn't sure. It would be easy for him to say that his connection with her started that morning seven months ago when she'd saved his life. But when did that connection become love? Because he did not doubt that he loved her. The thought of letting her go, of not having her in his life, of her being in danger kept him awake. He was frightened for Freya, and that's how he knew it was real. Losing Freya scared him as much as he hated to admit it but admitting it to himself meant he would make sure it never happened.

The ringing of the phone he'd just used moments ago to speak to Freya, pulled him out of his musing.

"Yes?" Leo listened to what his man had to say. "*Sì, grazie.*"

It didn't surprise him to hear that Dante was there. Leo had announced his intention to marry Freya at a meeting in one of their underground casinos earlier. Dante was the heir to the Vetrano family, but he was also Leo's cousin. Dante's mother was Giovanni Costa's sister. Leo took a scotch bottle from the bar and two glasses and brought them to the coffee table as he waited for Dante to arrive. He happily greeted his cousin, they may live at different ends of the country, but they had grown up as friends and family.

"You are serious about marrying an outsider."

"As serious as I'll ever be about anything."

"You know you have my support, but you will hear opposition from others."

"They have no say as to who I choose to spend my life with. She is not family business, and if I do bring her in, she will have proven herself, but I do not want that life for her. I want her to be safe."

"Sometimes we do not have that choice."

"If something comes, I will handle it."

***

"Leo is really going to marry that outsider." Filipe did not respond. Bartolo did not expect his loyal guard to. "She is going to taint their blood." *She would.* If she bore any children, they would not be a full-blooded Italian, and they would not be accepted to run

La Famiglia business.

Chapter Nineteen

He needed Leo dead. Luciano would be easy to kill, and Giovanni would be easy to overthrow once his heirs were gone. But Leo was a problem. Those idiots he'd hired had fucked up big time, and he knew they were most likely dead. He didn't care; he knew they couldn't tell Leo anything about him. He'd made sure of it. Their fuck up had caused him to take a step back for months, delaying his plans.

Leo's engagement, however, was another problem. If the bitch gives him an heir, *La Famiglia* will not let him take over. The Costa family had the backing of the Vetrano family, and if any Costa heir were available, the Vetrano family would never let him have it. The girl could be used against Leo though. He could see it. She was a weakness Leo hadn't expected, and he knew he could use her to lure Leo. Leo had no idea who he was, and that's what would get him what he wanted.

He dialed the number on his untraceable phone.

"Yes?" his weapon answered.

"Remember who you are speaking to."

"I am. I do not bow down to you. Not yet. You are not the boss yet and when you do become the Don I am your heir. We are equal. Remember who's doing your dirty work." He controlled his irritation over the insolence. He would deal with him when the time came, but for now, he was useful.

"He has announced that he is marrying her. Is she pregnant?"

"Not that I know of. If she is, they have not told anyone, but there has been no trip to the doctors as far as I can tell."

"She gets a brat in her; they'll never let me takeover."

"She gets a brat in her; I'll make sure it dies with her."

"Good." He hung up; he had what he wanted.

***

He stared at the phone. He was furious over the possibility of having what was dangling in front of him taken away again. Not when he's so close. He didn't want him making a move, but he was tired of waiting around. Something needed to happen. He'd been waiting his whole life. Maybe it was time to start planning on his own.

He meant what he said. If Freya ended up pregnant, he'd pull that baby out of her and watch it die with his hand wrapped around its neck. *No one* was going to take what should belong to him again.

Chapter Twenty

Freya and the girls were treated like royalty. Their every need was handled right away. Guess if you were the boss' woman, you get treated like the boss too. She was glad that Drago and the other bodyguards had stayed away, like bouncers. Though Drago did drive them, he and the others gave her space. A waitress was assigned to them, something she noticed was just for them. Leo probably didn't want another incident like the last time she'd been in his club.

For the first time ever, she felt carefree. She didn't worry about how she's getting home or how much she was drinking because she knew Drago would make sure she got home safely. After a couple of shots and cheers, celebrating her *fake* engagement with the girls, they headed back to the dance floor.

***

Leo had worked nonstop to get back as fast as he could.

She's dirty dancing...

Holy fuck, she was. Leo wasn't sure if he should be appalled or turned on by Freya's bumping and grinding with her friends. He noticed the difference right away. She was relaxed and having a great time. She knew that she would be taken care of and he imagined that for the first time in her life, she's letting go of her control and just enjoying herself.

"Her hot friend is with her. Score," Vito said from behind him. Vito had a thing for Freya's short friend, Lena. It was sickening watching his friend act like a damn dog trying to get her attention.

"Your pink pants will definitely catch her attention." Leo and Vito both looked down at Vito's obnoxious pants.

"This is called being fashion forward. Unlike you, I have taste."

"I have taste, just not pink pants."

"It's not really pink; it's pastel."

"It's pink." Leo didn't wait for a response. He headed to the dance floor to join his fiancé. He'd be lying if he said he couldn't wait to get back to her. It was crazy, how much he missed her and how much he felt for her. She'd taken over his life and broke his discipline.

***

Freya was having such a great time dancing to a New Kids on the Block song that she didn't notice anyone approaching until an arm wrapped around her waist. She froze, the alcohol dulling her senses before she quickly recognized it was Leo holding her. She turned to face him and happily jumped into his arms.

"I missed you!" she was sure she shouted.

"I can tell," he replied with a laugh. "Dance with me."

She had never felt confident enough to dance with men, especially this kind of dancing but something in his touch and probably the alcohol told her she could. And she did. She danced with him like how she'd seen people do in clubs and music videos. She ground against him, loving the feel of his hands on her, loving the feel of him against her. Everyone else forgotten, just her, Leo, and the music.

Chapter Twenty One

She groaned as sunlight blinded her. A chuckle next to her had her swatting the person before she remembered it was Leo. *He's back*!

"You're back!" she nearly cried as she jumped into his arms. She remembered him last night, but for a moment, when she woke up, she thought it was just a dream because the night had felt surreal. She'd danced and drank and danced and drank again with her girlfriends, and then Leo came. She didn't remember much after that, right now she just knew she had a wonderful time.

"I am," he replied as he kissed her forehead.

"I missed you," she told him as she settled on top of him.

"And I missed you," he replied before giving her a kiss on the lips.

"And I'm naked," she replied, realizing that they were both completely naked.

"So am I," he laughed as he gave her another kiss.

"I probably look like a hot mess," she told him before kissing him. This time it was a long kiss.

"You always look beautiful," he whispered against her lips.

She sat up and straddled his hips. She could feel his penis prodding against her.

"You always look beautiful," he repeated as his hands reached up and cupped her breasts. She moaned when he pinched her nipples. Her breasts felt heavy, and she knew she was getting wet. She hummed as she let herself enjoy his fingers working their magic on her nipples.

She rubbed herself against his length. His cock hardened and poked her. He started to sit up, but she stopped him with a hand on his chest. She moved and straddled his legs before she leaned down to lick the tip of his cock. It jumped at the touch of her tongue. She used her hands to guide it to her mouth. He groaned as she took the swollen head into her mouth and sucked. She ran her tongue over the slit, tasting the slightly salty pre-cum. She took more of him into her mouth, running her tongue over his length and sucking hard.

His hand delved into her hair before gripping a handful of it. He guided her, bobbing her head up and down on his cock. She savored his taste and loved the idea of making him lose control. He didn't give her a chance.

"Fuck! I'm about to cum. I want to be in that pussy, baby." He pulled her hair to pull her mouth off of him. She almost pouted, but he took her mouth into a searing kiss. She pushed him back down to his back and moved to straddle his waist again. She guided his penis into her and moaned as she sank down, one hard inch at a time.

He let her ride him, let her set the pace but soon began to meet her. She rode him, and he drove up to meet each thrust. Pretty soon she lost control and rode him harder, no rhythm just a need she wanted to satisfy. He surprised a cry out of her when he suddenly pulled out and flipped her under him before plunging back into her just as quickly. He fucked her hard, and she loved every second of it.

"Harder, please," she cried.

He gave it to her. She realized that he'd give her

anything she ever asked for. Her orgasm came with a cry of his name. It felt like a never-ending release as he pounded into her through it. He pounded her into another orgasm, quickly after her first one. The second orgasm drained her. He shouted his released.

***

"Valentina will be here soon," Freya reminded Leo. Valentina wanted to plan their engagement party.

"Plan it like its real," Leo quietly told her. She looked up at him from where she laid her head on his chest. He was watching her. She wondered if he wanted it to be real because she realized herself how much she wanted it too.

"I don't know where we're headed, but for now, I want to think of it as real," she explained.

"It is real. Everything we've done is real," Leo insisted as he pulled her up closer to him. He leaned over her and kissed her. "Every kiss and every touch is real. There's no deadline for this engagement. And I never expected it to be more than what it was, but I know that right now, probably tomorrow, and maybe a month from now, I want to wake up with you next to me. Just like this."

It was much more than she'd expected and even though he hadn't told her that he loved her, she knew he cared. She knew she mattered to him, and for now, that was enough for her.

***

"Dear, you look beautiful, but you do look like you need to sleep more," Valentina greeted as she pressed her cheek against Freya's. "Leo, you need to make sure she is getting enough rest," Valentina added as she did the same to Leo.

"I try mother, but she's stubborn," Leo replied with a wink to Freya.

"Well, you boys have fun. Freya and I will be busy. Luciano is taking Freya and I to Quinces," Valentina added as Luciano hugged Freya in greeting. Freya recognized the upscale French-Italian restaurant located at the center of the piers.

"I promise to take good care of them," Luciano joked.

"Marco will go with you," Leo replied. It was an order and was expected. Leo would normally have Romano, Vito, or Drago stay with Freya, but he trusted his brother.

Valentina had her own guards, much like Freya, she was never without one, but with Luciano being there, she had only taken one. Freya kissed Leo goodbye as they headed to separate cars in the garage. Freya and Valentina sat in the back of the black Mercedes while Leo headed to his BMW. Marco and Valentina's guard, Piero, followed in a black SUV while Luciano and his bodyguard, Antonio settled into the Mercedes.

Valentina was quickly recognized, and they were seated on the patio sitting area. Valentina chatted about what they needed to do for the engagement party and Luciano made quips to tease his mother over her enthusiasm. Marco and Piero occupied two other tables surrounding them while Antonio had stayed with the cars. Freya didn't understand the need for so much precaution but then reminded herself that Leo had been kidnapped and could have died.

Freya wasn't really interested in planning parties. Instead, she enjoyed the beautiful city while Valentina droned on about the engagement party. She knew it was rude of her, but the weather was perfect, the atmosphere cheerful, and the food delicious. She couldn't help but feel absolutely content at that moment. The only thing missing was Leo. She didn't know why but when she thought of Leo, she often looked around as if expecting him to appear. That's when she'd noticed a motorcycle approaching; its passengers were decked in all black. She thought about how hot they must feel being covered in leather and black when the sun was shining brightly. Luciano stood, excusing himself to use the restroom, just as she and Piero noticed there was something off about the couple on the motorcycle.

They had slowed down, and premonition warned her that something bad was about to happen. She shoved Luciano as hard as she could, causing him to fall before she heard a popping sound. Before she could react, Piero shoved both her and Valentina down and overturned the table as more popping sounds filled the air. Soon the screams drowned them out.

People were running and screaming, and it took her a moment to realize that someone had shot at them! She remembered Luciano and pushed away from the ground. He was down on the ground, dark liquid seeping through his white shirt. Someone grabbed her leg to stop her from moving. Not realizing it was for her safety, she kicked back. The moment she was released she crawled to Luciano, staring at the blood brought back memories of Leo. Their faces were so much alike. But Luciano was awake and talking.

"What the hell, get down, Freya," he demanded as he tried to push her down.

She ignored him, and as she'd done to Leo, she took her sweater off, bundled it and covered the wound on his shoulder. He groaned as she put pressure on it. She could hear the sirens, and the screaming seemed to fade. Piero was frantically speaking on the phone.

She glanced up as cops arrived at the same time Marco came to her side. Valentina pulled away from Piero and joined Freya at Luciano's side.

"Oh, my baby, my poor boy," Valentina said distraughtly

"I'm okay ma...go with Piero," Luciano replied in pain.

"No, I will stay with you," Valentina demanded.

"No ma, you need to go with Piero. Now," Luciano ordered. Piero grabbed for Valentina to force her up. "You too, Freya," Luciano added as Marco reached for her.

"NO!" Marco and Luciano were surprised by her outburst.

Paramedics came, and she was shuffled aside, away from Luciano and into Marco's arms. She refused to budge from their side, even going as far as to slap Marco's hands away when he tried to get her moving. The cops were trying to get some sort of order to piece together what happened.

When the cops ordered her away from Luciano and the paramedics, she didn't budge. They were about to forcefully move her when she heard her name being called. She looked up and saw Leo running towards her.

The cops tried to stop him from entering the scene, but he ignored them and the next thing she knew, she was throwing herself at him. He held her tight, and she knew everything was going to be okay.

Leo had run the whole six blocks to get to the restaurant, ignoring stop lights, dodging people and cars, depending on his men to deal with the consequences. The call from Marco had nearly stopped his heart. Someone had shot at them, and Luciano was down. Driving would have taken longer; the city wasn't made for cars, so he ran.

Marco told him that his mother was safe and in the car. Piero had followed procedure. Marco said Freya had refused to leave. He didn't bother responding or throwing out an order. He had to get to her and his brother. He ignored the cops that tried to stop him.

The sight of Freya with blood on her hands and clothes made it hard for him to breath. It wasn't until she was on his arm that he could finally take a full breath. He didn't care that she was staining his clothes, he was just so damn glad she was safe. He held her tight, assuring himself that she was okay. As she shook in his arms, and the paramedics worked on Luciano, he demanded an explanation from Marco.

"Go with Vito. I need to check on Luciano," he gently told her. She didn't let go right away, and he had to take hold of her arms to get her to listen to him. He gave her a quick kiss, to assure her, and himself, before handing her to Vito. He spoke to the paramedics to know where they were taking his brother and insisted that Drago go with them. The cops recognized him, of course they would, and helped convinced the paramedics to allow Drago into the ambulance. Luciano met Leo's eyes briefly before he passed out from blood loss.

Leo interfered before the cops could speak to Freya. He'd insisted that they speak to her at the hospital where, his mother and the bodyguards would also be. He needed to speak to them first before the cops did.

Leo led Freya to the waiting car, joining her in the back seat not only because he needed to speak with her, but also because she had a grip on him. He pulled her close to him, nearly sitting her on his lap. He worried she might go into shock. Pulling the details from her was like pulling hairs one by one.

When she finally managed to speak, despite her choppy explanation, he got the gist of what went down.

It was a nice day. The sound of a motorcycle made her look. She wondered why they were dressed in black and completely covered on such a warm day. She had a bad feeling, or maybe she was paranoid. Luciano was going to the restroom. Luciano fell. Piero turned the table over. There was a lot of screaming. Her knees and elbows hurt.

He held a curse when he checked her knees and elbows and found them badly scraped. He needed to talk to Piero and Marco as well. Marco was in the back row and had been facing the opposite direction of the shooter. He'd only turned when he heard a commotion, Luciano falling and then the shots that followed.

He called Antonio and ordered him to take his mother to the hospital instead. His mother needed to be checked too. Leo made a call to his father who, he had no doubt, was on his way to the hospital already.

***

Leo quietly left Freya's room when he saw his father on the other side of the window. Freya had started showing symptoms of shock as they neared the hospital and was quickly admitted. She began having trouble breathing, had begun to feel nauseated and complained of headaches. She'd suffered an acute stress reaction. Her blood pressure was high, and she was medicated to help control it and prevent further damage.

Luciano had gone into surgery, and though the bullet hadn't hit anything vital, it had shattered and scattered fragments that needed to be removed. Any remnants of the bullet could cause an infection and clearing the pieces of the bullets took time. Their parents had stayed in the waiting room during Luciano's surgery, and Leo had stayed with Freya.

Freya had saved Luciano's life. According to Piero, she seemed to be the first one to notice the shooter. She'd pushed Luciano before the attacker even lifted the gun. If she hadn't pushed him, the bullet would have hit something more vital. He wondered if she'd realized that she'd saved two Costa heirs, he thought bitterly. Of course, she wouldn't know that, wouldn't understand it. She'd been shot at twice since taking up with him and knowing her; she wouldn't blame him.

"How is she?" Giovanni Costa looked as cool and calm as ever, but Leo knew his father was simmering. There would be hell to pay for today's shooting. They had handled Leo's kidnapping carefully because Leo had wanted to make sure that he had the whole picture. Giovanni had a different idea. He'd been ready to shoot up everyone and anyone. Thirty years ago, that was how they did things. Today, Leo had worked hard to make sure nothing could lead back to them. Though he was tempted to let his father shoot every fucking one he felt might be responsible, he knew the result would just fuck with everything they'd worked hard to achieve.

"She's fine; they're just monitoring her blood pressure to make sure it's stable. We'll join you once they're finished with her," Leo answered.

"Luciano is out of surgery. They are preparing to transfer him to a room so that we can see him," Giovanni explained. "It seems, I owe Freya another 'thanks' for saving another son's life," Giovanni added gruffly.

"Maybe not now. They've just got her under control. I don't want to stress her out any more than she already is."

"You are going to marry her." It was a demand.

"Yes," Leo simply answered. He had planned on eventually marrying Freya; he'd announced his intention to *La Famiglia*. He thought he loved her like he did his family.

After today, he knew he was wrong. He'd never felt fear like he'd felt when he learned about the shooting. He'd never been so scared in his life at the thought of her being taken from him. She might not be ready to accept him, but he wasn't going to let her go. Not ever. She was his, and he'd make sure she understood that. He'd spend his life making sure she would never want to leave him.

"Good, good... I will see you both in a bit.

Antonio will let you know where Luciano's room will be."

"Dad," Leo called out to stop him from leaving. "I need you to hold off on taking any direct actions." The good old days no longer work in today's world.

"You want me to do nothing while your brother and your woman are hospitalized?" Giovanni Costa demanded.

"Yes, because we don't know who it is." Leo knew they couldn't just kill them all. The men that followed them after they'd left his parents' house were another bunch of low level hired help. Just like the man who'd shot up the BART train. None of them could tell him who hired them. None of them were connected either. All three groups that had attacked them were scattered, wannabe gangs who wanted money and didn't have enough brain.

"We'll talk about this later," Giovanni dismissed.

***

Freya sighed as they entered their bedroom. After she'd had an embarrassing nervous breakdown, the cops had insisted that she talked to them. Leo had wanted to wait, but she wanted it to be over with. She'd told them what happened. She didn't tell them that she had a feeling that told her to push Luciano before the shooter began shooting. She just told him that the noise from the motorcycle made her look and when she saw the gun, which she really didn't see, she pushed Luciano out of the way. She'd told them that that was all she could really remember, anything after was a blur, which was the truth. Piero and Marco were able to tell them what happened after she'd seen the shooter.

When pressed as to why a shooter wanted to shoot them, she insisted she had no idea. But she did have an idea. She had a feeling that it was all connected to Leo. She had been shot at twice, accused of murdering a man she couldn't remember and there was the car chase. She started to believe that the bodyguards weren't just to keep her safe from being mugged because of her ring. But did it matter to her?

She cared about Leo.

No, it was beyond caring for him.

She knew she loved Leo. But did she really know him? Did what she didn't know about him change the way she felt about him? She glanced at him, noticing the blood prints on his blue dress shirt. Blood she'd gotten on him when she'd seen him. They'd cleaned up the blood on her at the hospital, but she hadn't wanted to change into the hospital gown. She kept her dress on, blood and all. It had been one of her favorite dresses, but she wondered if she'd be able to wear it again, even if they managed to remove the blood stain.

At least Luciano was okay. She'd seen him herself, and he even joked that she needed a little more meat on her to push him harder next time. She didn't know whether to laugh or cry at the joke. She was pretty sure she did both.

Valentina couldn't stop hugging her either. Freya was just so glad that no one else was hurt. Once they were sure Luciano was okay, Leo had taken her home.

"How about a bath?" Leo asked her, pulling her out of her thoughts.

"Maybe just a shower. Join me?"

He helped her undress and quickly joined her after taking his clothes off. He'd been so gentle with her since the shooting, and yet she felt something darker in him.

"What's happening?" she asked him. He didn't respond. He continued to wash her, rinsing the shampoo from her hair. She didn't know if he trusted her enough to tell her the truth.

He didn't respond until after he'd dried them both, wrapped her in her bathrobe and carried her to bed. He sat on their bed and pulled her back against him. She didn't know if he was thinking about what to say to her or if he wasn't going to answer her at all. She sighed and relaxed against him, her wet hair pressed against his chest.

"If I tell you then there's no turning back," he finally answered. "You wouldn't be able to leave me. I wouldn't allow it. Neither will a lot of people."

She knew she loved him. But to never be able to leave him? Would she ever want to do that?

"It would go both ways though. If I couldn't leave you, you couldn't leave me either." She turned to look up at him. He stroked her face and then her hair, running his fingers through the wet strands.

"That doesn't sound so bad," he told her with a small smile. He leaned towards her as he pulled her closer to him. The kiss was soft and sweet. He angled her to her back as he settled on top of her. He kissed her lips several times before he moved to kiss her jaw, then her cheek, then her forehead and then the tip of her nose.

"Only ask what you can handle," he told her. "Don't ask about things you don't want to know."

Again, he understood her. He understood her thoughts even when she didn't voice them. He understood her hesitation at accepting what she already deduced on her own. Was she ready to face it?

"I love you," she replied. She hoped that was the right answer. She hoped it conveyed what she was ready for because she didn't know it herself.

"I know," he said. "My life froze when I got that call. All I could think about was getting to you. Making sure you were alright. It was the scariest moment of my life. Scarier than when I looked down the barrel of a gun knowing I was going to die."

"And all I could think about was that I wanted you there and you came. I just wanted you there because you always make things right. When I'm with you, I feel like I don't have to worry about anything. That I don't have to be afraid of anything," she replied. Freya, who never depended on anyone, trusted Leo with her life. She wasn't just trusting him; she depended on him when she never did in the past. She'd never needed anyone until Leo.

"The Costa family is more than hotels, nightclubs, and casinos. The Costa family is The Family," he explained, emphasizing The Family.

"The Family," she said, running the word through her mind. She understood what he meant.

"The Family...*La Famiglia* will always come first, but I promise that you will be my world and my life."

"And you would be mine," she replied. "Tell me what is happening," she solidified.

"Someone wants to be the next head of *La Famiglia*," he said as he lay back and pulled her against him. "We don't have enemies, at least not ones who are big enough to want a war and no one big enough to win a war against us. Someone from within wants to be the next Giovanni Costa. The only way to do that is to get rid of the heirs and any possible heirs."

"Your father is the head of *La Famiglia*?" she asked.

"Yes, but he's as good as retired. I've taken over. The best time to levy for the position is when there is a change in power. It's why they went after me first. I am the biggest threat. When they couldn't kill me, they went after you to use you against me."

"Use me against you?"

"You are important to me. They consider you my weakness. Outside of my family, I had no weakness, until you," Leo explained.

"I don't want to be the reason you get hurt."

"They want to hurt me, so they'll find a way, regardless of whether you are there or not. I've just made it easier for them by being with you."

"What will you do now?"

"I'm going to protect you and protect *La Famiglia*, and I'm going to get rid of the threat. It's best if you don't know the rest."

"I can't lose you," she confessed.

"And I can't lose you. Believe in that. I will do anything in my power to make sure that we get through this."

"I love you," she whispered as she settled her head against his shoulder. He held her tight against him. He didn't say it, but she felt it.

Chapter Twenty Two

The ringing of his phone jolted Leo awake. A glance at the clock showed that he'd only been asleep for a couple of hours. He answered the phone as soon as he saw who was calling. He wouldn't be calling at this hour unless it was an absolute emergency. The urgency in Bartolo's voice and the sound of a gunfight wiped the sleep from his mind.

"I'm on my way." He ended the call without waiting for a response and quickly dialed Vito's number. He dressed quickly as he gave orders and then called Romano to give him another set of commands as he holstered his gun.

Freya sat up and watched him as he ordered his men. He looked dangerous and ready for battle. When he saw her watching him, he headed to her, reached out and pulled her to him. He kissed her, and she held on to him.

"Stay safe," she whispered against his lips.

"Stay put," he replied. His hand cupped her head as he pulled her into another kiss, this one brief.

"Wait for me," Leo told her as he pulled away. He quickly headed out of their room, and she sat back, trying to control the turmoil inside her. She didn't understand what was happening but with the shooting just yesterday and the other incidents, she knew that Leo was heading somewhere dangerous. The gun told her that.

Leo met Drago in front of the elevator that would take them down to the garage where Romano was waiting with the cars. Leo had ordered Vito to gather men and meet them at the warehouse near Crockett. Though that side of the bay area was Bartolo's region, the Costa family owned the territory.

"Sandro, head up. Marco and Santi will stay here," Leo ordered the three remaining guards. He didn't want to leave Freya without his trusted men, but he needed them. With the attack on Luciano, Freya, and his mother yesterday, he knew he had a rat in La Famiglia. He didn't know if he really was walking into a rescue or an ambush. The only ones who would benefit from the removal of the Costa family were the Capos, and he knew the enemy was one of them. He didn't trust his Capos, but he couldn't very well let Bartolo be attacked if he wasn't the enemy. He had a responsibility as the boss of La Famiglia, and he couldn't leave them hanging.

***

Freya knew she wouldn't be able to go back to sleep, so she decided to get ready for the day. By the time she had showered and dressed, the clock read 4:45 AM. Leo had been gone for fifty minutes. She knew Paula would still be asleep, and she didn't want to bother her, so she stayed in her room, trying to distract herself with makeup. She'd done her makeup twice now and still hated how pale she looked. In the end, she settled on black eyeliner and mascara with dark red lipstick. She wanted to look good when Leo came back. If he didn't come back by noon, she decided she'd visit Luciano at the hospital and wait for Leo there. At least there, she would have someone to distract her. She–

Fast knocking on her bedroom door stopped her musing. The door opened before she could call them in.

"There's an emergency, I need you to come with me," Marco rushed out.

"What happened? What–"

"Boss's hurt. Let's go," Marco cut off her questions. She quickly followed him. He took hold of her arm and led her to the elevator. She wondered where Sandro was. Sandro had let her know that Leo had sent him up there earlier.

"Where's Sandro?" she asked as the elevator took them down to the garage.

"Boss needed him somewhere else," Marco answered. A black SUV was parked in front when the elevator doors opened. Marco quickly shuffled her into the passenger seat and hurried into the driver's seat.

"What happened to Leo?" she asked. Her imagination was going wild.

"Trouble at Bartolo's," Marco answered as he maneuvered the car through fairly empty streets. She noted that they were heading away from the city.

"Where are we going? Where's Leo?" she asked as Marco nearly entered the freeway on two wheels. Marco didn't respond. "Marco, where are we going?" she asked again.

She watched him grip the stirring wheel tightly. He gave her a look but didn't answer. Her gut was screaming at her, telling her she needed to get out. This was wrong. She needed Marco to talk and give her time to figure this out. "Where–"

***

Leo called Romano over as soon as he was sure that it was done. Most of the attackers were dead; six dead and two left alive to be questioned. The direct attack was brazen. The tattoos on the attackers told him that they were a part of gangs.

"Go back to Freya," Leo ordered Romano as soon as he was close enough. Romano nodded, didn't complain or whine that he'd been sent to babysit his boss' girlfriend. It was probably because he knew just how important Freya was to Leo. Babysitting the boss' woman was below Romano's worth but Freya wasn't just any woman, she was family now.

"Shit, Bartolo just killed one of them," Vito told Leo. *Fuck. God damn Bartolo.*

***

Freya blinked to clear her eyes. Her head and face were throbbing. She touched her face trying to relieve the pressure and winced as she touched her swollen side. She looked around the dark room; there was a dim light coming from a small window high up on the wall. Where was she? What happ-Marco punched her! Why? Was Leo alright? Was he really hurt? Or was it all a lie? But where was Sandro? Why would Marco take her?

She looked around the room. The walls were cement, and it seemed like the room hadn't been used in a while. There was nothing around her, no clutter, no furniture, no nothing. There was one door, and she slowly pushed herself up. She felt a bit faint. It was a bit hot in the room. The sun was shining brightly through the window. How late was it? She was thirsty. How long has she been in here?

She went to the door and tried the doorknob. The knob turned to her surprise, but the door did not budge as she pulled to open it. She tried pushing instead and realized that there must be something on the other side keeping it shut. She banged on the door with her palm, stinging her hand. The door was heavy and didn't seem to make that much sound when she banged her hands on it. It was then when she noticed that her engagement ring was gone. Her bare finger left her feeling naked. Why had he taken her? And why had he taken her ring? Sure, it was worth a lot of money but why not just take the ring? Was he ransoming her?

"Hello?" she called out loudly, hoping someone would hear her. "Is anyone there?" she called out. She heard nothing. Where was she?

"Hello?" she yelled out again. Still, no sounds were coming from the other side. The door was made of heavy metal. She looked around again hoping to find something to bang on the door, but the room was completely empty except for her.

She had nothing on her. Marco hadn't even let her grab her purse or phone. How could she have been so stupid to believe him? She should have questioned him more before they left. She should have tried calling Leo first! Leo told her to stay put. Why hadn't she listened?

"Marco?" she called out. "Hello?" She tried screaming louder. She tried shouting for someone. But no one was there. No one came. There was no noise. She was sweating from the afternoon heat. She felt claustrophobic. She sat on the floor, next to the door as she continued to try and make noise in case anyone comes by to hear her.

When her arms began to cramp, and her voice became hoarse, she leaned against the wall and stared at the ringless finger. Leo wouldn't leave her. She had to believe that he was okay. Leo would find her. She had to believe that.

***

Leo didn't let his reaction show. Romano's call had frozen him. Something latched on to his heart and squeezed it. It was almost hard to breathe. Paula and Sandro were hurt, Santi was dead, and Freya and Marco were missing. He'd made a mistake.

The warehouse was so far out in the middle of fucking nowhere that no one called the cops. No one heard the gunfire, no one heard the screams, and no one heard the shot that ended the life of the last survivor. He hadn't had anything useful to share. He was just paid to attack this place and kill anyone that wasn't one of them. When everyone was dead, they were supposed to burn the place to the ground. Something a rival family would have done in the past, kill the enemy and destroy their resources before taking over their territory. But Leo didn't believe it was another family. He knew it was someone from within.

Leo glanced at Bartolo Lombardi. He was a friend of his father; he'd started out as a soldier and made his way up to a capo for the Costa family. Many thought he was loyal to his bones and that was how he'd made it up to his position as a capo. Giovanni Costa thought he had a lot of potential and saw determination for his need to have more, to be bigger, to be higher in La Famiglia ranks. Leo saw him as too ambitious. Ambitious enough to think he could be the next boss. But would he really kill his own men? He would if it served a purpose.

But the last attacker had been told to kill anyone who wasn't theirs. That meant Bartolo would have been killed too if he'd been caught. When Leo and his men arrived, Bartolo had only one soldier left of his four.

Vito and Drago were never far from Leo. It was their duty to protect the Costa heir.

"What is it?" Vito demanded.

"Freya and Marco are missing. Paula and Sandro are on their way to the hospital. Santi is dead."

"Fuck. This was a diversion," Vito voiced what they were thinking.

"Take over here," Leo ordered Drago. "I don't trust him." Leo didn't need to tell Drago who he meant.

Leo and Vito left just as the cleanup crew arrived.

"Talk to me," Vito said as they left the compound and entered the freeway.

"I made a mistake. I shouldn't have left her without one of you."

"You're not psychic. You couldn't have known this would happen. You did what you were supposed to do."

"I should have known better, especially after yesterday," Leo insisted. "Fuck, I haven't even checked on Luciano."

Leo called his father.

***

"Tell me what you need," Giovanni said with conviction. He might not have liked how Freya came into their life, but she was family now. She had saved both of his sons, and that had earned her his love and loyalty. Even if she hadn't, she was Leo's, and he would do anything for his family.

"I need the family safe so that I can focus on finding Freya."

"Luciano is well protected. I will keep your mother with me."

"I will call you later." Leo hadn't accepted or asked for his help.

Leo had been raised to be the heir of the Costa family, and he had never failed to meet Giovanni's expectations, he often surpassed them. His son was hurting, and as much as he let his son take over the family, Giovanni was still the head of this family and had his fingers in everything.

"How can we help him, Gio?" Valentina asked.

"We find out who the rat is," Giovanni answered. He began making calls. He'd find the son of a bitch.

***

Leo was a patient man, but he wasn't now.

"Turn this whole city upside down. Everyone will answer to me. Find her." The order was clear. His men would be busting doors and gang hideaways until somebody fucking talked. He'd kill them all, wipe out their existence if he needed to. Someone was hiring these little fuckers, and Leo was going to get that name. Leo's way wasn't working, so, he'll do it his father's way. He would set this whole fucking city on fire if he needed to.

Chapter Twenty Three

Freya woke to the sound of metal scraping. The door of her prison swung open revealing a tall figure. She was hungry and thirsty. She'd spent the day in the room with no one answering her calls. When night had fallen, she was left all alone in the dark. She'd never been so frightened in her life. She hated the darkness. She'd cried herself to sleep. When she'd woken the next day, she felt dirty, and her stomach hurt. Her white jeans were dirty from sleeping on the ground, and her light sweater had barely kept the cold away. With nothing to do but wait, she'd slept her hunger and thirst away. Night had fallen again, and there was no light in the room to show her who he was. The light shining brightly behind the figure hid his identity.

"What do you want?" she asked as she slowly sat up. She tried to see behind the figure but saw no one else.

"What do I want? I want the world. But for now, I'll settle for everything the Costa family owes me," Marco answered. She recognized his voice even if she couldn't see his face. He came closer and crouched down near her. Not close enough for her to attack, but still close enough to the exit to stop her from escaping.

"It should have been mine, to begin with, you know," he casually told her.

"What should have been yours?" she asked, wanting to understand why she'd been taken.

"I should have been the one to take over La Famiglia. I dedicated my whole life to the damn family. Leo stole it from me."

"How?" she asked.

"My mother was Camilla Rossi. She was Giovanni's mistress."

Was he saying he was Giovanni's son?

"I was born a month before Leo. I am the oldest. I should be the one taking over!"

"I didn't know–"

"Because Giovanni never admitted it! My own

father never acknowledged me!"

"Does he know?" Freya asked. She couldn't imagine Giovanni ignoring his own child. It didn't seem like he would be the type to ignore family. Family was more important to Giovanni than anything else.

"Of course, he knows! He'd been with my mother before he married Valentina! That woman stole him from my mother! He should have married my mother. I am his heir!" Marco ranted as he got up and paced.

"Why did you take me?" Freya asked as she got up on unsteady feet. If he stayed distracted with his ranting, she could make it out of there. Keep him distracted.

"Because Leo will come for you. I never thought that son of a bitch would settle down. He was the only one who was in the way, you know. Luciano would have been easy to get rid of. We almost had him the other day, but you ruined that. You seem to be ruining everything, Freya." His gazed suddenly focused on her.

"Leo is too cocky to see what's staring him in the face. Leo should be dead by now, but you came along and ruined it," he accused her as he slowly stalked towards her. A menacing look crossed his face. "What a little hero you are, Freya...always there to save the Costa boys."

"Say you get rid of Leo and Luciano. How would you become the heir? Drago, Vito or even Romano would be the more obvious choice for Giovanni. You can't kill them all." Marco's stalking backed her into the far wall, away from the door.

"I won't need to. Giovanni lost his chance. Giovanni has weakened La Famiglia. Once Leo and Luciano are gone, Giovanni will be easy to overthrow. He's an old man, and he's handed most of the family business to Leo. He'll be too sick with grief for his precious sons." Marco backed her against the wall, caging her with his body.

"Why wouldn't you need to? Who–"

"With the boss and underboss gone, the capos will fight for the position, but he'll easily defeat them. He'll be the logical choice. I'm his heir. Once he's in power, maybe I'll get rid of him too. He doesn't deserve it. He's just as greedy and useless as Giovanni."

"Who is he?" Freya tried to get away from him, but Marco pressed against her, and she tried to fight him off. He easily caught her hands and locked her wrists in a tight grip.

"That's for me to know," Marco told her. Freya tried to pull away from his painful hold, but Marco probably outweighed her by a hundred pounds. Her struggle felt useless. She tried stomping on his foot, but he laughed at her before he threw her against the wall with a flick of his hand.

Freya struggled to get up. He'd knock the breath out of her and pain radiated through her body from being slammed against the wall. Marco came closer, crouched in front of her. Through the hazy pain, Freya saw a crazed look in his eyes. Marco wasn't just hell-bent on revenge, Freya realized. Marco was unstable. Revenge or not, Marco was crazy, and he was watching her like he wanted to play with his food.

Chapter Twenty Four

"Here you go, boss." Vito grabbed the man's head and forced the heavily tattooed man to look at Leo.

"*Cabron.*" Asshole. Enrique Garcia was the leader of the fuck heads who'd tried to kill him the first time. He'd convinced Leo that he didn't know who hired the three dumbasses, low ranking members of his gang, but Leo was going to force every connection they knew out of this asshole.

"Mr. Costa. I have told you, we do not know who they were dealing with."

"I want the name of every single connection they knew, or I will blow the head off of every single member of your family."

"This is not our war." He was sweating because

he knew that Leo would do exactly as he'd said.

"It became yours when you got sloppy and connected yourself to them." This was why these gangs never worked. They had no quality. They wanted quantity, but you could have a thousand sheep, and a single Lion could eat them all.

Chapter Twenty Five

Leo stepped into the underground Chinese parlor like he owned the place. Men and women cried out in surprise. The men fled, not wanting to be caught in the crosshairs, and the women, prostitutes, ran or hid as Leo and his men headed to the back office. Drago kicked the closed door, ripping it open. The men inside jumped and quickly grabbed their guns, ready to fight. Drago stepped into the room, and Leo followed behind him. Weapons were lowered rapidly the moment they saw Leo. The Costa family let this triad stay in San Francisco as long as they remained in Chinatown. There were a lot of little gangs in the bay area, but they were no match for the Costa. Only gangs with money, size, and respect could prosper. Many of these gangs died out and formed new ones because none of them had all three. The La Famiglia and Costa family had that and more. Though this Triad was powerful, they all bowed to the Costa. You bow, or you die, it's as simple as that.

"Mr. Costa," Leland Fong, the current leader of this little Triad, said. "What can we do for you?"

Leo waltzed in like he owned the place, which he did. The Costa owned San Francisco. He took a seat on an empty couch, looking like he's about to take a fucking nap even though he was raging inside. He had a reputation to keep. No one would see how he's really losing it.

"Don't play stupid Leland; you know what I'm looking for." Every crooked cop and criminal knew who he was looking for. Leo had been turning the whole region upside down, trying to find Freya. The biggest gossip bitches were the crime family, so Leo had been kicking down doors, lighting a fire under everyone's ass.

"We do not have your woman." They wouldn't dare. Only a man with a death wish would.

"But you can tell me something."

"Nothing that will lead to your woman."

"I'm not hearing what I want to hear, Leland." He saw one of them twitch and it was enough for Drago to take the man down. Before anyone could blink, Drago had the man's head in his hands. "Drago is not a patient man, Leland; you know that. You got two seconds before he rips your guy's head off."

A burst of Cantonese filled the room, the men talking over one another, and telling shit to Leland.

"A man approached one of my prospects, wanting to put a hit out on you, months ago."

"And you didn't feel the need to tell me, huh? Maybe it should be your head Drago's holding."

"We didn't take it seriously. They'd have to be crazy to hit you. The prospect did not make it in."

"Leland, I'm about to burn this building to the ground with all of you in it."

"That's all I know. The prospect died in a knife fight."

"You have two options, Leland, you go find the fucker who tried to hire your guy, or you and your little crew get the fuck out of this city and don't come back." He didn't have to tell them 'or else.' They knew it meant, get out, get what Leo wanted, or die. Leo was nice enough to give them a choice. He got up and headed for the door. He heard a thud and a cry but didn't turn. He imagined Drago probably slammed the fucker against the wall. *Leo didn't fucking care.* All he cared about was finding Freya, even if it meant he'd need to kick down every fucking door and kill any fucker who didn't give him the answer he wanted.

Chapter Twenty Six

Her husband was angry and in a hurry. She hadn't meant to listen, but he'd left the door partially opened as he stormed into his office to take the call. He was angry and speaking in Italian to someone on the phone. Anna was born and raised in San Francisco, any Italian she knew, she'd learned from being married to Bartolo. She didn't like him, didn't want to marry him, but her father had forced her to. Bartolo was not a kind man despite the façade he presented to everyone as the jolly Italian restaurant owner. He was cruel. If he caught her eavesdropping, he'd beat her, but something told her she had to.

She understood that someone had taken something too early. Bartolo was good at never mentioning names when it came to his dealings, but he'd said the only one that mattered. Leo. The only Leo that mattered was Leo Costa. Someone had taken something from Leo and had taken it to one of Bartolo's warehouses. *Which one?* The longer she stayed, the sweatier her hands got. He'd kill her if he knew she heard. *Tell me where.*

Martinez.

She hurried back to their bedroom. Something had been taken from Leo Costa, and it was in Bartolo's Martinez Warehouse. This could be her escape, or this could be her death. If she hadn't understood it correctly, she'd not only have to deal with Bartolo; she'd be at the mercy of Giovanni Costa. Should she go? She had to take the chance. Bianca was in school and in no danger at the moment. She wasn't just doing this for herself; she was doing this for Bianca too, before Bartolo married her off to some old man who'd abuse her.

She dressed quickly but made sure she looked impeccable. Bartolo would be angry if she looked sloppy. She waited at least forty minutes before approaching him, so he wouldn't be suspicious of her sudden departure. She plastered a smile on her face and knocked on his office door. It was risky, but it would be more dangerous if she just left without telling him. She had to pretend she knew nothing.

"What?"

"Honey, I'm going to Valentina's."

"Valentina?" He was frazzled.

"Yes, remember I had mentioned that she wanted me to help her plan Leo's engagement party." She did no such thing, but she knew he wouldn't question Valentina. Bartolo believed that women knew nothing of their husbands' business, but they knew much more than their husbands would imagine.

"Why would she ask you? You have no taste." Bartolo was staring at her; she could see the suspicion. She kept the bright smile on her face and exaggerated her excitement. "She loved your birthday party last year, she told me, and had asked me to go over who we had used for the party."

"Valentina might not be up to it today. There is something going on."

"But Valentina hadn't called to cancel with me. In fact, she'd called me yesterday to confirm that I was still coming today. She even promised *Sfogliatella*." Bartolo stared at her, taking note of every inch. Trying to find a hint of a lie in her mannerisms. He wouldn't dare call Valentina to confirm with her; he knew that that would insult Valentina who believed herself to be highly independent.

"Fine. Be home by the time Bianca is home."

"I will dear. Goodbye." She came closer, leaned in, and kissed his cheek. For some reason, it felt like she was really saying goodbye to him.

She hurried to her car, no bodyguard followed her, and if they had, she didn't care. She drove to Piedmont, exactly where she said she was going, straight to the Costa mansion. The guard at the gate was expected, and she told them that she was there to speak to Giovanni, that it was imperative. The fact that she had asked for Giovanni and not Valentina was what she was counting on getting her into the Costa house without an appointment. She, being a wife and an outsider of La Famiglia, would have no reason to speak to him. After the car was inspected, she was asked to move to the passenger seat, while one of the bodyguards drove her to the front of the mansion. She was searched upon exiting the car. Giovanni greeted her with a dark look and Anna was suddenly afraid that she would die today.

Chapter Twenty Seven

Marco was raging. How dare Filipe come here and tell him what he could or couldn't do? He was Bartolo's dog, not someone who should be talking to him like this.

"You acted against orders. Bartolo wasn't ready. He didn't have everything in place." Marco had had enough. Filipe might be a fucking giant, but he was ugly as fuck. He was a fucking troll, that's what he was, *a fucking troll*. Trolls deserved to die. Marco didn't even blink as he picked up the gun on the table and shot the fucking troll in the chest. The shocked look on his face was enough to make Marco giddy. Filipe fell to his knees, trying to grab the gun from his holster at the same time he tried to stop the bleeding in his chest. "Didn't see that coming did you, Ugly? Well, fuck you and Bartolo. Bartolo is next!" Marco pointed the gun and emptied it into Filipe's face and chest. *No fucking way he's going to come back from that.*

He reloaded his gun and turned to the back room. Freya would have heard that. It would have scared her. The thought of her fear aroused him. The adrenaline was rushing straight to his dick. She wasn't his type, but she was fuckable. He could even say he liked her a little. She showed him respect. Wouldn't it just piss Leo off if he knew Marco fucked his woman? Maybe he'd choke her with his dick. Maybe she'd enjoy it more than fucking Leo. He was better than Leo after all.

He had enjoyed hurting her yesterday, but Bartolo's call had interrupted his pleasure. He had to clean up some problems, and then he was too fucking tired to beat her some more. Today he was going to do a different kind of beating. Maybe he should record it, record himself fucking her, tearing that pussy and face up, and then send it to Leo.

***

She woke to the sound of arguing. She was still in the dark, alone, with nothing to protect her, but she was alive. Pain ran through her body. A phone call had saved her from more beating from Marco, and she nearly wept in relief when he slammed the door and locked her in there alone. But she dreaded his return. She'd spent three days locked in the room with no food or water. She felt weak but tried to conserve her energy. Nothing gave her comfort except the thought of Leo coming for her, but she couldn't sit around waiting. She had to get out on her own. Leo wouldn't always be there to save her, and he'd want her to fight her way out.

Whoever Marco was arguing with; she couldn't hear, was keeping his voice low. Loud popping sounds had her jumping. *Gunshots.* She'd never forget the sound of it. Who was dead? Was Marco dead? She could hear someone moving; then she heard the door being unlocked. Someone was there. She hoped they killed Marco and came to save her. She backed away from the door, pressing herself against the far wall.

To her disappointment and horror, it was Marco who entered. He came to her with a purpose in his stride. He pressed his body against her. "You know, I like you. It's too bad I can't keep you." He pressed his bulge against her stomach, terrifying her. "You're really pretty and small. I bet you're nice and tight," he taunted her.

She struggled against him. "You know what they say? When they're small on the outside, they're small on the inside too. I bet Leo tears that pussy up. I know I would." He tried to kiss her, but she resisted. She fought to get away from him. Her struggles were ineffective. She hurt everywhere, but she wasn't going to let him do that to her. She didn't have a weapon; she only had

252

herself. She decided to use her head.

She banged her head as hard as she could against his. It worked. She felt dazed, but he had let go of her. His scream seemed more in anger than pain. She saw enough to see blood. She used her knees and felt him completely let go of her. She stumbled away from him and made it out of the door. She was in a warehouse. She saw some tables and chairs and looked for a door. She ran toward one that she hoped would get her out. She nearly stumbled over a big body, whom she recognized as Felipe. She didn't dwell on it. Instead, she kept going, running hard, as far as she could and was surprised to find herself in the middle of nowhere.

Oh, dear God, there was nowhere to run! All she could see were hills and dry grass with a few scattered trees. She ran. She hoped she'd eventually find a road; there had to be one. She could hear him shouting, hear him coming after her. She ran as fast as her legs would take her, ignoring the pain, and the hunger and thirst. She needed to save herself.

***

Vito gunned the car towards the warehouse in Martinez. Another warehouse in the middle of fucking nowhere, just twenty minutes from where he had been when she was taken! Leo swore he was going to burn down every fucking warehouse he owned that's in the middle of nowhere, once he got Freya back.

The answer had come from a surprising source. Anna had heard Bartolo talking to someone about something being taken from Leo, and she'd run to Giovanni in hopes of protecting her daughter, Bianca. Giovanni had immediately called Leo. While Leo went to get Freya, his father went for Bartolo.

He could see the light on in the warehouse. They didn't bother to hide their arrival. From what Anna had heard, it was only Marco with Freya, but Leo made sure to take as many trusted men as he could. The warehouse was empty, but they'd found the missing SUV that Marco had taken. Marco had taken one of the untraceable cars, cars that were used for family business. It couldn't be tracked.

"No one's here–" Romano's announcement was cut off by the sound of a gunshot.

***

Freya tried not to duck when she heard the shot. He was shooting at her! She was panting, her chest ready to explode but she couldn't stop. He was almost there; she could feel him. She heard another gunshot at the same time she saw dirt near her explode. She continued running and saw a fence coming up. Good God she was trapped! The chain fence was high; she wouldn't be able to climb it. She stopped, looked left and right, both sides showed nothing but hills and dry grass. She went right, which seemed to slant down, she could run faster. She heard another shot and ducked in reaction before continuing to run as fast as she could. She could hear him coming. The pounding of his steps was as loud as her breathing to her ears.

He was so close; she could almost hear him breathing.

Closer than she thought.

She was tackled from behind.

***

Leo could hear the gunshots, and the grip that held his heart tightened with every shot. He'd been the first one to run towards the shots and was ahead of his men. He heard the yells from Vito, but he ignored him. He needed to get to Freya. He could see them running now, and he screamed at Marco to try and get him to focus on him. Marco was too far gone. He was too focused on Freya.

***

Freya's body hurt. The collision with Marco knocked the breath out of her. She fought him, but he was strong and angry. He yanked her back down as she tried to get up, before straddling her body. She tried to fight him, but his hand wrapped around her neck and squeezed.

He was going to kill her! She could see it in his eyes. She tried to dislodge his hands, but he held on tight. Tears spilled from her eyes as she fought to breathe. Her chest burned. Her vision started to fade when he suddenly let go. She felt another body hit them before they rolled off of her.

Her air deprived lungs kept her on the ground as she struggled to breath. She could hear shouts as she turned to her side. She let out a cry when she felt a hand on her shoulder. She tried to get away, thinking it was Marco until she heard her name being called. She recognized Romano's voice.

Romano! Leo trusted him, and she knew Romano wouldn't hurt her. She clung to him as he helped her up.

"Leo. I want-" She wanted Leo.

"It's okay, he's here," Romano assured her as he helped her see where he was.

Vito had just pulled Leo away from Marco and Leo was struggling against Vito to go after Marco again.

"Leo," Romano called him but to no effect.

"Leo," she called him, and this time Leo seemed to stop struggling. Vito seemed to say something, and they both turned towards her. When Leo wrestled away, Vito let go. "Leo," she called him again.

***

Leo went to her. He'd seen Marco strangling Freya and had tackled him to get him away from her. All Leo could think of was killing Marco for putting his hand on her. Vito had pulled him off of Marco, but Leo wanted to pummel him dead. It was Freya that got through to him, her voice. He'd turned to her, and he realized he needed to be with her, more than he needed to kill Marco. He'd finish him later. Right now, Freya needed him.

He pulled her into his arms and held her tight. She had to be alright. She had to be. He held her tightly before remembering he needed to check her. He pulled away and looked her over.

"Where are you hurt?" he asked as he touched her body, checking her, making sure she was really okay.

"I'm okay...I'm okay," she replied. "I'm so happy to see you," she added tearfully.

He pulled her to him, kissed her head before kissing her mouth. He savored her taste.

"I love you," he told her.

"I know," she replied as she looked up at him with a wobbly smile.

"I want to go home now," she told him. He wasn't close to being done with Marco, but Freya came first. He took a step to head back, but she didn't move with him.

"What's wrong?" he asked, concerned. She seemed to be grounded to the spot.

"I'm not sure I can walk anymore," she answered with a shaky smile. "My legs feel like Jell-O. I'm afraid that if I move they'll–"

He picked her up. It would be a long walk back.

Chapter Twenty Eight

Leo checked on Freya, making sure she was asleep before he left to deal with that son of a bitch. The doctor that he'd had come to check on Freya told him that she was dehydrated and that her injuries were superficial. Leo wanted to avoid bringing Freya to a hospital because they would ask questions and he didn't want that to complicate matters more than it already was with the cops. The doctor had left instructions to keep Freya hydrated and which drinks would be best to help her recover faster. She had cuts, mostly from running and falling, but it was the bruises that worried Leo. She had a lot of them. He was able to get the story from her before she was lightly sedated so that she could rest.

After assuring himself that she was okay, he headed out. His mother was there waiting. She understood what needed to be done. "I'll take care of her, don't worry," she promised him. She kissed him on the head, something she hadn't done in a while. "You make them pay," she added as she pulled away. His mother might not have done work for La Famiglia, but she was a mobster's daughter, wife, and mother.

The drive to the warehouse...yes, another fucking warehouse, where Marco was being kept wasn't far. Less than a ten-minute drive from his parents' mansion. His father was there. Bartolo had gotten away, Filipe was dead, but they had Marco. Giovanni and Drago had been asked by Leo to leave Marco to him. Marco remained seated, tied to a chair, with trigger-happy men surrounding him.

"You're not mine; you could never be. I would not produce such a coward rat like you." Leo heard his father say as he joined them. Freya had told him what Marco had told her, but Leo chose to believe his father.

"Fuck you, old man."

"If it weren't for Leo's request, I'd show you exactly what this old man can do."

"This one is mine." Marco looked the same as he did when Leo had last seen him. He was beaten up from Leo's beating earlier but not more. "Let him up." Leo could tell his father wasn't happy with that decision but said nothing. This was Leo's fight. Drago untied him. "This is your chance to talk before I kill you."

"Fuck you." Marco charged at him, but Leo was ready. Leo's fist hit him straight in the face, sending him backward, falling hard down to the concrete floor. Leo kicked him once, twice, and five more times. He already knew that Marco wasn't going to talk. Not if it helped the Costa family in anyway. Leo felt a rage in him that he tried hard to control. He could kill Marco with his bare hands.

"Should have killed that bitch the first night you told me to watch her." Leo snapped. He lunged at Marco, got on top of him, and punched his face over and over again. He felt the blood pounding through his veins, felt Marco's blood spurting everywhere, but there was a monster raging in him that wouldn't stop. He kept punching him, not feeling anything, but fury towards Marco for daring to touch Freya. If Marco had just betrayed him, it would have been a bullet to the head. But he'd touched Freya, and that was unforgivable. Marco would receive no mercy from Leo.

"Leo, he's done." He barely registered his father's voice. Leo picked up the lifeless body and threw it across the room. The blood in his ears wasn't ready to calm. Leo screamed, his rage taking control of him. His target was done, there was no one else within reach to destroy. He picked up the chair that Marco had been tied to and threw that at the motionless body. Then he reached for the table and overturned it.

Leo fought his need to annihilate anything and anyone else. He didn't let the monster in him out for good reasons. It was what allowed him to tear a man apart limb by limb. He had to lock it tight, control it, and hide it. He paced, avoiding any contact with anyone, trying to rein it in. When he was sure he had control of himself, he looked at his father. His father didn't show it, but Leo could see it in his eyes. *Leo had scared Giovanni Costa.*

Leo headed to the sink, cleaned his hands, and face, which were splattered with blood. Vito handed him a towel. He didn't look at the rest of the men, but he knew they were probably shitting themselves. If the monster in him had the ability to scare his father, he knew that none of them stood a chance against it. Drago laid folded clothes on the counter, something Leo always had in his car just in case blood was spilled. Leo took off his shirt; the blood had seeped through to his skin. He wet the towel to clean it from his skin. Then he stripped the rest of clothes, even his socks and shoes. He stood there naked, not giving a damn, as he put the clean clothes on. His old clothes would be burnt, leaving no evidence of Marco. The warehouse would be cleaned. When this warehouse becomes a club, there would be no evidence that he'd beat a man to death here.

He looked at himself in the mirror one last time. He would need to thoroughly shower before he touched Freya. He wouldn't taint her with this. He turned to his men. Some still had a shocked look to them. He knew they would talk, and it would get out to their enemies, and their own people that Leo could kill a man with his bare hands, in minutes. Marco was taller than him, bigger, and he wasn't weak, but Leo killed him in minutes with his fists. They would fear him more, not only for the power he held over them but for what he could do.

"Get rid of him," Leo ordered, nodding towards Marco's lifeless body. "Find me, Bartolo." Leo didn't wait, he walked out of the warehouse, followed by Vito and Romano. Drago would make sure that his orders were followed and that cleanup was complete.

As a rule, Giovanni and Leo never rode in the same car. Leo sat in the back of his SUV and let Vito and Romano take him back to his parents' house where Freya was. His father would be heading home too, and he'd probably beat them home because Romano was driving. Romano, the most law-abiding driver ever. Leo didn't mind. He needed the extra time. The monster in him was still furious, and he didn't want to come anywhere near Freya until he had it completely under control. He let Romano and Vito's bickering drown out the roaring in his ears.

Chapter Twenty Nine

It had been two weeks since her kidnapping and Leo had refused to make love to her until he was sure she was fully recovered. Paula was home; she had a mild concussion from being hit on the head. Sandro was still in the hospital recovering from several gunshot wounds, but he was in stable condition and would make a full recovery. Santi had been found dead in one of the cars, and his funeral was held earlier this week.

There was a video of Marco shooting Santi in the garage. There was no way of controlling the situation once the police had gotten involved. Paula had told the police that she had no idea what happened, she had been walking out of the room, the next, being awoken by the paramedics. Sandro said that he'd just rounded the corner after doing rounds in the penthouse when Marco surprised him and shot him.

According to Paula and Sandro, Freya had been with Leo at the time. There were no videos of Marco leaving the building, according to security, Marco must have taken them and forgot about the one of him shooting Santi. Because there were no videos of Marco leaving, they had no idea what car he'd used and therefore didn't know what car to look for in traffic videos. No cars belonging to Leo were missing.

Paula and Sandro had pointed their fingers at Marco, and with the damning video of Santi's murder, Marco was the only bad guy in this story. Marco's whereabouts were unknown. Leo reported that several pieces of jewelry, worth over three million dollars, were missing and suggested that the possible motive was robbery. Detective Wilson and Detective Davis who had come along with the detectives investigating the attack in Leo's penthouse made a snide comment about hiding evidence. Leo, taking offense, ordered them to leave.

Leo had wanted to keep Freya away from the detectives, but they wanted to confirm that she had been with Leo the whole time and had no idea what happened at home. Freya had told them that she and Leo had spent the night at his parents' house after having a family dinner which his parents collaborated. Freya had been missing for three days, and Leo had been able to hold off any interview with the detectives for a week. She didn't like being thought of as weak, but for this instance it was necessary, and she needed it. Physically recovering from the kidnapping was surprisingly fast. Freya had sported several cuts and bruises during her interview with the detectives and told them she'd fallen while hiking. The detectives easily accepted her excuse making her wonder if they were really interested in her statement.

Three days since Freya's initial kidnapping, Anna Lombardi reported her husband missing. Bartolo Lombardi had gone to work and didn't return home. Though the cops initially suspected Anna, it was eventually speculated that Bartolo must have gone into hiding because of tax problems with the IRS, who were getting ready to arrest him. Bartolo just like Marco was now both wanted and missing.

Freya knew the real story. Leo had told her when she'd asked. Anna had helped saved Freya when she overheard her husband and had gone to Giovanni with the information. Anna had done it to protect Bianca. Bianca was told the same story the police heard, and she was devastated by her father's disappearance. Though she didn't ask and Leo didn't offer her any information, Freya knew that both Marco and Bartolo were probably dead. It bothered her a little that she didn't feel strongly opposed to their punishment. She should have. She should have wanted the law to deal with them, but she understood that there were rules. If she wanted to be a part of this family, she had to follow the rules. Her love for Leo and his family was enough to pacify her. She didn't agree on how they handled crimes against them, but she wouldn't trade the Costa family for anything. She'd finally found a place where she belonged, where she felt complete.

She sighed as she glanced over at Leo. She loved watching him sleep. She was also horny. She decided that she was tired of waiting for him. She ran her finger down his chest, knowing he'd waken by her mere touch. He was a light sleeper, while she slept like the dead.

She circled his nipple with the tip of her finger. His hand snapped around hers, surprising her, but his hold was gentle. She looked up to find him staring at her intensely.

"Good morning," she whispered as she moved closer to him.

"We shouldn't–"

"I am a hundred percent recovered Leo, but if you don't touch me soon, I might just die from horniness and–"

Her statement was cut off by the touch of his lips. There was no working up to it; the kiss was deep and wanting. His hands were on her body, already working on her clothes. Though Leo normally slept naked, he hadn't since bringing her home. Her hand wandered into his sweatpants and found his hardening member. She gripped his length and ran her thumb across the seeping head. He groaned into her mouth. She gasped as his hand delved between her legs, his fingers probing her lips before penetrating her. It didn't take long for her to start riding his fingers, wanting more. "More Leo, I want more," she begged.

The sheets and clothes were quickly thrown aside, and Leo was thrusting into her. She moaned with his swift and deep penetration. There was no finesse to it, no build up; it was fierce and intense fucking. Freya gave as good as she got, meeting his rough and hard thrusts. She'd missed this, missed his body, missed this connection with him. She held onto him as he pounded into her. Her release was quick and explosive. His release followed. He emptied himself into her body, groaning loudly with each thrust.

***

Leo held her against him as she slept after their fierce lovemaking. He'd never imagined his life would take such a drastic change in less than a year. He had never expected to be attacked. Who would have thought that being kidnapped would be the best thing that's ever happened to him? He was certain that he would never have met Freya if he hadn't been kidnapped. It would have been impossible. They belonged to different circles and when she had made it into one of his clubs;

he never would have looked for her if she hadn't saved him. She'd saved him in more ways than she knew.

He knew that what he'd asked her to do went against her moral beliefs. He asked her to live with the knowledge that he was a killer. He asked her to let him deal justice how La Famiglia expected him to. Marco was dead. It was too bad that his bitch of a mother was dead too because Leo wanted to kill her for the poison she'd filled Marco's head with. Marco wasn't a Costa; Giovanni had gotten a paternity test done a long time ago to make sure. Camilla and Bartolo had filled Marco's head with lies and festered his hate for Leo and Giovanni. Leo wasn't making excuses for Marco; he was adding blame to Camilla and Bartolo. Camilla was dead, and Leo made sure Marco was too, but Bartolo had gotten away.

He didn't think Bartolo would go to the feds to make a deal. He had no proof, and because of him, the operation had changed. Bartolo was also guilty of plenty of murders that could be proven. He wouldn't run to the feds. He might try to run to the other families, but they wouldn't want to create problems with the Vetrano and Costa by helping him. Bartolo's only option was to get out and stay out. Leo wasn't going to let him get away. Bartolo had been one of Giovanni's longest friend, and he'd betrayed him. There would be no forgiveness; there will only be death for him.

Chapter Thirty

August

Freya's cheeks hurt from smiling so much. Valentina had said that there would only be about a hundred guests for their engagement party. What she failed to mention was that it was a hundred guests other than their family members and by family members, she meant La Famiglia. The 'one hundred guests' were people who were not connected to La Famiglia. The only people from Freya's side to attend their engagement party, and probably for their wedding too, were her friends. Her diverse group of friends ranged from Lao, Vietnamese, Filipino, Mexican, El Salvadorian and Nigerian stood out among the large group of Italians. This was the first of several formal parties that Valentina was putting together. The next one would be Leo's birthday, in less than a month, and then the holiday season. Though she seemed to have permanently moved in with Leo, she continued to work on the other side of the bay. She thought about looking for a new job in the city, but she was unsure about her future. She loved Leo and Leo loved her, but she didn't know if this engagement was real or if they were simply dating. Leo had insisted that they let Valentina plan this engagement party and that made Freya think that he did intend to marry her eventually.

"You look like you need a break," Leo whispered next to her ear. The party was in full swing, and many people joined them on the dance floor. The slow songs had brought out the couples and joined Leo and Freya.

"I loved meeting everyone, but your family is very large."

"They're your family now too."

"I know. Thank you."

"For?"

"For giving me a family." He didn't respond for a while.

"Come with me." He took her hand, and the two of them slipped out onto the balcony of his parent's mansion, facing the courtyard. The party noise faded as he closed the door to give them privacy.

"What's going on?" she asked as he looked at her with uncertainty.

"I know this life isn't what you signed up for. It goes beyond friendship and temporary engagement. You've been through shit that most people couldn't even imagine, and not once have you asked me to let you go."

"Are you–are you breaking up with me?" At their engagement party? She might just shoot him with the gun he usually had tucked against his back.

"No. I'm saying I never gave you a choice."

"But I did, I could have said 'no.'"

"You couldn't have. I wouldn't have let you."

"So, what are you saying now?" She was afraid that he wanted to get away from her now that the danger seemed to be over.

"I'm giving you a choice. I realized I never asked. So, I'm asking now." Leo stepped back and then he bent down on one knee. He pulled a small black box from his pocket, opened it, and held it out to her. "Freya, will you marry me?" The large oval diamond shined bright, the lights reflecting from the party on the other side of the glass doors made it sparkle. Her first engagement ring had never been found. "Say something."

She realized she stood there gaping at him. "You didn't need to get me another ring. I'm sorry I lost-"

Leo cut her off by getting up and pulling her into a kiss.

"None of that was your fault. I don't ever want you to apologize for it. Now, answer my question."

"Yes," she answered almost tearfully.

"Good." Leo slipped the new ring on her finger, this one was a little smaller than her last ring, but it seemed to sparkle more. Maybe because it was for real this time. "I love you."

"I love you, too," she replied with an almost tearful laugh. He pulled her in for a kiss.

"You are everything I have ever wanted and more than I thought I ever would."

***

Bianca was miserable. She hated being here. Hated the people here. Most of all, she hated the reason for this party. She was an outcast now, and she didn't want to attend the stupid engagement party of the people who ruined her life, but Big Old Giovanni decided she was going to attend. She hated him—hated his whole family. She even hated her mother. She glanced at her mother, sitting mutely at their table. *Circondata da puttanefinte.* Surrounded by fake bitches who were pretending they were better than Bianca and her mother when they were just as pathetic. They were at the beck and call of the Costa family and the Don, simpering for attention from made men who see them as nothing but whores.

She didn't feel bad for her mother. This was her fault too. If Anna Lombardi had just kept her mouth shut, maybe Bianca's father would be here, and maybe Bartolo Lombardi would be the one running this city instead. But her mother had betrayed her father, and now he's hiding not just from the *La Famiglia,* but also, from the federal agents who keep coming around harassing her and her mother.

If Freya had died, maybe Bianca would be the one celebrating her engagement to Leo. Not that she wanted him now. *Leo è stupido.* Leo was too stupid to realize that Freya was all wrong for him. She was an outsider. She didn't deserve him. He was the heir of the Don, and he settles for a nobody with a trashy mother. He should have been with someone like Bianca.

Disgusted, Bianca stood up, stomped away from their table, and went onto the balcony. The fresh air did nothing to cool her anger. Not caringabout her expensive silk gown, she sat on the floor in the far corner. Out here in the darkness, the sound of the party was muted, and for a moment, she found peace in the silence.

She wasn't sure how long she sat there stewing when she heard the doors to the balcony open. She hoped no one would see her, so she stayed quiet. She was well hidden in the dark, her black dress and long black hair covering her skin, blending her into the darkened corner.

Just fucking fantastic. Leo and Freya stepped onto the balcony, completely oblivious to her. She could shoot Freya right now, and no one would be able to stop her. Her father had taught her how to use a gun. She could handle it. As she watched Leo bend on one knee, proposing, lowering himself to someone like that trash, Bianca really wished she had a gun. She hated Freya. Bianca's misery was Freya's fault. She needs to pay.

***

Freya wasn't one to show off, but she couldn't hide the happiness radiating from her even if she tried. How her and Leo got together was very unusual, and what started out as a fake engagement, had turned into something she could have never imagined. Leo and Freya had saved each other in many ways: she'd save his life, though technically it was her dog who saw him first, and he'd given her life.

Her tremulous childhood led her to live an overly cautious and too routine adulthood. She hadn't realized how dull her life had gotten until Leo had turned her world upside down. Looking back, she wouldn't change a thing that's happened since they met... *Okay,* maybe she'd change a few things like Luciano not being shot, Santi not being killed, and her not being kidnapped. It had been a very eventful nine months or so.

She couldn't believe she'd only known Leo for such a short amount of time, but she couldn't imagine her life without him, or his family. Giovanni and Valentina had become the doting parents she'd never had and Luciano, though only months separated them in age, had become the mischievous little brother. Even Drago, Vito, and Romano, though they weren't immediate family, were treated like brothers, and she wouldn't have anyone else watch her and Leo's back beside them.

Though her cheeks felt sore from smiling so much, she happily continued as she showed her friends her new engagement ring, replacing the one that had been lost. It was her engagement party, and for once in her life, she wanted to show off, beginning with the ring Leo had given her just moments ago. It was a beautiful ring.

"Geez, I think I can do my make-up in front of

that rock," Nicole joked.

"Right, I'm pretty sure there's enough diamond in there to split between all of us," Lena added. Lena, another close and longtime friend, as well as a coworker, was going to be Freya's maid of honor, but she hadn't asked yet. Freya was pretty sure Lena would agree but hadn't asked considering she wasn't exactly sure when the wedding would happen until about twenty minutes ago.

Freya hadn't voiced it, but she'd secretly planned her wedding in her head. She hadn't dared to hope it would happen and convinced herself it was for fun, but she always loved the idea of a winter wedding. Now that she was actually getting married, she's wondering if it would be possible to have it in January, less than five months away. It might be costly, but she didn't think Leo would mind considering he throws money around like it's nothing.

Would it be possible? She hoped so. *Unless Leo wanted a long engagement.* A girl only gets married once...well, at least Freya hopes she's only going to get married once.

"We should test that theory, Lena," Vi responded, getting a laugh from the other girls at the table.

Her 'side' would have a lot less people than

Leo's. She didn't have all that many friends, most of them were coworkers, and the only family member she had was her mother, who she decided not to invite. Freya was ashamed to admit that she was embarrassed of her mother. *Was she turning into a snob?* Leo's family was just so great that she hated the idea of embarrassing them in front of their friends and family. Knowing Mariana, she would do something to embarrass not just Freya, but the Costa family as well. No one questioned her decision not to invite her mother, her friends knew about her, and Leo...well, he'd seen what she was like.

"Have you done any wedding planning yet?" Stefanie, another co-worker,and possible bride's maid candidate, asked.

"Not really. I–"

"Freya?" Leo's call was soft but captured her attention. She turned to find him coming toward her. She smiled and heard her friends sigh as they watched him swagger towards them. He really was too good looking. Just watching him walk was sexy.

"Hello, ladies," Leo greeted. "Would you mind if I borrow my fiancé for a moment?" He didn't wait for an answer. He held out his hand knowing she'd take it and do his bidding. She would have rolled her eyes at the silliness of it, but she didn't mind. She would do anything for Leo. "Excuse us."

Ever so polite.

"Dante is here, I'd like you to meet him."

Ah, Dante, the big boss. Freya was a little nervous about meeting him. Dante Vetrano was the head of the Vetrano mafia, and he's supposedly related to some big guns in Sicily, Italy. Freya had done an internet search on him and found that he was popular in New York for being a businessman and a bit of a playboy. Adding 'mafia' to her search had resulted in a vague connection to Sicilian mobs and the tragic massacre of several prominent Italian families less than twenty years ago. There was very little information regarding the death of the Italians and their family, but she recognized a couple of the names, Donati, Vetrano, and Accardi... Romano, Drago, and Vito.

Drago, Vito, and Romano never really talked about their families and after what she'd discovered, Freya realized that perhaps they didn't have family left. Maybe the only family they had left were Giovanni and Valentina. She'd seen the photos all over her soon to be in-laws' home. In every room, there were photos of families, though most of them had photos of boys and teens growing up. She recognized Leo, Luciano, Drago, Vito, and Romano, but there were more of them.

Leo led her to a table occupied by Giovanni,

Valentina, and several people she somewhat recognized. A handsome man, she instinctively knew as Dante, was with them. Something about Dante exuded power. He dominated others around him without trying. It showed in the way others around him responded to his movement. He moves his arm, and the person next to him moves away to give him space, as if there was a force that makes the others move with him. Freya expected someone younger, around Leo's age, but Dante appeared to be closer in age to Romano.

He must be one of the boys she hadn't recognized in the photos. She noticed that many of the photos stopped in their late teen years. She figured they must not have liked taking pictures as adults, but now she wondered if it was because of who they were.

"Here she is!" Giovanni announced their arrival boisterously.

Everyone looked, and it seemed that they were all in a good mood. Dante was the first to stand up, prompting the other men to remember their manners. Leo led her to the seat next to Valentina, pulled the chair back, and helped her sit down. Rather than sitting on the empty chair between her and Dante, he introduced them.

"Freya meet Dante, he is family. Dante, my fiancé, Freya."

Freya held her hand out to Dante, and he surprised her by taking her hand and placing a kiss on her knuckles instead of shaking it.

"All right, that's enough," Leo grumbled as he pulled her hand away from Dante and sat down between them.

Dante flashed her a smile before teasing Leo, "You are a beauty. If you decide you don't want Leo, call me."

Leo glared at him before pulling Freya's hand into his and holding it tightly, shoving it off to the table. "She won't want anyone else."

Valentina looked exasperated before giving her a warm smile. "These boys; they never grow up. Always fighting over everything. Don't pay them any attention, dear."

"You grew up together?" Freya asked, turning to Dante who was still grinning at Leo.

"Practically like brothers," Dante answered. She liked his voice. It was smooth and soothing. He was so different from what she expected. He was suave, young, and sophisticated—not at all what she was picturing for a mobster boss...but then, neither did Leo. Dante didn't scream danger, at least not to her. After almost being murdered she would know what real danger looked like, right? Or she was fooled once before, so how would she know?

"Have you met my sister and brother?" Dante asked.

"No, I haven't." Her answer cued one of the men standing behind Dante to leave.

"You will soon. Stefano is a flirt, and Caterina might come off as rude, but you'll like them both." It sounded like an order, that she *will* like them.

***

She heard the doors open just as she was cleaning herself. The dress was a little complicated and required extra attention getting back on. She hadn't paid them any attention until she heard Leo's name.

"Can't believe Leo's lowering himself to that." The comment was said snidely.

Another giggled at the comment.

"She doesn't belong," someone else added. "Leo is too good for her."

"Did you see her friends?" More giggles followed. Some Italian she didn't understand was said with more laughter, but she was sure they were about her.

She paused, taking in the meanness. She shouldn't listen to what they were saying, but it didn't stop her from being hurt by the ugly words. She waited for the women to leave before she left the bathroom stall. She tried to convince herself to brush it off while she washed her hands, then headed out.

Romano, as usual, was waiting for her. She gave him a smile, that she hoped hid her turmoil, but it slipped when she saw the girls, not too far off, looking at her. One of them, Irene if she remembered correctly, said something to the other two women while looking at her, pulling laughter from them. She tried her best to ignore it. She was a woman, and this was her party. She shouldn't let school girl antics get to her.

"Everything all right, Freya?" Romano asked, looking between her and the women.

"Yeah, everything's okay." Somehow, it sounded hollow to her.

Chapter Thirty One

Knowing Sandro, he was going to balk at her unscheduled trip. She notified work that she would be leaving early but didn't mention it to Leo or her bodyguards because it was a surprise. She sent the last email she needed to answer before shutting off her computer. She already had an idea on how she'd get her hulking bodyguard out of sight once they got to Alice's house. She was planning on telling him that they were practicing makeup and hair for the wedding. Nothing like feminine madness to make the big, tough, Sandro squirm away and leave them to their photo session.

She was going to pose naked for Alice. Freya knew that her friend had a long waiting list, and she really appreciated Alice fitting her in as a last-minute client. Leo's birthday was coming up, and Freya had no idea what to get him. What do you get a man who already has everything? Every time she asked him what he wanted, he'd tell her that all he wanted was her. It was sweet but completely unhelpful. He just wanted her...so, she decided to give *her* to him...well, photos of her at least.

Blown up photos of her.

Blown up *naked* photos of her.

The only person she felt comfortable enough to take those kinds of pictures with was Alice. Alice had been there for her when Freya's mother had her moments. You know, when her mother was on her drunk binges and would disappear for days at a time. Alice had shared her family with Freya while they were in school. They had even been roommates.

Freya's first instinct was to ask Alice to be her Maid of Honor, but she knew that Alice would be a lot happier and more comfortable behind the camera. Alice had always hated having the attention on her, it was one of the reasons she got so good at hiding behind the camera. Freya was going to insist on having Alice as her wedding photographer, even if she had to throw a fit. She was letting Valentina do most of the planning since she wanted to, probably from boredom, and Freya was glad for her help, but somethings Freya wanted to go her way.

She stood up and began gathering her things,

causing Sandro to look up from his phone. When Leo had first insisted she have a bodyguard, she argued, but after everything that's happened, she felt safer with one. Her first bodyguard, Romano, had been replaced by Sandro because Leo needed Romano for *family* work. *Yes, that family—the one that could totally get them all arrested.*

Freya, and obviously Leo, trusted Sandro with her safety, but she did miss having the more social Romano following her around all day. Sandro was a Hulk and wasn't much for chatting. He was also a bit impatient, one of the reasons Romano was the one who drove her to and from work. The first time Freya had met Sandro, she thought he was going to mug her. Turned out, he only wanted to tell her she was done walking her dog because Leo wanted to talk to her.

"We're going to do an errand," she told him, acting like it was no big deal.

Sandro glared at her, knowing she's about to cause him trouble, and tersely replied, "That's not planned."

"I planned it."

"But you didn't tell the boss."

That sounded like a complaint.

"Leo doesn't tell me what to do."

Sandro gave her a look that screamed bullshit. "What kind of errand?" he asked as he got up to block her doorway, preventing her from leaving.

"We're going to my friend Alice's house. We're going to do some makeup and hair looks for the wedding." She lied casually, almost real enough to be believable.

Sandro stared at her as if he was trying to catch the lie.

"Alice what? Last name? Is she approved?"

Now it was her turn to glare. "Approved? What do you mean?"

"Boss has a list of approved people you're allowed to see." He grinned knowingly.

"What?! Since when?!" she demanded.

He shrugged, infuriating her more.

"Listen, I'll see whoever I want,whenever I want. And since you'll tattle to Leo, I'm going to tell him where he can shove that approved list." She stormed past Sandro, brushing by him. She knew he'd move enough to let her go because he wouldn't want her to get hurt if she decided to run into him. She heard him quickly shuffle before stepping in front of her. One thing she'd gotten used to was walking behind a bodyguard, and she automatically stopped to let Sandro lead the way. She gave a quick wave to coworkers she passed by, and briefly chatted with Lena before they finally made it to the BMW they had taken to work.

Sandro tucked his phone into his pocket, taking a momentary reprieve from tattling on her to open the passenger side door. Another battle she'd won. They used to insist she sit in the back, but she hated being back there by herself. When possible, she sat in the passenger seat. She pulled her phone out knowing Leo would be calling.

"Where are you going?" Leo greeted. He seemed stressed.

"Hello to you too."

"Sorry." He sounded distracted, and she started to feel a little guilty about adding to his worries. "It's been busy. Where are you headed?"

"Alice's house."

"You should have let me know so I could have Romano there." With everything that had happened, Leo had insisted that she always travel with back up. Romano drove her to and from work while Sandro followed in another car. Leo preferred Romano drive her since he was a meticulous driver. Leo was okay with her going out to lunch with coworkers with just Sandro as long as they didn't go far, and they sat indoors only. After being shot at, at an outdoor restaurant, Freya agreed.

"Not everything can be planned in advance, Leo."

"It's for your safety."

"Marco is gone."

"He's not the only enemy out there."

"Leo...you can't protect me from everything."

"I can damn well try."

"I'm going to see my friend, and unless you tell Sandro to tie me down, I'm going." She wanted to be firm. Freya was annoyed since she was technically doing the photoshoot for him. There was a long silence, and she realized he might actually be contemplating it. "Don't you dare," she threatened.

He sighed loudly and overly exaggerated. "Fine. Only her house. When will you be done?"

"Not sure. A couple of hours." The drive to

Alice's house was going to take about an hour as it is, and she imagined the session would probably take at least two hours. It would still be plenty of time to beat the rush hour traffic on the way home.

"I'll see you when you get home." He hung up.

Rude.

Sandro got a text, no doubt Leo's approval. He started the car, entered Alice's address on the navigation, and then drove them out of the lot. It wasn't until they were halfway to Alice's house that Freya realized she hadn't given Sandro the address. She sighed. Leo had probably already done a more thorough background check on Alice than the FBI would have. He'd have known Alice and Freya went back nearly fifteen years.

Freya had been disappointed that Alice wasn't able to make it to Freya's engagement party because she'd had a wedding client. Valentina had done the planning, and Freya just had to show up, that was her mistake. Valentina had picked a date Alice wasn't able to attend.

She stared out the window as the thoughts of her engagement party popped into her head. Meeting the *extended family* at their engagement party had been a trial, especially the women. Freya had wanted them to like her, and as hard as she tried to forget what they said, it still hurt her feelings and made her feel inferior. Leo *was* a catch, even with his baggage, but Irene had her questioning her self-worth. Growing up, all she wanted was stability and security. Now she had more money and more security than she ever dreamed of, yet she allowed Irene's callous remarks to stir up her old insecurities. It frustrated her.

Now wasn't the time to think about these things. She needed to look more confident than she felt in the photos. Since there was no traffic in the middle of the day, the drive to Alice's house was quick, and Freya opened her car door as soon as Sandro parked the car in front of the small house. It was an older home, but it was well kept. The instant she stepped out of the air-conditioned car, the Sacramento heat hit her hard and the sweat started to build at the back of her neck.

"Wait," Sandro ordered.

She stopped and waited by the car.

He checked their surroundings before heading toward the house.

Before they reached the front of the house, Alice opened the door, greeting them, "It's so good to finally see you!" She passed Sandro and headed straight to Freya, wrapping her arms around her friend and squeezing her tight.

"I know. Six months is way too long."

The hug was much needed. Though they texted and talked to each other regularly, it wasn't anything close to being able to hug her friend. There hadn't really been an opportunity for them to get together. On top of managing her business, Alice was also having problems controlling her sister, Claudia, who had an addiction problem and was in and out of trouble with the law. Freya hadn't told Alice, or really anyone about what had happened to her in the last six months. She hadn't wanted to add to Alice's worries, and to be fair, she didn't think she should be sharing that kind of information with anyone besides Leo.

They headed inside, but Sandro gave her a look. She waylaid Alice at the entrance of the house with questions while Sandro cleared the house. Though she'd warned Alice about him, she wanted to minimize the questions by distracting her friend. It wasn't until Sandro stopped by the door, indicating the house met his inspection, that she decided it was time to get rid of him.

"We're going to be in her room. You can stay here."

Sandro looked like he wanted to argue, but Freya glared. "Fine."

"So, what did you tell him you were doing?" Alice

asked as soon as the door to the studio closed. Freya had called it Alice's room because at a glance it was a bedroom, a sensual one, that Alice used as a studio for her boudoir sessions. Alice's actual bedroom was the plain one that looked like a guest room.

"I said hair and makeup test," Freya answered as she pulled out some lingerie from her oversized purse.

"Smart."

"It'll keep Sandro out of my hair for a while."

"Must be serious if you're getting naked for my camera," Alice joked.

"Well, I *am* marrying him," Freya replied with a grin. What she loved about Alice was that no matter how much time passed, whenever they did get together it seemed like no time had passed at all.

"Can't wait to meet him."

"I'm sure you'll meet him as soon as he sees the photos."

"Oh?" Alice began working on her hair.

"Yeah...probably to threaten to break your legs if anyone else sees these photos," Freya said it as a joke, but she wasn't sure she was joking.

"He sounds charming."

Freya applied the makeup while Alice worked on her hair, or as Alice liked to refer to it, *sexing her up*.

"So, really. Is everything okay? You looked like you were about to cry when you saw me. He isn't like holding you hostage, is he? Cause if he was, I'm sure Claudia has friends who could threaten him."

The thought was hilarious. Even Claudia wouldn't know anyone who could go up against Leo, but she loved her friend for offering her sister's less than stellar goons. "I've just missed you and the past six months just seemed so long. A lot has happened, and I'm just nervous about getting married."

"Are you really ready to get married?" Alice asked the question no one had asked her. "Are you really sure he's the one? I mean, it has only been six months, and you're getting married in less than five months. I know you rescued him when he was mugged before you guys started dating, but are you really sure he's it?"

Freya was more sure about it than anything else. "Leo is the one. I can't imagine my life without him."

"Then I'm happy for you."

"Can you come for a girl's night?" Freya asked, changing the topic. "Lena wants to celebrate my engagement for the fifteenth time. It's next Friday." The day before Leo's birthday and subsequent party. The only reason Freya agreed to it was because she knew she needed to destress before she had to face *La Famiglia* again. Freya knew that Alice was busy and didn't really like clubbing, but she always asked just in case her friend needed a break too.

"Yes, I'm actually free next weekend."

"Great! You might finally meet Leo! And you can totally spend the night at his hotel, it's amazing! You could stay for the weekend if you want." It would be crazy for Alice to drive home after a night of partying considering the distance and Freya wouldn't let her. If Alice really wanted to go home, Freya would have Leo send one of his people to drive her.

"You ready to take the photos?"

Freya looked in the mirror. Her hair was curled in soft waves, and her makeup was darker and heavier than normal in order to show up on the photos.

"Let me show Sandro, so he knows I'm doing what I said I was before he comes to check on me."

Alice went to check on her camera and set up the lights and reflectors while Freya went back into the living room. She hid her lingerie under a thick robe, making sure she was completely covered before heading out to where Sandro was waiting.

"What do you think?" Freya asked.

"Boss won't like it. Too dark and unnatural."

Freya expected that answer but pretended to be offended, making a face, to mess with him. "Fine." She headed back into the studio, closing the door and locking it to keep anyone from barging in, in the middle of her session.

"Okay, I'm ready."

"Great, take off your clothes."

***

The photo session lasted almost two hours, but it was worth it. Alice let her peek at some of the photos, and once they're edited, Freya will get to pick which two photos will be printed in large copies. She tied her hair up but kept her makeup on before she switched back to her work clothes.

Romano had joined Sandro by the time she'd finished taking photos, which didn't surprise her.

Romano drove her home as usual while Sandro went in the backup car. Taking and doing photo sessions can get exhausting and Freya slept on the way home. She also wasn't interested in being scolded about making unscheduled plans, so sleeping seemed like a great idea. The drive home was fast since they were going the opposite direction of traffic and leaving earlier than peak rush hour.

Romano actually had to shake her awake once they were home. She thanked him and took the private elevator up to the penthouse she now called home. Honey and Lestat greeted her. They were on their way out with Anthony, another one of Leo's men who happened to love animals, for a walk. She had never tried walking her cat before, but Anthony tried it when he took over the task after what happened with Marco. It turned out that her cat loved walking on a leash and once he was tired, Anthony would carry him the rest of the way while Honey finished her walk. Outside of the three amigos—as Freya liked to call Drago, Vito, and Romano—Anthony was her favorite of Leo's men because he treated her pets well.

Freya said a quick hello to Paula who was in the kitchen working on dinner before she went looking for Leo. She figured he was probably busy since he normally came to greet her if he was home before her. Freya found him asleep on the black leather lounge chair in his home office. *She'd never get over how handsome he was.*

She stopped at the doorway just watching him for a moment. Freya had just decided to leave him alone when he woke up. He gave her a sleepy smile. He was about to get up, but she stopped him by walking to him. He reached out to touch her, as she stopped in front of him, and took it as an invitation to join him. Freya surprised him when she decided to straddle him. She'd worn a loose dress to avoid getting lines on her skin for the photo shoot. It came in handy right now.

"How'd it go with your friend?" Leo asked as his hands settled on her hips, pulling her closer to him.

She leaned in and kissed him before answering, "It was great. I really missed her." She kissed him again, deeper, trying to distract him.

His hand moved from her hip to her waist and then around her back. She could feel him stirring beneath her. His cock hardened as his hand explored her covered body.

Her arms went around his neck as his slipped under her dress and cradled her behind. Each hand rested on the globes of her ass, massaging them. Her hands started working on the buttons of his shirt. His fingers slipped into her thong, and she gasped as they worked her. Each stroke of his finger had her temperature rising. She pulled back, putting distance between them as her hands went to his belt and pants. She released his hard length, freeing him, stroking him. Precum seeped from the tip of his hard cock.

"Ride me." She didn't need to be told twice. She moved, guiding his cock to her entrance. His fingers pushed her underwear aside, helping her sit on him. She slid down his cock, earning a groan from him and a sigh from her. She loved the feel of him.

"So, fucking perfect," he whispered as he guided her up and down his length.

Her hands delved into his hair, pulling him close to kiss him.

He kissed like he fucked. Demanding and explosive. Setting her skin on fire, as his hands guided her hips up and down his cock.

"Ah, hell," he groaned out as he suddenly switched their position. Without disconnecting their joined parts, he flipped her onto her back on the couch, withdrew, and then thrust in hard. He pushed her dress up, letting it flow around her waist, and spread her legs wider, watching his cock slide in and out of her. "I love watching you take me—all of me."

"Only you," she replied because she couldn't imagine being with anyone else.

His finger worked her clit, instantly pushing her over the edge. She whimpered with her release, toes curling, and a burst of lightning flowing through her. His thrusts grew harder, pounding into her before his own release followed.

***

"We need to talk about your unscheduled trips, Freya," Leo said after taking his first bite of their meal. Though they'd just made love minutes ago, there was tension between them. The glow from their intimacy had faded by the time they sat down for dinner. It didn't help that the guys, who normally joined them, were out of sight.

"I just went to see a friend, Leo. I have a life outside of you and work." She hadn't meant to snap, but lately she'd been feeling suffocated by his overprotectiveness. She could understand his fear for her safety—considering she almost died—but he was smothering her.

"I'm not saying you can't see your friends, I'm saying these outings need to be planned. It's for your own damn protection. I don't want a repeat of what happened with Marco, or the BART train incident. I wish you'd be more cooperative when it came to your safety."

"I am doing the best I can, Leo, but this is hard.

I have taken care of myself since the moment I could. Letting anyone dictate my life is not easy."

"I'm not dictating your life, I'm trying to protect you. Depending on me is part of being in a family. You can be independent and still depend on me to keep you safe."

"You're being overprotective."

"Because you are careless about your safety. If you weren't, you'd have left your job already. It's hard to protect you from a distance. It's even harder when you're disregarding my orders."

"You don't get to tell me what to do just because you're fucking me." She knew it was the wrong thing to say.

His hand tightened around his fork, his knuckles went white, and his jaw ticked. He was fighting his anger too. "I'm more than fucking you; I'm trying to keep you alive long enough to finally marry you. You don't even like working at your job. You're just being stubborn and looking for a fight. It needs to end, Freya. It will only cause more problems in the future."

"I'm done talking about this." Freya didn't like confrontations, and she especially did not like arguing with Leo. He was half right, but she was irritated with his high-handedness. She wasn't fighting for her independence. She was fighting her fear of losing herself. *What would happen if she depended on him and it all ended?* She'd be left with nothing... Like her mother.

"You're good at running away from problems, Freya, but this isn't going to go away." Leo put his fork down and then took a drink of his water. "I'm going to work." And with that, he pushed his chair back, stood up, and left her alone with their half-eaten dinner.

Chapter Thirty Two

Bartolo Lombardi was a dead man walking. Once upon a time, he was loyal to the Italian mafia down to his soul...but things have changed. His plan had been brilliant, but Marco ruined it. If everything had gone according to plan, he'd be the head of the San Francisco Mafia. *Damn Marco for fucking up his plans.*

Life had been against him since his birth, but he had always come out on top. His own mother had not wanted him, but he showed her—he left her with a broken leg, set that shitty house on fire, and burned her and everything about his past with it. The stench of her burning flesh and the sound of her shrill screams as the fire melted her skin still brought him pleasure—intense satisfaction. She deserved the pain, as did his betraying wife. He wanted to wrap his hands around her neck and squeeze the life out of her. Just like wife deserved to be burned alive. He didn't make it to the top just to be taken down by his betraying wife.

Anna had turned on him and gave him up to Giovanni. He couldn't even think about that bitch without seeing red. He wanted her blood. He could have fixed what Marco had fucked up, but his own god damned wife betrayed him! If it wasn't for her, he could have still gotten away with it. Leo and his bitch would be gone. He would never be here, at the mercy of these Russian rats. Anna was the biggest betrayer of them all. That whore was never loyal to him.

He'll make her pay soon enough. For now, he had to make a deal. The only reason Fedor Ivanov kept Bartolo alive was to thumb his nose at the Italian Mafia. The Bratva and La Famiglia have warred for many years. The war between the Bratva and the Mafia resulted in many deaths, but the Italians won. Now, these Russian rats content themselves with what little they have. Bartolo always knew that he'd use Fedor to gain control of the West Coast operation.

It would have benefited them both. Bartolo would control the west, and he would have given Fedor more freedom in the north as long as he did Bartolo's dirty work. La Famiglia was too closed off and wanted to stay Italian. Their country pride is strong, but they don't know how to manipulate their enemies into doing the work for them. Bartolo was smarter than all of them.

That's why he was still alive. Now he just needed to push Fedor.

Bartolo walked with purpose toward the lounge room where he knew Fedor and his men lazily wasted time. Fedor was the second child in the Ivanov family, and therefore, not the one in power, but he wanted to be. Fedor would love nothing more than to get out of his older brother's shadow. Czar ran the Bratva, but if Fedor eliminated the ruling Mafia, he'd gain his independence and rule the west. Bratva will get rid of the Costa family and then Bartolo will take control and make a deal.

"Fedor, I have a plan." That was the wrong thing to say, and Bartolo didn't care.

"You don't tell me what to do. You are a guest here," Fedor told him before tipping the vodka bottle into his mouth. *No manners.* He could never be a good leader. This is why his brother has control. At least Czar sets good examples for his men to follow.

"Guest I may be, but we had a deal. You help me, I help you." Bartolo wouldn't cower to this Russian scum.

"I am helping you by keeping you alive. Where else would a rat like you be hiding if it wasn't for me? I keep you in my home, share my food with you, and yet you are very ungracious." Fedor was trying to get him riled up, but Bartolo wasn't going to fall for it.

"You are not keeping your end of the deal by sitting here drinking all day," Bartolo accused.

"It's better than you moping around all day."

"I am not moping. I have a plan."

"Your plans don't work too well as you are *here*," Fedor emphasized the *here* by gesturing around his home with the bottle in hand.

Disgusting slob. "If it had not been for–"

"Yes, yes...I have heard it enough" Fedor cut him off flippantly. "Your whore of a wife, and useless soldiers are to blame." Fedor sighs, exaggerating his boredom with the conversation. "So, tell me. What is your new plan?"

Fedor was a good actor. He pretended to drink all day and act careless, but he was a calculating bastard. Bartolo thought that he was in control, but Fedor is only letting him live long enough to get what he wanted. He understood Bartolo from the moment the rat had started making a deal with him. Bartolo was just a selfish man who wanted power he didn't deserve. Fedor deserved the power he wanted.

Czar was only the leader because he had been

born first, but he was weak. He had let the Italians push the Bratva around since their father's death. Fedor also has a plan: take out the mafia from the west coast, gain his rightful respect and power, and then one day, get rid of Czar. His younger brothers would not have issues with Fedor taking out Czar. Czar had too tight of a leash on their family, like a dictator trying to keep hold of his power. Soon, Fedor will get rid of his dear older brother...and any siblings who would challenge him.

"We use Bianca."

"Your daughter. She is pretty but useless, no?" Fedor knew everything about Bartolo, including his slut of a daughter. Bianca Lombardi was as beautiful as her traitorous mother. He wouldn't mind fucking her before he killed her. *A woman's only role was to please him,* as far as he was concerned.

"She is pretty and can get inside information." Bartolo was a ruthless man who had no problem using anyone, and Fedor appreciated that in a man. It was one of the very few reasons Fedor let him live; the other was exactly what he knew Bartolo was getting to—inside information.

Fedor has been waiting for this day. Call him dramatic, but he liked a good bloodbath and drama. Lots of drama. When the Costa heir announced his marriage, Fedor came up with an idea. Originally, he had in mind to copy a red wedding from some show his men were obsessed with and blow them all up, but his new plan was better—bloodier. There'll be a surprise and no pretense of fake peace. *He wanted to kill them all.*

Leonardo's wedding was bound to bring all the mafia bosses together, and rather than take out just the Costas, he'd take them all out at once. He will make sure that everyone will remember this wedding.

"How will she get this inside information? She is related to you. I imagine that your wife and child are no longer welcome." He knew the word wife would pull a string. He could see Bartolo trying to control his temper. *Such a silly little man.*

"Get rid of her mother. Giovanni will take her in. They are too soft. She can easily get the information we need to hit them."

"And I suppose you want me to get rid of your wife?" Fedor asked lazily, pushing Bartolo's buttons.

"That bitch is no wife of mine. She is a traitor and should die."

"Fine...fine... I will take care of your wife. You take care of the other bitch."

"Bianca will be easy to convince. She is loyal to

me."

"If you say so, Bartolo."

"I know so. As for Anna, I would like to kill her myself."

"No, a pretty woman like her will be useful in other ways."

"She's too old to be in one of your whore houses."

"But not too old to be a whore. She may have betrayed you, but she is still beautiful. I will enjoy her as will my men. If you're a good boy, I may let you taste her one last time too."

He watched Bartolo stomp off like a child. Fedor did not like the man, but he needed him.

"He's too self-important. You are playing a dangerous game, big brother." Fedor turned toward the voice and found his youngest brother, Dimitri, the only brother he could stand, leaning against the doorway.

"I am simply finishing what our father started."

"Czar will have kittens if he knew you were rattling the cage."

"It is better to ask for forgiveness than to ask for

permission, little brother."

Chapter Thirty Three

September

Leo entered La Veranda, the Italian Restaurant, with an entourage of bodyguards. He wasn't a fan of the number of people following him around, but it was necessary. He was the heir to the Costa family and recent events concerning his family members meant they were targets. Though Leo had pretty much taken the reins on most of the *family business*, his father was still the head of La Famiglia, and when he wanted something, it was done. Giovanni Costa wanted more protection for everyone, and Leo agreed, but it didn't mean he had to like it. Having Vito and Drago at his side at all times was bad enough, but now he traveled with no less than four men to ensure his safety. The days when a single bodyguard was enough were gone...at least until Bartolo and any other rats that follow him were gone.

As usual, people looked when he entered the room, except in this room, most of the people knew him as either a business associate or *their boss*. He knew most of them, it was part of the business. You want to survive in this life? You needed to know who your friends were, who your enemies were, and who your enemies' friends were. La Famiglia was exclusive but large. It helped that most of the people at La Veranda were loyal to the family and grew up as a part of it. If he didn't know someone, chances were, he'd know which of his men they belonged to.

He had a purpose for being there, but another reason just presented itself and was coming toward him. Irene Ricci. He'd known her since she was in diapers. She grew up in privilege, like most of them, and she was a snob. Leo didn't care that she was a spoiled brat, but he did care about her knowing her place and respecting ranks.

She smiled at him—a flirtatious smile aimed at making him appreciate her beauty. *She was beautiful, no doubt about that*. But he wasn't interested. Not in her tiny waist, not in the large breasts, not in the long legs, and not on her innocent face.

He made eye contact with her, giving her permission to approach him. Though he wasn't as strict as his father when it came to his people, some rules don't ever change. There were only a few people who could talk to him without his permission. Even then, it was only because they'd grown up like brothers. They knew the rules still applied when there were others around.

Irene approached him. As she got closer and went to give him a kiss on the cheek she said, "Leo, it's so nice to see–"

Before she could finish her greeting or touch her lips to his cheek, his hand gripped a fist full of hair and tugged hard. Those kinds of greetings were reserved for close family and friends. She wasn't one of them, and she should know better than to approach him with such familiarity, especially since she'd just attended his engagement party.

His men surrounded him, keeping prying eyes off him of them.

He held her face close to his, so she'd hear everything he told her clearly. "I do not tolerate disrespect from my people, especially women who don't know their place. You disrespect my wife, you disrespect me." He didn't bother to ask Irene if she understood, he knew she did. Freya hadn't told him about her comments, but others have. Romano, who didn't know what occurred in the ladies' room, reported Freya's strange reaction, and for some brownie points, one of Leo's men told him about what his wife overheard in the restroom.

Before letting go, he pulled her away from him with a hard tug to emphasize his point.

The color left her face.

He turned away and continued on to his original business matter. He'd given her the warning. It was up to her to heed it.

He headed toward the corner table—the same table that he takes Freya to whenever they come here for a date—it was reserved only for him and his business and was the best location in the restaurant. It provided privacy, plenty of it, without being locked in a room. It had a beautiful view of the bay on one side and was close to both front and back exits in case the occasion arose. His business was already there.

"Still threatening little girls, I see," Castello Moretti greeted him with a grin.

Leo ignored his comment and greeted his longtime friend, and practically brother, with an affectionate hug and some hard back pounding, as men do. "Castle, it's good to see you. It's been a while. You didn't even visit me when I was in the hospital!" He feigned disappointment. He wasn't really upset, and

Castle had visited, just not when Leo was awake.

"I did visit, but you were sleeping like a baby, and Angelo got himself in trouble. I had to get home. You look good for someone who almost died though." Castle and his younger brother had come to live with the Costa family, just as the Vetrano children had. Tragedy and war had brought them all together, and as much as Leo wouldn't trade the time they'd grown up together, he was sure his friends would rather have their families back. A war between the Russian Bratva and the Italian Mafia took the lives of a lot of people, most importantly, took a lot of parents from them. At the time, the safest place for the young heirs was with the Costa family.

"How is Angelo?" Leo asked as he sat in the chair across from Castle. He didn't even have to order, Lorenzo had the food—the regular twenty-two-course meal he liked—ready.

"Trouble like always. Sorry to have missed your engagement party. I was in Mexico trying to get his ass back home." Castle sounded frustrated, and Leo didn't blame him. Angelo had always managed to get himself into trouble and expected his older brother to fix things for him. Leo would let Angelo rot in whatever hell he got himself into, but he knew Castle wouldn't. After their parents, older brother, and older sister had all been murdered by the Bratva a little over twenty years ago, he'd protect the last remaining family member, but knew he couldn't wrap him up in a bubble and lock him in a room.

"It's alright. You'll be at the wedding... And my birthday party, I hope." His mother had insisted on a birthday party. Leo wasn't a fan of parties, but his mother was, and she took any opportunity to plan a party. His mother was probably the happiest person, next to Leo, about Freya joining their family. Valentina had always wanted a daughter but only had Leo and Luciano, and a bunch of orphaned boys to raise. Though Caterina was there, she hadn't been interested in being a girl and doing girly things. Caterina had grown up with boys and wanted to be treated as one of the boys. His mother had Freya now. As much as his mother drove Freya nuts with party planning, Freya loved having a *real* mother. He hadn't known he could love his mother more until she welcomed Freya into their family without condition.

"Of course." They enjoyed each other's company and their meals before they got to the purpose of their meeting.

"Your contact can be trusted?" Leo inquired.

"As much as you can trust anyone." *Which means never trust anyone.* They had all learned this as children.

"So, let me get this straight. Bratva may or may not have Bartolo, and they may or may not be planning something?"

"Yep, that about sums it up."

Chapter Thirty Four

September 21

"Freya meet Castle. Castle, Freya, my wife...well fiancé, same thing." Leo's introduction was light-hearted,and Freya could tell that Leo genuinely meant it. The same couldn't be said about the man Leo had just introduced to her. Leo told her that Castle was a very close friend who had grown up with him. The man smiled, even held out his hand for her to shake, but something about him told her he was a dangerous man. It wasn't in his manners, for they were impeccable, like the rest of La Famiglia, it was just the man himself. Castle Moretti had an aura that warned *'not to be fucked with.'*

"Happy to finally meet you, Freya," he said her name slower than usual, as if he was familiarizing himself with it. Meeting the rest of *La Famiglia* had nothing on how Castle made her feel. He was handsome, tall, and fit, someone a lot of people would be attracted to, but something about him screamed *get away.* "Sorry to have missed your engagement party."

She gave the right answers, played the polite and attentive host, but as soon as she had the chance to escape, she couldn't get away fast enough. While she felt comfortable and loved by Leo and his immediate family, the rest of La Famiglia made her feel like she didn't belong. They never said anything, besides the girls in the ladies' room during their engagement party, but she could feel an invisible wall blocking her from being accepted. She didn't want to know all the illegal stuff they did because then she'd have to face her guilt over it, but she felt like it was keeping her from being part of their inner circle. For once in her life, she wanted to be part of something, but she couldn't figure out how to do it.

Since this was Leo's birthday party, she had decided not to invite her friends knowing who would be here. They'd stand out, and she didn't want her friends to feel how she when surrounded by them. She played host with Leo and his parents while they greeted everyone arriving but escaped to Leo's old bedroom as soon as she could. Though she knew her in-laws had a couple of full-time housekeepers that kept the mansion clean, something told her that Leo's room was probably spotless to begin with.

There were no teenage posters of rock bands, cars, or even half-naked women. The room looked like a guest room: minimal and clean. The only reason she knew this was Leo's room were the few picture frames on the shelves of a young Leo with family and friends, and the fact that she'd seen Luciano's room, which was a mess. It screamed hormonal and angsty teenager every day of the week.

Freya wandered closer to the photos. Now that she'd met more of La Famiglia, she began to recognize the boys in the photos with Leo. Dante and his siblings were in many of the photos throughout the house, but they were in just one of the photos in Leo's room, which told her Leo wasn't as close to Dante as he was to Vito and Castle. Almost every photo included at least Castle or Vito, if not both. She hardly ever saw Leo relaxed. Her lover had too much on his shoulders to be like the carefree boy in the photos.

She barely registered the sound of the door opening as she focused on the photos.

"Hiding?" the voice wasn't who she was expecting. She gasped in surprise and turned to face Luciano. Her soon to be brother in law was the opposite of Leo. Where Leo was serious, Luciano was always up to trouble.

"You made it!" Freya greeted him happily as she accepted his embrace. Though Luciano was only three months younger than her at twenty-nine, he'd felt like the mischievous little brother she'd never had.

"Told you I would...just late," he replied as he fondly messed with her perfectly styled hair. She didn't mind.

After playing nice with a bunch of people who didn't really care for her, it was wonderful to have someone who genuinely liked her. "Only thirty minutes. That's not even late considering the party is going to go all night."

"If I'm not there at least ten minutes early, it's late according to Dad."

"I'm glad you're here," Freya confessed. For a moment, she thought she'd said too much since his smile disappeared. She didn't want to offend one of her very few allies.

"Don't worry. I don't like half of them and most of them probably find me really annoying."

She sighed, happy to have a teammate. Her and Luciano's relationship was good from the very beginning, but after the shooting at the restaurant earlier this year, they've both become protective of each other. Luciano ran La Famiglia business in Las Vegas, which meant he spent most of his time there. Leo had promised to take her to Las Vegas since she has never been to Sin City, but work had kept both of them from traveling.

"They're not bad...I just don't think they like me," she told him as she made her way to Leo's bed and sat down on the edge. Luciano walked toward the desk, pulled out the rolling chair, and sat on it, facing her.

"Their loss." His loyalty made her smile. "Seriously, sis, they don't like anyone they don't know. It makes them weak. They refuse to adapt. And honestly," he gave her a grin, "I don't think half of them like us; they just come for the free booze and Mom's artichokes."

Ah, yes! Valentina's specialty: Artichoke *Gratinata*. Freya had a serious grievance against artichokes from a childhood incident when her mother had forced her to eat artichokes. She still couldn't eat them without gagging. *Too bad it was her mother-in-law's favorite*. She shared a smile with Luciano. She was feeling better now. Not as suffocated.

"Is this where the cool kids hang out?" Vito's voice had them both looking toward the door. Leo's best friend and second, as Leo often called him, stood in the doorway looking too handsome and up to a lot of trouble. He strutted into the room with four beer bottles

– two in each hand. He handed one to Luciano and one to Freya before sitting on the bed next to her.

"No, this is where the adults hang out." Romano joined them. "That means you need to go back to the playground." The comment was funny coming from Romano since he was the youngest of the group at twenty-six. He took the other beer from Vito without asking and leaned against the desk, halfway sitting on it.

"I couldn't help but overhear–"

"Lie, you were eavesdropping," Romano cut off Vito who glared back at him.

"As I was saying, I overheard you and Lucky talking, and I gotta say, I don't like half of them either." Lucky, she had learned was Luciano's childhood nickname because he never seemed to get in trouble, even though he'd most likely started the trouble. She didn't like calling him by his nickname because she liked his actual name.

"I don't think half of them likes half of them," Luciano added before taking a sip of his beer.

"I don't think any of them actually likes any of them," came from Romano.

"I like *some* of them," Vito conceded.

"Yeah, the women who aren't related to you," Romano teased.

"I can't help it if the ladies love me," Vito bragged, spreading his arms out in a motion that said, '*look at me*.'

He was too handsome for sure. Vito was a heartbreaker. Loyal to his bones, charismatic, and outrageously flirtatious. And he was one of Freya's favorite people.

***

Leo saw Freya slip away. He wanted to follow her. As much as Freya believed that Leo could do whatever the fuck he wanted, he did have to answer to people. He couldn't abruptly leave this conversation to sneak away with her, not that she had invited him. He knew something wasn't right between them, but he didn't know how to fix it without making it worse. Her safety was his priority, and her independent nature was making it harder for him to ensure it. Transitioning into their world was hard, he knew that. Some rules didn't make sense to her.

He excused himself as soon as he had the chance. Maybe they couldn't work out their issues tonight, but he wanted to be with her - needed to be with her. He missed her. They both had a job that kept them apart most days, and even if they slept skin to skin, he missed their closeness.

He walked with purpose to put off anyone who thought about catching his attention. She probably escaped to his old room. She often hid there when she needed a break. Freya was a solitary woman and being engulfed into his large family took a toll on her. He rounded the corner just in time to see Romano enter his room. *What the hell?*

"No, this is where the adults hang out," he heard Romano say. Apparently, his old room was the hangout spot like it had been when they were younger. So much for having a little alone time with his future wife.

The conversation in the room stopped him in his tracks.

"I don't think half of them likes half of them," his brother added.

He knew Freya was having a hard time fitting into his word, but his brother and cousin's words made him realize that it was worse than he'd thought. She'd gone to his room to hide...and as proud and happy as he was that his family were rallying around her, he had to admit that he'd messed up. He hadn't paid enough attention to her. Hadn't considered her position enough. Sometimes he could get so blinded by his need to control shit that he missed what was important.

Leo considered going in there, kicking the men out, and hashing it out with Freya right then and there, but he dismissed the idea. He needed to do it when they were alone and weren't going to be interrupted. His birthday party, that he didn't even want, wasn't the time to do it. Not when people were demanding his attention.

Tomorrow. Before anything else. They needed to talk, and he needed to figure out how he could help her. Maybe tonight, he needed to make sure the rest of *his family* understood that she was his, and she was staying with or without them. He turned around and headed back down to the great hall. It was time to flex his muscles and shoot anyone who didn't agree.

***

Freya rounded the corner and regretted her decision in an instant. She usually preferred not having a bodyguard dogging her every step, but right now wasn't the time. Irene, with the legs up to her armpits, was coming toward her. *Why was this woman everywhere all of a sudden?*

Freya kept her head up and looked straight ahead with every intention of walking by her. She was Leo's woman, and Irene was just jealous. She'd dealt with girls like her in school. If she paid her attention, she'd get worse. The hallway was wide enough for them to pass each other without having to turn their bodies.

Freya kept her gaze at the end of the hallway, not giving the bitch a glance.

They neared, Freya could smell the strong, fruity perfume coming from Irene. The closer they were, the more nervous she felt. It was so unusual for her to feel so insecure but just being near Irene made Freya's skin crawl. She felt her shoulders droop.

They passed, air brushing against her skin, raising the hair on her arms. The perfume overwhelmed her, like it was engulfing her in an invisible wall that was closing in on her. She held her breath, keeping this woman out of her head and out of her senses as much as she could. She couldn't let Irene get to her.

She was almost free, nearly passed this obstacle when she felt the grip on her wrist stop her. It took her a moment to realize that Irene had a hold of her left wrist. Freya looked down at the dark red manicured fingers wrapped around her wrist. Her gaze followed the hand up her thin arm to very long neck and stopped on a pair of glaring brown-green eyes.

Freya pulled her hand away. "You have something to say?"

Irene briefly gripped it tighter before letting it go. "I have a lot to say. I'll start by telling you that you're nothing but a gold digger. You think you got the Costa family wrapped around your finger? It's only a matter of time 'til he realizes what a mistake you are," Irene accused her.

"You're wrong. Leo loves me, and I love him. I'm–"

"You don't belong with us!" Irene cut her off. "You are not one of–" Irene's tirade was cut off by an arm appearing over Freya's shoulder. The hand wrapped around Irene's neck, before it slammed her against the wall, pulling a small cry out of her.

Freya recognized Castle as the man pinning Irene to the wall by the hand on her neck. Irene struggled to breathe and made small crying noises. Freya went to stop Castle – an immediate reaction to someone in distress.

"Castle," she called to him, as she placed her hand on his arm. She was ignored.

Castle said a tirade of words in Italian. Freya had no idea what Castle was saying, but he wasn't letting up on his grip.

Irene's hand wrapped around Castle's hand, trying to loosen his hold. "I will not tolerate disrespect toward the Don."

"Castle, let her go. She can't–" Freya tried to pull

on his arm to catch his attention when he suddenly let go of Irene, nearly flinging her away from him.

Irene stumbled against the wall before she gathered herself together and ran away from them. Her heels clicked loudly on the hardwood floor as her dress flew around her legs. Irene was several steps away before Castle turned his attention to Freya.

By the look of menace on Castle's face, Freya should've been afraid, but she faced monsters before. After Marco, it was hard for her to be afraid of physical pain, and subconsciously she knew that Castle wouldn't hurt her. Not physically.

"If you're going to be his woman then you need to start playing the part. You're going to be a Costa. Act like it. Don't become an embarrassment to that name." Castle's comment wasn't said in anger. In fact, it was almost a complete turnabout from his angry comments to Irene. He said it calmly and without a hint of emotion.

He didn't wait for her response. He turned away from her and walked in the same direction as Irene had just scampered through. She didn't need him to stay. She had other thoughts to keep her occupied. *Was she too weak for Leo? Did she seem like a meek little woman next to him? Was that what everyone of them sees when they see her with him? Why Irene felt like she could say those rude and mean things about her? Was she enabling them?*

She was used to being alone and only worrying about what she thought of herself. She thought her and Leo would just keep being themselves, and everyone else would accept it, but maybe she would need to accept that being with Leo meant being in the spotlight. She couldn't hide behind him, and she didn't want to. *Was that how Leo was seeing her? Why he's overly protective of her and too controlling of her life? Did he see her as weak? That she needed more protection than necessary?*

Funny how it takes other people to make you see what your problems are.

Chapter Thirty Five

September 22

Freya stood alone in the middle of Valentina's Great Hall, surrounded by all of *them*. There seemed to be more people now than there was before. They were all talking to each other, completely ignoring her. Some laughed too loud, some whispered like they were gossiping with each other. No one paid attention to her. She saw Luciano coming toward her and smiled, happy to find a friendly face in the crowd. She moved toward him, but he just passed by her, not acknowledging her. She called his name, but he didn't seem to hear. Romano followed close behind. She went to ask him what was wrong with Luciano, but he too just walked by her, as if he didn't see her. She called their names again but neither turned.

What the hell was happening? She looked around searched for familiar faces. She went to them, but over and over no one acknowledged her. She grabbed on to Valentina's arm and pulled, shaking it to get her future mother-in-law to face her, but she was ignored.

Leo. She needed Leo.

She turned to look for him, but the crowd seemed to move closer and closer. They were crowding her now. Boxing her in. Bodies pressed together, tightening around her. She felt like she was slowly being swallowed into a black hole.

She called Leo's name. Over and over until she finally heard him calling hers. *"Freya, Freya, Freya..."*

She woke in a startle, her heart racing fast. Sweat had formed on her forehead and back. She was hot and cold at the same time.

"Freya, sweetheart...it's okay. It's just a dream," Leo's voice brought her comfort.

A dream...only a dream.

"You're all right. I'm here."

"Just a bad dream," she told him. She glanced at the clock on the nightstand and realized it was Leo's birthday. She took a couple of breaths, trying to calm herself. This was his day, she didn't want to ruin it with her problems.

"Happy birthday," she greeted him as she leaned in for a kiss.

"Thank you...are you all right?" He pulled her into his arms, as they laid back in bed.

"I'm fine. Just a dream." *A dream about her suffocating.* It was a representation of how she was feeling about being part of La Famiglia. Overwhelmed and afraid to lose herself, she needed to come to terms with it if she was really going to be a part of this family.

"Wish we could just stay here all day," he told her and emphasized by giving her a small squeeze. It would be great if they could stay home and do nothing all day—just be with each other. There was always some kind of function to go to, or they were both working. She missed him and—

"Your present!" she remembered. She untangled herself from his arms and left the bed to go to her closet, where the two photos she had chosen were framed and wrapped. She took them back to the bed but slowed her steps as she got closer; her shyness rearing its ugly head.

"I told you, you are all the present I need."

"I know...so I thought...well...just open them." She carefully laid the photos on the bed. She'd hadn't chosen an expensive, heavy frame, just one that protected the photos. Leo gave her a curious smile before tearing the wrapping paper. The anticipation of his reaction was killing her, as he slowly revealed the first photo. She was naked with her private parts covered by a soft, white blanket. She was seductively gazing at the camera, looking sultry. She barely recognized herself.

He stared at it; his face unreadable. She began doubting her choice of gift. He moved to the other photo and unwrapped it, and then sat there staring at both of them, speechless.

"You...don't like them?" she asked hesitantly

"Freya, I fucking love them. They're perfect." He looked up, his face in awe. She'd misread his speechless reaction. He stood up from the bed, carefully stacked the pictures, and put them on the floor, leaning them against the nightstand. He then went to her, pulling her to his body. "They are the best present anyone could have given me. You are the best present I've ever had."

He took her mouth in a hungry kiss. At the same time, he picked her up. Freya wrapped her legs around his waist, and her hands delved into his hair, pulling him closer. The feel of her body against his, the curves, the perfect fit to his, burned him from the inside. *God, he loved the feel of her.*

He carried her to the bed, and gently laid her down. He spread her legs, settling his body between them. Her softness against his hard body felt like being wrapped in silk. With all the shit he's done, all his sins...Leo imagined that this was the closest to heaven he'd ever get, and he was perfectly okay with it. As long as he had Freya.

***

"I wish you wouldn't bring up our issues in front of your family." It was the first words she'd spoken to him since dinner. *Happy fucking birthday to him.* What had started out as a promising day had turned into another argument. He hadn't meant to push it, but he'd been drinking. As happy as he was celebrating with his family, the topic of their wedding and her work brought back the same recurrent argument.

"Why wouldn't I? They are family...an important part of our lives. Our future. You know, the one you seem to not want to be a part of." *There, he'd said it.* He thought they were getting this fixed, but now he doubted it.

"I never said I don't want them to be a part of it. I just wish you wouldn't air our dirty laundry in front of them."

"If I didn't, then you'd just continue avoiding it." He wasn't backing down anymore. Things needed to be said. "I'm tired of coddling you. I love you, and I want to marry you. When I asked you to marry me, you knew what that meant. After everything we've been through, all I ask is for you to trust me. Let me take care of you."

"What you want is for me to depend on you!" she accused. Her voice raised, egging him on.

"What the fuck is wrong with that?!" He couldn't help but yell over her outburst. "That's how it should be! I'm going to be your husband.I'm supposed to take care of you. You don't even like your job!"

"Who are you to say that I don't like my job?" she demanded. "And it's not the job, Leo. I want to be able to take care of myself."

"I keep telling you that you don't have to. That's what I am here for!"

"And what? Treat me like a child?!"

"If you think wanting you safe and happy is treating you like a child, then you have some fucked up ideas of what lovers and family do."

"You already knew that. You've seen my

mother!"

"There's going to have to be a point when you own up to your own issues and quit blaming your mother for everything!" *And that hurt her.* He could see it the moment the last syllable was out. *Fuck.* He hated it. He wasn't even sure how to take it back because he *meant* it.

Silence.

She sat there, staring at him. Her face now void of all thoughts and feelings. She was good at hiding how she really felt, but not this time. "Freya..."

She turned and walked away from him.

He felt helpless. "Freya, talk to me."

She did what she did best, ignored him. She hid herself from him and avoided him.

He felt like a jackass. He watched her get ready for bed, not saying a word. She'll need time to get over her hurt. He wished she would rage at him, but she never did. If she raged at him or even had an outburst of any sort, he wouldn't be sitting there wondering what the hell she was thinking.

"Are you going to ignore me all night?"

She paused but showed no other reaction.

It was what he expected. *Fuck it.* It was his birthday. They had to figure this shit out, but maybe it won't be tonight. They avoided each other as they prepared to head to bed...not that it was hard, they had a huge bathroom.

She got into bed before him, wearing a silk, barely there nightgown. She laid on her usual side, facing the windows, her back to him. He sighed as he made his way to bed. Normally, he'd sleep naked, but the way things have been between them, he'd been sleeping in sweatpants. The strain in their relationship is ripping them apart. It never occurred to him that maybe it was them and not everyone else. That just maybe, there was something wrong between them. He'll admit that he'd been a little blind about her situation, thinking that she could handle the changes after everything that's happened.

Chapter Thirty Six

September 28

"So, have you started planning your wedding?" Lena's question intensified the throbbing in Freya's head. It wasn't about Lena asking questions, it was the topic of the question: her wedding. That was all everyone wanted to talk about. It's not that she wasn't looking forward to being married to Leo...she just wanted to get it over with. She wanted to get to the settling down with Leo part and skip all the La Famiglia and parties in between. Every time they were around, Freya was reminded that Leo and his family were a powerhouse.

And her? Well, she was the result of one of her mother's Johns. Her only family was a mother who only wanted money for alcohol. She couldn't even remember celebrating her birthday as a child...while Leo's family threw him a God damn ball. Freya Santos was a nobody, raised in a trailer park by a mother who didn't want her. It depressed her. She knew she had it much better than a lot of people, but her lack of family or background made her feel inadequate.

"No, not yet. It's just been very hectic lately," Freya answered.

"Oh man, if it were me, I'd be quitting and planning a huge wedding. I would have..."

Freya drowned out Lena's dream wedding. The pounding in her head was getting worse. She also felt a little nauseated. The stress of work, on top of everything else, was not helping. Though they haven't argued about it again, she knew Leo wanted her to quit her job and dedicate her life to being a Costa. *And she wanted that.* She was just afraid to give him complete control of her life. Quitting her job felt like another chip from her independence. It wasn't like she liked the stress of her job. Reading government regulations and standards all day made her want to stab her eyes out. It was boring and tedious—worse than reading a car manual.

"...I'd have peonies..." Lena rattled.

"Mmhmm," Freya answered distracted with her own thoughts.

"...Probably some biscuits and gravy..."

"Yeah," Freya responded noncommittally.

"Some happy meals for the old bitches and a side of snails."

"Yeah...ok...wait what?" *Snail*? *Old bitches*? Freya turned to her friend, who grinned at her. Freya smiled. This was one of the reasons she loved Lena. *Always there to lighten the mood.*

"I'm sorry, I'm just so distracted with this," Freya explained, pointing at the new regulations she had to study in order to make sure the company complied. The problem with government regulations was that they change. A minor tweak in wording could disqualify a company from being able to sell their products.

"It's okay. Tell me what else is going on?" Lena might seem like a ditzy, perky person, but she was smart, and she always knew when something was bothering Freya.

"Just...Leo and I are not agreeing on things."

"That's normal. It would not be normal if you guys agreed on everything. That would just be a little freakish. What aren't you guys agreeing on?"

"He wants me to quit working."

"Honestly, I would too if I was him. The commute alone is killing you, I can tell you've been tired a lot lately. Especially this past month alone. You've been slacking." Lena gave her a wink to tell her she was kidding.

"I am a little tired, but it's probably from the stress of meeting all of his family and friends... It's just been really busy when it comes to the social front. We're always making an appearance at some campaign or party. And I know I sound really shitty complaining about going to parties, but it's hard for me to smile and pretend they're not judging me."

"I don't really think your issue is that they're judging you. You never cared about that before."

"I know. It's just harder now. There are always eyes on us. I am so afraid of embarrassing him and his family."

"Honey, you saved his life. As far as I'm concerned,or anyone else should be, they should be kissing your feet. The fact that you two fell in love is a fairytale story. Yeah, sure the rest of his family seems a bit snobbish, but your in-laws adore you to death. That's who you'll be spending time with once it's all settled down. That's who your family will be. I know you've never had a big family, but snobby bitches and judgmental assholes are normal. There's always an aunt who tells you you're getting fat even though she's the size of a cow herself, and there's always an uncle who is just a little inappropriate, and a spoiled ass cousin who thinks she's better than everyone. It's normal Freya. You just have to not let them get to you. At the end of the day, it's the ones closest to you who matter. Everyone else is just entertainment."

Maybe Lena was right. Freya could pretend that *La Famiglia* was the extended family she could keep at a distance.

"Tell you what, why don't we have a girls' night? It's been a while since we had one. Invite Alice too. It would be great to finally meet her."

Maybe a girls' night was just what she needed.

"Yeah, I'll ask her." And while they're chatting... "By the way...I was wondering..."

"Yeah?" Lena asked, turning to face Freya from her seat. The two of them now shared an office, with their backs to each other. Freya had convinced their boss that Lena would be perfect for the position, but in reality, Freya was preparing the company for when she eventually did leave. She'd grown up in this company, and she wouldn't just leave without properly training someone to take over her job.

"You don't have to answer now...and I don't have

any plans yet, but you're one of my closest friends and–
"

"Yes, I'll be your bridesmaid," Lena cut her off with a laugh. "I was wondering how long it would take you to ask." Lena got up from her seat, and Freya accepted the hug her friend loved giving.

"I actually was wondering if you'd be my Maid of Honor." When it came down to it, it would have been between Lena and Alice. Though Alice was one of Freya's longest friend, Alice didn't like being the center of attention which was why Freya decided to pick Lena as her Maid of Honor.

***

Leo walked straight to the front door of the small house. He made sure she'd be home when he finally made the visit. This was an important visit. He rang the doorbell, waited, and listened. After a moment of hearing nothing, he pressed the doorbell again, and followed it with a loud knock on the door.

"Okay, okay, I'm coming," a disgruntled voice yelled.

He kept his patience in check. This woman was important to Freya, and he wasn't going to do anything that would keep him in the doghouse even longer, but he needed to make sure that they were protected.

The door swung open, revealing a woman he'd only seen in photos. She was a little taller than Freya, but not by much. The dark, thick hair wasn't quite as dark as Freya's black hair, but it fell in waves he would have found attractive had he been a single man. Nowadays, he finds that he compares every woman to Freya. There was simply no one like *his* Freya. Her casual appearance was much more relaxed than Freya's, but he could see the same intelligence behind those brown eyes. Alice Flores in many ways reminded him of Freya based on what the background check told him. The difference between Alice and Freya was that Alice had no problem staring him down.

"You must be the fiancé." Alice held out her hand to him.

He shook it with a firm handshake.

She didn't blink, she didn't hesitate, and she was all business. "Come in. I wasn't expecting anyone, so it's a bit of a mess. I'm working on a new set..." She was already walking away from him, leaving the front door wide open, expecting him to follow.

He needs to teach her better safety habits. If anything happened to her, Freya would be devastated. Maybe he should put a watcher on her like he'd done to Freya in the beginning. Someone to just watch from a distance, and call for backup if there was trouble, not that he expected it, but it pays to be prepared.

Leo didn't have to tell his men to stand guard. Drago followed him inside while Romano stayed at the front door. Though he'd been giving Romano more responsibilities, he wanted him nearby in case Freya made another unscheduled stop. Once they leave here, he'll be sending Romano to check on several businesses closer to Freya. *Just in case.* The house was clean, though things were cluttered such as lights and fabrics. No dirty dishes were lying around. He supposed if you run a business in your house, you'd keep it clean too. He followed her down the hallway where he guessed the studio was.

"Back here. I have the originals." The studio turned out to be the master bedroom. He recognized the fancy bed set on one side of the room surrounded by props and lights. He could picture Freya on that bed, posing for the camera. Knowing Freya, she would have been shy, but Alice had done a fantastic job at capturing her essence. She was a subtle beauty—a quiet nature— with a strong back bone. The photos were beautiful.

Alice searched through a stack of CDs on her desk before turning to face him, holding up a CD case. The label read Freya's name with a date—a date he recognized. The unscheduled trip that had started their fight. Alice also included Freya's number and email address. *An organized chick.*

"This is the only copy of the photos." She handed it to him. He held it. It was what he wanted yes, but he also wanted something else.

"Miss Flores, I want to emphasize that if anyone else sees these photos, or if they are published in any way to the public, I–"

"Yeah, I know, I know. You'll break my legs. Freya already told me."

He liked her bluntness.

"But really Mr. Costa." The way she said his name let him know that she was challenging him. "Freya and I have been best friends a hell of a lot longer than you and her have known each other. We've been through a lot together. You might be there now, but she knows that she can always turn to me. I wouldn't do anything that would hurt her, can you say the same?"

There was steel in her voice and posture. There was a threat there that warned him she wasn't afraid of him. *She should be*, but she was loyal to Freya, and he respected her for that.

He controlled his temper, which flared at her insinuation. He would never purposely hurt Freya. "Your warning is noted but unnecessary. I love Freya and will do everything I can to make sure she is happy and safe."

"As long as we understand each other, Mr. Costa." Alice gave him a small grin, appeased. "I would hate to have to talk to my sister's shady friends to have them break *your* legs."

He found that humorous considering those *shady friends* were nothing but thugs that would never get close enough to him and what's his. His background check on Alice extended to her sister, Claudia Flores.

"You may call me Leo since you are important to Freya and we will probably be seeing each other often enough. While I did come here for the originals, I also came to request a couple more prints of her photos in larger sizes."

"Okay." Alice hit a key to wake her computer before taking the CD back from his hand. If he was big on manners, it would have irritated him. He watched her load the CD and open the files for him. "You probably haven't seen them all, Freya only picked two. I'll give you some time to look through it, and you can choose which ones you want." Alice set up the photos on the computer for his viewing before pushing the chair back and leaving the seat for him.

He hadn't thought about picking the photos, he wanted the two he'd already received larger. He hadn't told Freya he was coming here or that he wanted more photos of her printed. He also hadn't told her what he planned to do with the photos he was requesting. She'll see them soon enough, he just hopes she doesn't make an issue of them.

"What size did you want?" Alice asked.

He sat and browsed through the photos. "Five by seven." He wanted Freya's photos blown up to cover walls in his offices.

"Unfortunately, that size will have to be contracted out to someone else. The widest my printer will print is two feet. I can give you some recommendations–"

"Tell Romano–I believe you've met him–he'll get you whatever you need."

"That's crazy! The printer size you want is going to cost at least twenty thousand–"

"He will get you what you need." He didn't give her time to argue. "I want this, this, this, and this." He selected the photos he wanted. The two Freya had given him were already up; one in his walk-in closet and the other in his home office. He plans to display the four he had chosen in his offices at the hotel and club.

Chapter Thirty Seven

October

Bartolo knew that Bianca was most likely being monitored. He'd decided that the best way to approach her was in school. It took some fast money to convince the custodian to pretend he was a new employee until he could get a chance to talk to his daughter. It didn't take long. He waited for lunch break and watched the hallway fill with students. He found her right away. She had a confidence that matched his. People parted to let her through.

He made eye contact with her, and he knew the instant she recognized him. She nearly stopped at the shock of seeing him. He nodded his head toward an empty classroom, indicating he wanted to meet with her. He'd waited nearly six minutes before she finally joined him.

"Daddy?" she called out. She was beautiful and tall. He hadn't had a son, but she did him proud. She always looked perfect, something he was proud of.

"Hey, baby."

"Oh my God, it is you!" She went to him and hugged him. "How...why?"

"That's not important."

"They will kill you if they see you."

"They won't find me."

"What are you doing here?"

"Do you want to make them pay for what they did to me? For what they did to us?" *There was no time to waste.*

"Of course, I do! This is all Mom's fault. She did this to us! She should have kept her mouth shut. Now, we're always being watched. That Drago guy is always there asking her questions about you. And Leo and his family! I can't stand them!"

"Good. We'll get our payback soon, but I need your help." He handed her a phone. It was untraceable. If she hid it well, no one would know they were ever in contact. "It's time to make the Lombardi name proud, Bianca. We're going to make them pay."

Chapter Thirty Eight

She never thought she would ever be one of those people. A rocky childhood made her crave stability, security, and control, but it didn't make her want to be rich and famous. She wasn't exactly either, but she was treated like it. It was a perk of being with Leo. She was rich because she was marrying into a wealthy family, and she lived accordingly, as most people could probably tell by her clothes, the car she came out of, and the fact that she had bodyguards everywhere she went. They were treated like royalty.

The Friday night crowd was out in full swing. The city was alive, buzzing with all the night owls, and party goers. Freya had never really been into clubbing before, but when you're about to marry a man who owned several prominent nightclubs, you tend to like clubbing a bit more. She never has to pay for anything, and she and her girlfriends were always given the VIP booths. They also didn't have to worry about how they were going to get home. They were well protected and catered to, from beginning to end. Freya and her friends arrived at Elite, the best and most exclusive nightclub in San Francisco, in a black Mercedes SUV escorted by Romano and Sandro. Since Leo owned the place, it had become the go-to location for her and her friends when they wanted a girls' night out. The car pulled up at the entrance of the club. A long line of people watched as she and her friends exited the vehicle. Sandro blocked the sidewalk to make sure no one – as if anyone would dare – got to them.

Freya could feel the weight of the crowd's stare, and the contempt and curiosity at their special treatment. She had gotten used to it. She simply ignored it as the velvet ropes opened for them. They were quickly ushered into the club, where they were welcomed by lights and loud music. Each thump of the song seemed to beat with her heart. They were led to their booth where drinks were already waiting for them. Freya waved off the waitress assigned to them, and let the girls pour their own drinks. Romano handed her a blue drink, something she arranged in advance.

Leo and her had gotten together because she'd been drugged by another patron, so Leo insists that her drinks are specially handled by his trusted people. She did the obligatory toasting and cheers with her friends, taking several sips of her mixed drink before heading to the dance floor. She danced to a couple of songs with her friends before Anthony, another bodyguard watching over her and her friends, tapped her on the shoulder and nodded toward the office that overlooked the dance floor, indicating Leo was there.

Freya excused herself, knowing her friends wouldn't miss her too much. Romano stayed close to her, nearly shoving people out of the way as he cleared the path toward the back rooms and stairs. She stopped Romano from following her once she reached the stairs that led to Leo's office. She knocked on the door and entered once she heard his permission. He looked up as she was closing the door and stood up to greet her. The one-way glass that looked over the dance floor flashed a small amount of changing colored lights into the office. He came around his desk as she walked closer to him.

"I told you to just come in; you don't have to knock," he told her as he pulled her body toward his and dropped a sweet kiss on her lips. "I see you've already started," he whispered against her mouth before he licked her bottom lip.

He must mean the alcohol. "I just took a sip or two," she replied as her arms went around his neck. Her heels gave her much needed height, but Leo was tall, and she ended up settling her hands on his shoulders.

"You look beautiful."

She stepped back to let him see her whole outfit. She gave a quick twirl before going back into his arms.

"If you bend over even a little, your ass is going to be on display," he complained, making her smile. He leaned back against his desk and pulled her between his legs.

"It's not *that* short," she insisted. She knew he didn't really mind as long as the *goods* weren't actually showing.

His hand went to her rear, slipping under her dress to cup her cheeks. He gave them a small squeeze to make a point.

"You look really hot yourself, Mister Costa. Red looks good on you," she teased as her fingers played with the buttons of his shirt.

"Why thank you, Miss Santos. My fiancé insisted I needed to add color into my wardrobe, so here I am."

Freya let out a small giggle. She did complain that almost everything he owned was black. She'd bought him the red shirt to add color into his closet.

"Red is a great color on you," she replied before kissing him. With him sitting on his desk, she was able to wrap her arms around his neck to pull him closer. His hands were almost lifting her by the ass as he held her tighter against him.

She was so lost in their kiss, she hadn't realized they had switched position until the cold table touched her skin. Her dress bunched up around her waist, and her cheeks rested on the cool top of the table. She shivered at the first touch. Leo pulled her body closer to the edge, locking their bodies together. She could feel his bulge against the thin fabric of her underwear. He kissed his way down to her neck as he pushed the thin straps of her gold dress off of her shoulders, pushing it further down to reveal her braless breasts.

"So fucking perfect," he whispered before bending down to take a hardened nipple into his mouth. She gasped at the first suck. His hand went to her other breast, kneading and pinching her nipple. Arousal cruised through her body, sending tingles of pleasure to her core and to the tips of her fingers.

Her hands found the buttons of his shirt, nearly tearing it open with her need to feel his bare flesh. Once opened, she shoved his shirt off his shoulders, and let her hands roam his hot skin. *She loved the feel of his muscles.* Running her fingers through the ridges of his shoulders and chest, she made her way down to his abdominal muscles.

His mouth on her made it hard to focus as she struggled to undo his belt. His mouth attacked her other breast as his hands helped hers. Freya's hands delved into his boxer briefs, seeking the hard flesh. His cock was heavy and hot in her hand. Leo moaned against her breast, and then gently bit her nipple, eliciting her own moan. He pulled back, giving her space to play with him. She stroked him, loving the way his breath hitched as she caressed his cock.

He was as close to the edge as she was. He discarded his shirt somewhere behind him and dropped his underwear and pants down with one hand while his other dipped in between her legs. His fingers pushed her flimsy underwear aside and entered her, testing her. She was wet and ready for him. *Always ready for him.* He kissed her again, loving her taste. She reminded him of mint and sugar. It was addicting. His hands roamed her body, loving every perfect, soft, curve. Her dress bunched at her waist as he pushed it further up, revealing delicate, lace underwear, he had it in mind to fuck her with it on but had enough sense not to ruin them. He pulled the scrap of underwear off, loving the feel of her skin as he slid it down her legs.

"This is going to be fast," he warned her. Not just because he was close, but he had something to do after. He knew he did, just couldn't remember it at that moment.

"Good." She nearly jumped him, pulling him down to kiss him, locking him between her legs.

He angled her body as his cock sought to be buried in her heat. He thrust in one long and hard push, burying himself as deep as he could.

She cried out at his forceful penetration.

He didn't stop, couldn't stop. He pulled back and then surged back in. Again and again. Her body clung to his, trying to keep him in her. With each thrust, he owned her body and demanded her pleasure.

Her orgasm pushed his. Her inner muscles squeezed his cock. He emptied himself in her, barely stopping himself from collapsing over her. Her arms and legs were still wrapped around him, as they both fought for air. He let himself soften in her, not ready to be separated. It seemed like hours before she finally broke the haze they had fallen into.

"I love you," she said.

It was all he needed to hear to know that they would be okay. The past two months had put a strain between them. Their fight on his birthday had been the talking they needed to do, but even after they'd said their apologies and vowed to work it out, there has been a thread of sting that kept them apart. He'd felt that thread break tonight. Felt the connection come back.

He leaned his head against hers, studying her flushed face, her eyes closed, feeling her breath on his skin. He loved this woman more than life itself.

She didn't open her eyes until he pulled away. Her eyes told him she felt it too. Their commitment to each other was back and stronger. Those beautiful brown eyes told him all he needed to know. He kissed her just to see her smile. He pulled his underwear and pants back up, leaving the zipper undone, and reached for the handkerchief in his pocket. He went to clean her before she took it from him and wiped herself. He watched the intimate procedure as he worked to right his own clothes. He picked up her tiny underwear from his desk and insisted on helping her put it back on. Her hair, which she left hanging loose, looked like he'd been running his hands through it and he liked it. He wanted everyone who saw her to know she was a taken woman.

"I'll see you at home?" she asked him as she used the mirror on the east wall of his office. The mirror was there for the exact same reason she was using it for now. Placed there by his father for his mother, for when they did the exact same thing that he and Freya had just done...not that he wanted to think about his parents' sex life. He'd kept the office exactly like his father had kept it, except for the new addition that Freya hadn't noticed yet.

"If you stay here for the night, I will take you

home. I'll be having some meetings here." He walked up behind her, wrapped his arms around her small waist, and pulled her back against his body. She leaned against him, as they watched their reflection in the mirror. "I'll be thinking about you and what we just did on that desk while I have those meetings."

"You are a naughty man, Mister Costa," she teased.

"Just for you." He kissed the back of her head. She turned to face him but froze halfway through the turn, and he knew the moment she noticed the new addition.

"Oh my God, Leo! You're crazy!" She pulled away from him as she moved closer to the large portrait of her, barely dressed. It was one of the photos he'd chosen to have enlarged. It covered a large portion of the wall. It wasn't the first thing you'd see when you walked into his office, but it definitely wasn't hiding. In this photo, her face was somewhat obscure since she wasn't looking at the camera, but anyone who knew him would know it was her.

He didn't fucking care; he loved seeing it anytime he looked up from his work.

"I can't...How did you even...You didn't scare Alice, did you?" She turned a heated look at him. He couldn't help but grin.

"No, I just asked her to make a couple of them for my offices." He pulled her to him, loving her shyness. He loved those photos, they were the best birthday present he had ever received.

"A couple?" She hit his chest to make him look at her. "Don't tell me you have one in every office?!" The glow from her recent orgasm turned into a blush from embarrassment.

"I love them. I love seeing you every time I am in my office."

"I honestly thought you'd just leave them hanging in like...your closet or something." She played with the buttons of his shirt.

"You are not meant to be hidden. I want every man to see that and be jealous of me. They are beautiful, and I love showing you off."

"What if your parents' see it? They're going to think I'm a sl-"

"Don't even finish that. My parents would never think that. Mom will say you look beautiful, and Dad will appreciate your beauty. I don't ever want to hear you say that about yourself...unless of course, you're saying you're a slut for me." She melted at his dimpled grin.

"Fine...I just...Everyone's going to see it."

"And they'll either appreciate it or be jealous of it. They are beautiful. You are perfect to me." He kissed her. Sensing someone behind him, he remembered his meeting and that kept him from taking her on his desk all over again.

"Come get me when you're ready to go. I'll be here all night." He walked her to the door, gave her one last kiss, and watched her head down the stairs before returning to his forgotten guest.

"Didn't know you were into voyeurism," Leo said to Castle, who leaned against the door of the bathroom. Leo had completely forgotten that Castle had gone to the restroom in his office when Freya had walked in looking like a sexy vixen in a barely there gold dress. *If Freya had gone into the restroom, she would have had the shock of her life.* Leo made his way back to his chair as Castle strolled over to the couch.

"Love it, always been a fan," Castle drawled. He stopped to appreciate Freya's portrait.

Leo felt a momentary jealous reaction at Castle appreciating Freya's body. *Castle probably jacked himself off in the restroom while we fucked,* he thought. The only thing keeping Leo from going full caveman was the fact that he knew Castle would never go after Freya or treat her any less than a sister.

"You're hooked and sunk buddy," Castle teased.

Leo wasn't at all embarrassed about being completely enthralled by Freya. "I love that woman with every breath in me," Leo answered seriously.

"And I will protect her for as long as I live." Castle hadn't needed to make the promise since Leo knew he would protect his family with his life if he needed to. Freya becoming Leo's life made her Castle's family too.

Chapter Thirty Nine

Maybe it was because she was constantly surrounded by Leo's family, but Freya had been thinking about her mother a lot lately, enough to make her attempt to call her, but the number had been disconnected. Freya had called her mother's neighbor just to check, but she had unfortunately moved and no longer lived in the same mobile park. Freya knew that Leo would be upset, but something was nagging her to check on her mother. She called Leo.

***

Leo was tempted to tell Freya no, but he didn't. He'll just have to adjust. She seemed determined to do what she wanted regardless of what he wished. It wasn't worth arguing over, especially since they had just patched things up. He was headed out of his office to tell Romano to go meet Freya at her mother's when the call came.

"My mom's missing!" Bianca's shrill cry over the phone nearly blistered his ear. The teenager wasn't making much sense as she babbled on, but he got the gist of it. Leo had never thought that Anna and Bianca had gotten along. Bianca was more like her father, spoiled and entitled, but they were still *his* people. *His responsibility.*

He had a man assigned to Anna for several reasons, one of which was for her protection. Leo wouldn't have gotten to Freya on time if Anna hadn't betrayed her own husband. Her husband had been a high-ranking member of *La Famiglia*, and he betrayed them. Leo had also wanted Anna and Bianca watched in case Bartolo decided to take his family while on the run from Leo and his men. No member of the Italian mafia will take Bartolo knowing the consequences would mean war with the Costa and Vetrano family along with their allies. Which left Bartolo seeking help from other factions. Leo would bet the Russian Bratva, their rival.

"Go to Freya," Leo told Romano as soon as he entered the lounge where his men were. Romano didn't ask questions, or where to go, he knew to get the answer from Sandro. Leo turned to Vito and Drago, his head of security. "Take me to the Lombardi residence." His men didn't ask questions, they did their jobs. Vito gave orders to have transportation set up, and Drago arranged base protection.

***

Freya felt anxious as she and Sandro drove into the trailer park. She hoped that her mother was still there because if she wasn't then Freya had no idea how she'd find her. Her and Mariana's relationship had always been rocky, but she was Freya's only relative. Freya had tried for years to get her mother sober, but you can't force someone to get better if they don't want to. As an adult, her mother had only wanted money to feed her addiction, which often led to fights between her and Freya. Freya hadn't spoken to Mariana since introducing Leo to her. Her mother had embarrassed Freya after seeing what Leo's family was like.

Did it make her a snob?

Maybe.

She let out the breath she was holding when she saw the same rundown trailer parked where she had last seen it. Knowing Sandro would want to follow procedure since she'd made another unscheduled trip, she waited for him to open her door.

She hesitated walking to her mom's door for a moment, unsure of what to say. She was going to get married, and she hoped that her mother could be there.

She slowly went to the trailer and knocked on the feeble metal door.

"What?" her mother yelled through the door before it swung open. "Oh, you." Rather than ask her what she was doing there, her mother left the door opened, expecting her to come in.

Freya hesitated for a second and looked back at Sandro who started to walk toward her. She shook her head, telling him to stay. She could see the indecision; he wanted to follow procedure, but she was technically the boss. She didn't wait for him to make up his mind, she followed her mother into the beat-up trailer, and left the door slightly ajar.

The trailer looked worse than she remembered. It smelled of smoke, the small sink overflowed with dirty dishes, beer cans and alcohol bottles littered every nook and table. Her mother sat at the built-in booth and proceeded to light a cigarette. Mariana Santos looked worse than the last time she had seen her nearly six months ago. She looked older, her hair looked thinner, and she looked like she was doing more drugs now.

"Are you on drugs again?" The question came out like a sharp sting, and Freya knew it was the wrong thing to say, but she didn't hold back. Her mother was slowly killing herself, and nothing Freya did ever worked.

"None of your fucking business!" her mother snapped back.

Freya marched closer and tried to grab her mother's arm to look for needle marks. A short struggle ensued, but Freya was stronger than her mother's weakened frame. She managed to pull her mother's arm out enough to see the marks.

"Don't fucking touch me!"

Freya flung Mariana's arm back at her. Freya's anger at her mother wasn't new, but the hurt she felt didn't make sense to her. She and her mother didn't have a good relationship. She'd known since she was a child that her mother was a selfish woman who only cared about what felt good for her. Her disappointment at her mother was stronger than she was used to. Maybe it was because she'd been surrounded by Leo's loving family and she just wanted to feel just a fraction of that with her mother. "Do you ever think about how much better your life could be if you weren't a fucking addict?" It was cruel and very unlike her, but Freya's emotions were getting the best of her lately.

"What? Like you? Miss fancy-ass-snobby-bitch who can't even help her mother?" her mother spat back.

"I made something of myself before I met Leo. Something you had nothing to do with."

"I gave birth to you; you wouldn't be anywhere without me!" her mother screamed as she got up from the booth, going toe to toe with her.

Freya wasn't afraid and wasn't backing down. "You're the worst mother a child could have. You're nothing but a selfish bitch!" Freya raised her voice to be heard over her mother's.

"A selfish bitch? Yet you keep coming back here, looking like a lost little girl. Looking–"

"I was trying to help you! One day you're going to wake up a lonely old woman, still chasing a dick in order to feed your addiction!" Freya and her mother screamed at each other, back and forth, each one talking over the other. Freya felt the blood running through her veins, urging her to keep going – instigating and pushing her mother.

"I hate you! You ruined everything!" Mariana hit her before she could even finish her sentence, slapping Freya hard. Freya barely caught herself on the counter before her mother was on her, pulling at her hair. Dishes and cans fell on the floor as they struggled with each other.

***

Sandro contacted Romano to let him know what was happening. He could hear the screaming match, though mostly one-sided between the women. He'd been assured by the person assigned to watch Freya's mother that the woman was alone in the trailer, and he didn't want to argue with Freya about it. His gut told him she would be fine. It wasn't his business. His job was to make sure the boss's woman was safe. He was ready, the moment he heard sounds of struggle, he ran in. *That woman wasn't going to hurt Freya on his watch.*

Sandro came bursting in through the door and saw the women locked in a struggle. He put himself between them, but the two women didn't stop. Mariana yanked at Freya's hair. At the same time, Freya hit Mariana's arm to get her to let go. Sandro grabbed Mariana's arm, gripping it with enough force to hurt her and force her to release Freya's hair. The trailer was too small, and Sandro effectively separated the two women with his body.

Mariana screamed and beat Sandro's back. He barely felt her hits, he was more concerned about Freya.

"Enough!" he nearly yelled the order.

Freya heard it and stopped struggling with him.

He let Freya go, keeping her away from her waste of a life mother. Once he was sure she wasn't going to try and continue the fight, he turned around. He didn't bother being gentle when he faced the rabid woman behind him. His hand went to her neck, and held tight, scaring her but not leaving a mark—enough to stop her struggling. It quickly caught her attention, and he could see the fear radiating off of the useless woman. "You lay a hand on her again, and that'll be the last thing you'll do." His words were low, menacing, and a promise.

"Sandro, let her go. She didn't mean to...it's the drugs."

Sandro refrained from rolling his eyes. He was pissed. He liked Freya, but she was too soft for this kind of shit. He couldn't understand how the fuck she ended up being so forgiving when she was raised by the hellion he held by the neck.

"We're leaving now." It was an order.

Freya didn't argue with him, she could probably tell he wasn't in the mood, and he could tell she was a little shaken up.

"You touch her again, and I'll break your neck," he said in a low voice to Freya's mother. He meant it. He barely managed not to fling the woman across the tiny trailer. Hurting her in front of Freya would make the problem worse.

He could do his job alone, but times like this they needed two people. One to be in front of Freya and one behind her to keep her mother away. Sandro didn't like laying a hand on Freya; she was the boss's woman, and Leo was a little overzealous about other men touching her, but it was needed. He kept his body between the two women and had to squeeze between the tight space to get to the door first. He kept a hand on Freya's arm to keep her from stepping out before he was sure it was safe.

A few curious neighbors eyed the car, but that was expected because the expensive car stood out in the park. He made sure the coast was clear before letting Freya step out of the shitty trailer. He quickly shuffled her into the back seat of the car.

He didn't like the idea of leaving without back up but staying would just bring more attention. He sent a quick text to Romano to let him know the situation. The GPS tracked them, and Romano agreed to meet up with him. He looked back to make sure Freya was buckled in. It pissed him off to see a red mark on her face. *She got hurt under his watch.*

***

Freya was embarrassed by what happened. She couldn't even look at Sandro without feeling ashamed for getting into a fight with her mother. This whole trip suddenly seemed so stupid. *Why did she even bother? Why couldn't she just leave it alone?* She and her mother weren't meant to have a relationship. *Why couldn't she accept that?* Freya was glad that Sandro hadn't said something like 'I told you so' to shove it in her face. She was pretty sure he was going to tattle to Leo, and Leo would be even more upset over another unscheduled trip.

She sighed and looked out the window. They were entering the winding road that would take them to the highway. The one-lane road went over the mountain that separated the rich, the middle class, and the poor. If you had a house in the hills you had money, if you lived on the north side of the mountain, you were middle class, and if you lived on the east side of the mountain...well that was where trouble lived. That was where she'd grown up. Freya had always found it ironic that you had to drive through calendar-worthy scenery to enter the bad part of town. The winding road wasn't busy since most people didn't go outside of their environment. There was no reason for someone who lived in the north or the hills to cross over to the east side...and the people on the east side couldn't afford to get out.

Sandro spoke, pulling Freya out of her musings. At first, she thought he was talking to her, but quickly realized he was on the phone.

"Coming in hot. On the hills. It's clear."

Freya turned to look out the back window after

hearing the conversation. A car barreled toward them. The slick black car was either out of control or crazy because this was a dangerous road – popular for accidents. It drove recklessly.

"Freya, head down!" Sandro's order barely registered as she watched the car come closer and closer. Sandro swerved, causing her to be jerked aside, and pulling her out of her daze. "Freya, down!" She ducked down toward the seat, fighting with the seat belt.

She barely lowered her head before she heard the sound of glass shattering. She wasn't sure, but she thought she might have screamed. *Oh God, what was happening*? She was being jolted all over the back seat, as Sandro swerved the car.

More popping sounds.

More shattered glass.

They were being shot at. She'd never forget the sound of guns, not since she'd runaway from someone who was shooting at her.

What the hell? The only sound she could focus on was the gun.

"Keep your head down!" Sandro yelled just as she felt a sudden jolt that sent the car veering hard.

Were they hitting the car? What were they trying to do? She screamed as the cars hit again, whiplashing her forward. She covered her head with her arms and held onto the seat as best as she could.

The sound of metals scrapping raised the hair all over her body.

Then suddenly the car was flying, and she was being lifted off her seat, only to bet caught by her seatbelt.

***

Leo barely put his car in park before he jumped out of it, leaving it on and the door wide open. No one stopped him. *No one would dare.* His own bodyguards barely managed to keep up with him. Vito would give him hell, but he didn't give a fuck. Freya was in danger. He'd gotten the call and ran for his car. Romano had a twenty-minute head start but Leo had been right at his tail. He walked through the crowd, ignoring the cops, and headed straight toward the mangled car. The SUV was on its side.

Jesus fuck! He looked for Sandro, Freya, or Romano, and found Sandro arguing with the paramedics near an ambulance, surrounded by cops.

A cop tried to stop him, but he pushed him aside. The paramedics were trying to get Sandro to sit.

His face was covered in cuts and blood.

"Freya–" Leo barely got his question out before Sandro answered.

"Hospital with Romano."

"Sandro, go with them!" Leo ordered before turning to the cop he'd shoved aside. "Which hospital?"

"Sir, I'm going to need you–"

"Which fucking hospital?" he demanded.

"Sir–"

"It's alright. The one on North Hill, Mr. Costa. She's with her bodyguard," a voice answered from behind the damn cop.

He turned and recognized a detective he'd previously worked with. Leo took off back to his car as soon as he had his answer. Vito and Drago had just exited their own car when Leo ran back to his car.

"Drago, handle this!" Leo ordered just as Vito jumped into his car with him. There was no need to give instructions, his men knew their jobs. Leo drove to the hospital and then parked right in front, not giving a fuck.

"God damn it, Leo. Wait!"

Leo ignored Vito and ran for the hospital doors. He was quickly given direction to where Freya was and hurried there. He walked right into the room, bypassing the nurses' station and found Romano standing guard at the door.

"Hold on. You need to let them finish." Romano tried to stop him.

Leo ignored him too. He needed to see for himself.

Romano stepped in his path, the action was bold and Leo, for a second, lost his mind.

He grabbed Romano and shoved him out of his way; their struggle caused a scene alarming the nurses. He was grabbed from behind.

"Calm the fuck down! You're not going to help her like this!" Vito snapped from behind him. Vito's words penetrated Leo's foggy mind. He realized what he was doing and immediately stopped struggling.

"I'm good." He only had to say it once before Romano and Vito let go of him. He needed to fucking calm down and think straight. He took a deep breath. His need to see Freya and assure himself she was still with him had taken control of him.

"I'll take care of the car," Vita informed.

Leo barely acknowledged Vito as he turned to Romano. "Tell me."

***

Leo pulled the chair closer to Freya's bed. She had bruises and cuts on her face. She'd been wearing her seatbelt, and that kept her from being thrown around or out of the car when it rolled. Though there was no swelling on her brain or any internal damage that they can tell, she hadn't woken since being brought in. The doctors have assured him that she'll wake up on her own time, but he wanted to see her eyes open. He wanted her to look at him. He wanted the assurance that she was still with him.

There was a fire burning in his gut. It was dangerous. It made him reckless. That monster in him wanted to go out and punish everyone. His men were out looking for a target. He wanted to know who was out for his family. The attack had to have been planned in advance, and they just waited for an opportunity to carry it out. As far as he could tell, Freya had decided to visit her mother on her own, and whoever attacked had been watching.

There was no way to keep the incident hidden since there were too many locals involved. A cop happened to arrive as the SUV had gone rolling. They're calling it a road rage hit and run. The cop hadn't gone after the culprit because he needed to help the injured. Though shell casings were found, Sandro's story was that it was road rage. Guns would bring bigger problems and more questions. Leo hated to make Freya lie, but she'd need to keep Sandro's story.

Romano had arrived at the same time as the paramedics and had insisted on going with Freya, as he should have. Sandro had wanted to stay until back up arrived, and then was brought to the hospital. He had a possible mild concussion, and a hell of a lot of cuts and bruises, but he was fine. His body was used to taking hard hits, but Freya's wasn't, and she was still unconscious from the trauma of the accident.

And it didn't end there. He didn't think Freya would keep it from him, not something this important. Since Freya was not able to answer their questions, they had tested her for pregnancy to be safe. It was a miracle that their baby was unharmed, but it was still touch and go with the trauma her body had just experienced.

A baby.

It changed everything.

Chapter Forty

Her first thought as she woke up was that it was too bright, and she'd overslept. Her mouth was dry, and she felt like she was floating.

"Freya..." her name was soft, and she turned her head toward the sound.

"Leo," she croaked as he leaned closer to her. She quickly realized that she was in an unfamiliar place. "What..." She tried to remember how she got there. It was difficult at first, but it came back to her, and she wished it hadn't. They'd been shot at...attacked. She could hear the sounds of gunfire.

"It's alright," Leo whispered softly as he took her hand. "You're safe."

***

Leo helped Freya into her coat as they prepared to leave the hospital. He'd convinced her to stay for at least two days before she'd threatened to walk out of the hospital on her own. He had wanted her to stay for as long as the doctors wanted her to stay, but he didn't argue since he'd already asked her to lie to the detectives that came to take her statement. He had coached her into saying that she wasn't completely sure about what happened,except that the other driver seemed to have had wanted to make trouble.

He hadn't talked to her about the pregnancy. He knew her doctor had told her, but he hadn't brought it up himself. He wanted her to tell him. She was moving slow. She had bruises all over her body but nothing that wouldn't heal with rest and time.

"Are you sure you won't stay another day?" he asked in a sigh.

"I want to go home, Leo," she answered as she lifted her hair out of her coat.

Part of the reason she wanted to go home so quickly was because he'd promised to tell her everything – why she was attacked, why she had to lie to the police, and the truth about Bartolo and Marco. He wasn't looking forward to it, but she needed to know so she'd stop fighting him and make it easier for him to protect her.

She had refused to take a wheelchair down to the car. They had already checked out and her medications, including prenatal vitamins, had been picked up and taken to the car by Romano. Though she was moving on her own, it was a slow walk to the elevator. Vito silently followed behind them, with Drago in front, leading the way. It wasn't until the elevator doors had closed that she sighed and leaned against him. His arm went around her waist, keeping her anchored to him, ready to support her in any way he could. There was a somberness between them.

Freya didn't pull away from Leo as they exited the elevator and made their way to the waiting car in front of the hospital. Relief flooded her as she stepped in the fresh, cold air and lifted her mood. She hurt all over, but she was okay. The ride home was quiet but comfortable. She hadn't taken her medication to help her rest because she wanted to talk. *It was important they talk.* The incident wasn't the only thing they had to talk about. *There was something more important, something much bigger.* She couldn't even wrap her head around it. She'd been on the pill for years, and took it on schedule everyday...but somehow she was pregnant. She couldn't believe it. She hadn't told Leo, but she was pretty sure he already knew. It wasn't that she was against it, she just hadn't thought about it.

Six weeks pregnant and she had no idea how to react. She'd been shocked when her doctor told her. She felt like she was still in shock, but now the fear was setting in. What kind of mother would she be? Her mother was a terrible example. *Would she know what to do? Would Leo get even more protective? Would she feel suffocated by his protectiveness? Were they ready to be parents?* She was almost thirty with a good career, but she had no idea how to be a good parent or even what to do with a baby.

It was midafternoon, but she headed straight to their room when they arrived home. Leo followed close behind. They were going to talk about the past, the present, and the future. She sat on the edge of their bed.

"Why don't we get you comfortable first, and maybe some food, so you can take your–"

"I'm pregnant," she cut him off. *There. It was out,* and it hung between them like a heavy burden...or so she thought.

"I know." He surprised her, not by his words, but his actions. He took her hands in his, and kneeled in front of her, lowering himself. He brought her hands to his lips, kissed her fingers, and then gently held them against his chest. "I know," he said again.

"I'm scared," she confessed.

"I am too," he answered honestly. "But I will be here every step of the way. You'll have everything you'll need. I will not let anyone hurt you again."

"You can't guarantee that...and I don't expect you to." She pulled him up and indicated that he sit next to her. She didn't want to look down at him, she wanted them to be equal in this conversation. *They needed to do this together.* "I need you to tell me everything, Leo. If we're really going to be partners and parents, I need everything, not just what you think I need to know. I can't...I can't keep becoming a casualty to a war I don't understand."

"I won't let that happen." He took her face between his hands. "I'd die before you got hurt again. Not you. Not our baby. Not our family. I will end this."

"But what is it? Why does this keep happening?"

He stared at her as if deciding what he should say. She didn't want any more secrets.

"Let's get you changed and in bed before we talk about this. I will answer whatever questions you have, I promise. But you have to rest and take your medication. That's the deal."

She agreed, and Leo helped her into soft pajamas before tucking her into bed. He changed into sweatpants before joining her. She went into his arms, resting her head against his shoulder.

"Tell me."

"Bartolo is alive...and he wants the same thing he wanted and failed to get last time. Power."

"I just – I thought he was, you know, gone, like Marco." She'd always assumed that Bartolo had met the same end as Marco. When she'd asked Leo about Marco, all he'd told her was that Marco would never be a problem again. *She knew what it had meant.* She just hadn't wanted to think about it because she hadn't felt bad about it. Marco had hurt her and scared her, and deep down she wanted him punished.

Bartolo, on the other hand, hadn't been the one to directly hurt her, even if he was the one behind it. It was harder for her to think about him as an evil man because she'd only seen him as a father and husband to his family and a friend of Giovanni's. She hadn't seen him as the monster he was. But now she has...and a part of her wanted him to die – wanted him gone from being a threat to her family...to her baby.

"He was gone by the time we got to his place. We've been looking for him since." She could hear the frustration in his tone.

"Was he responsible for my accident?"

"Yes, I think he is... But I think he has help from another...entity."

"Who?" She wanted to know who her enemies were.

"The Russian Bratva."

"The what?" she asked, sitting up to face him.

"Bratva. They are like us but Russian."

"They are your enemies?"

"They are *our* enemies, Freya." He emphasized 'ours,' looking at her straight in the eyes and letting it sink in.

Yes, she was part of them now. And if they had anything to do with putting her baby in harm's way, then they were her enemies too. "What else haven't you told me?"

"I will tell you what you want to know."

"If I had known..."

"You would have thought I was being overbearing."

She would have. She wouldn't have believed it if the attack hadn't happened.

"I don't want to smother you, Freya. I just want to keep you safe. I have done what I thought was best to keep you safe and let you have your freedom...but this changes everything."

She knew that. She accepted it. *She felt the same way.*

"You are the most important person to me. I cannot lose you." Leo's words echoed her thoughts. Her first and last thought has always been Leo, and it was time that she started being what she was. *His woman.* A Costa.

Chapter Forty One

November

Freya felt as nervous as she had the first time she and Leo had driven up the long driveway of his parents' mansion. She'd been here for what feels like hundreds of times, but today was different. Today was the beginning of their future. A commitment she's taking to heart. The moment she found out she had another life to protect, she knew she needed to decide who she was going to be. She wasn't Freya Santos, the girl who refused to depend on anyone but herself. She was Leo's woman and about to become a mother. She would do whatever it took to protect her baby. Her baby's needs were more important than hers.

They had kept the news of her pregnancy to themselves. They needed to get used to the news. She had follow-up appointments both from the accident and her pregnancy. All was well, and she took it as a sign that what she was doing was right. She turned in her resignation letter by email after speaking to her boss on the phone. She had used her accident as an excuse for her abrupt resignation but agreed to provide support remotely until they found someone to replace her. With the danger hanging over their head, she didn't want to take the risk.

Though her in-laws-to-be had visited her a couple of times during the last two weeks to check on her recovery, she was nervous about her announcement. She'd been holding herself back for a while, afraid that all of it would slip away from her like it always had in the past, but she was ready to be completely part of this family. Tonight, she'd be announcing her pregnancy and their future plans.

Leo waited for Drago to open the door before stepping out. Until their enemy was gone, they were going to do everything by the book. Leo stepped out of the car first and looked around before letting her out. He helped her out of the car, being extra cautious about every step. The cold, early November air stung her face. Leo straightened her coat, before taking her hand, and walked her to the front door.

They were greeted by Giovanni and Valentina as usual. Leo had insisted on this formal family luncheon and had asked Luciano to come home. Freya hadn't wanted to make Luciano travel back and forth between San Francisco and Las Vegas, since he'd just recently visited after hearing about the attack, but Leo had insisted that this announcement should be done in person. Luciano greeted her with an affectionate hug that left her warm and feeling well loved. *She couldn't believe she tried to fight this.*

"Romano, dear, can you please call Bianca down, so we can start lunch?" Valentina asked Romano who followed close behind them.

Freya had forgotten about Bianca. She'd been so focused on herself that she'd completely forgotten that Anna was missing. She felt a moment of selfishness and wondered if it was a good idea to make this announcement when Bianca was there, missing her mother. Bianca hadn't wanted to stay in her home alone even with several full-time bodyguards. If it was Freya, she probably would have felt the same way. She couldn't imagine how Bianca was feeling with both of her parents missing.

As if reading her mind, Leo whispered, "It'll be alright."

They headed to the dining room they often used for big family dinners. Since they only filled two-thirds of the table, everyone sat close together. Freya sat next to Valentina, who was at Giovanni's right side, and Leo sat next to her. Luciano took the seat next to Leo, while Drago, Vito, Romano, and Bianca sat across from them.

Bianca looked beautiful as usual. Youthful and perfectly made up.

Lunch was happy, and Freya couldn't help but feel like the change in her own attitude had made her more receptive. Everything felt more real, more sincere, more loving. She placed her hand on Leo's thigh when she was ready. He looked at her, understood what she wanted, and captured everyone's attention.

"Freya and I would just like to say a couple of things," Leo started as he stood up. He held out his hand, and Freya took it as she stood next to him. "First, we would like to thank Mom and Dad for hosting lunch."

"You know you never have to thank us for that. We love it when all you boys, and girls, come home," Valentina fondly replied.

"We also wanted to say 'thank you' to the family, Drago, Vito, Romano included, for watching our back. If it wasn't for you, Freya and I would be in a lot more trouble."

"We love watching your ass. Hers more than yours," Vito quipped, pulling laughs from everyone.

"Lastly, we wanted the family together because we wanted to share some exciting news with you."

"You're finally coming out of the closet?" Luciano joked.

"That happened a long time ago," Romano added.

"You're finally moving into a real house?" Giovanni asked. He'd been telling them that a penthouse was not a place for family.

"You've finally set a wedding date?" Valentina asked hopefully.

"Maybe, and kinda," Freya answered with a smile.

"Don't keep us in suspense," Drago said sarcastically, but he had a hint of a smile.

"Freya and I are..." Leo stopped as if he was getting choked up with his announcement.

"I'm pregnant," Freya announced, continuing where Leo stopped.

The reaction was as expected, excitement, congratulatory, and happy.

***

Romano said his goodbyes to everyone and then headed out to do Leo's bidding.

"Romano, hold up," he heard a voice call behind him.

"What's up?" he asked the gorgeous woman walking toward him. *Girl,* he corrected himself. Bianca might be eighteen and looked like a full-grown woman with curves, but he shouldn't be admiring her. She was just a girl, playing grown-up games. She's been a flirt for as long as he's known her.

"Nothing. Can't I just talk to you? Why are you leaving so soon?"

"I have some things to do for Leo."

She rolled her eyes. "You're his cousin, but he treats you like you're at his beck and call."

"I am both. Did you need something?"

"Oh my God, Romano. I'm just trying to make friends. I'm all alone now. My mother is missing, and my father is a criminal."

He instantly felt bad for being short with her. "I'm sorry. I just need to get things done. I know this is probably really difficult for you. Is there anything I can do for you?"

She threw herself onto him. He nearly fell from the impact but managed to regain his balance. She wrapped her arms around his neck and rested her head on his chest. At first, he was unsure of what he should do, then he realized she was crying. He patted her back, trying to comfort her, but it was hard for him to ignore the soft curves pressing against his body.

***

Leo tucked Freya close to him in the back seat of the SUV. Though he usually preferred to drive, it was too dangerous for them to travel alone. Drago and Vito drove them. He'd decided to do lunch for their announcement so that he could take Freya to his surprise. He hadn't thought about them starting a family right way, but he wouldn't say he wasn't happy. The pregnancy was an unexpected gift in all the troubles they'd been facing.

Freya had dozed off after leaving his parents' home. She was around eight weeks, but he'd noticed the changes in her. She was sleeping a lot more, which he was happy about since she was also recovering from the attack. He woke her up as they approached the gate.

"Where are we?" she asked sleepily, not recognizing their surroundings.

"Sausalito." The small city was just north of San Francisco, crossing the Golden Gate Bridge, it was known for its wealth. It was just a half an hour drive to San Francisco making his commute bearable if Freya likes it. He'd thought it was the perfect place to start their family.

"Why?"

"I want you to see something." He pointed at the large house they were approaching. The luxurious contemporary home had five bedrooms and six bathrooms with several units on the property to house staff and guests. The house had a panoramic view of San Francisco Bay and plenty of privacy. The black gates opened as soon as they pulled up.

"Whose house is this?" Freya asked.

"Ours, if you like it."

She looked at him in surprise. "Really?"

"Yes. A real house...for our family."

"Can we see the inside?" she asked excitedly.

"Yes." He half laughed. The real estate agent was there with instructions for what he wanted. He'd sent Romano ahead of time to make sure it was ready for Freya and to secure the location.

"Wow," Freya said breathlessly as soon as she

stepped in. He'd felt the same way the first time he'd seen it. Upon entering they were immediately greeted by a beautiful view of San Francisco Bay. Even under fog, the view was breathtaking.

"It's ours?" she turned to ask him.

"If you want it, yes."

"I want to see all of it!"

It was part of their new beginning. This was where they'll raise their family. A home, a real house. Not his bachelor penthouse.

***

"She's pregnant. They're going to push the wedding to January, so she doesn't look fat and obvious." Bianca kept her voice low as she relayed the news to her father. She couldn't wait to get their revenge on the Costa family. They've been sickeningly nice to her. She was, of course, a great actress. They ruined her life, she was going to ruin theirs.

"You need to be part of that wedding. Offer to help plan it. That no-name bitch will need your help. We need as much information as possible about the wedding."

"You're going to hit the wedding?" she asked

excitedly. *Ruin what is supposed to be the best day of her life?* She couldn't wait for Freya to suffer.

"Just stay close and get as much information as you can. Sleep with the bodyguard. Do whatever you need to do to get the information for the wedding."

"Was that you? The one who tried to kill her?" Bianca asked.

"That wasn't me...That was an associate."

"She should have died."

"She will. They all will."

***

Bartolo hung up on Bianca. His daughter was at least good for something, unlike her mother. *That traitorous bitch.* He hoped she was dead. Fedor wouldn't tell him what he had done with Anna, and the damn Russian had dismissed him when he questioned the attack on Freya. Fedor had wanted to hurt Leo but had only managed to make Leo more on guard.

The wedding will be the perfect target to hit. Fedor didn't mind sending his men on a suicide mission, and it will be. Everyone who needs to die in order for him to takeover will be at that wedding. Blood will run, and he'll be there to make sure of it.

Chapter Forty Two

Mariana Santos would do anything for easy money. Even if it meant selling out her own child. Not that the bitch was worth anything. She didn't know how the fuck she raised such a judgmental bitch. That ungrateful whore wouldn't even give her own flesh and blood money, but she lives in that fancy building with that billionaire dickhead. It felt nice to smack that snobby bitch around to remind her she was nothing, even with all that money she's whoring herself for. It was even better that she finally made some money off of her.

She didn't give a fuck who they were and why they wanted to know when Freya came to visit, but they paid her well. She was almost tempted to call the bitch to tell her to come if it meant more money. It had been three weeks since they paid her, and she was hurting for more. What if she invited Freya? Made her come to see her mama. Maybe the Russians can kill off that son of a bitch bodyguard too. That fucker put his hand on Mariana, and she doesn't like that shit. Maybe she should call them to give them the idea? They're probably too stupid to think of it on their own.

***

"Take care of that suka, she is more trouble than she's worth," Fedor ordered Makar. Makar Pavlov has been his closest friend and ally since they were children. He was more loyal to Fedor than Fedor's own brothers were to him. Blood ties didn't mean shit in his own family.

Fedor had wanted Leo to hurt. Killing his woman would have accomplished that. Fedor had killed his own men for failing the mission. Men who do not get the job done, do not deserve to serve him.

"We will hit the wedding. It will be spectacular. Make sure the little rat does not make his own plans. He will die with them. He belongs with them."

***

Romano answered the insistent knocking on his door. He looked through the peep hole and quickly opened the door as soon as he recognized his midnight visitor.

"What the hell are you doing here?" he demanded as he swung the door open. He looked around behind her to make sure she was alone before he pulled her in.

"Did you come here alone? It isn't safe for you to be out at night by yourself."

"I know...but I didn't want to be alone."

"Bianca, this isn't right."

"I'm an adult, Romano."

"So you think."

"So I know."

"We can't do this," he insisted.

Bianca unbuttoned her coat, revealing a tiny dress.

"Jesus Christ."

"I'm lonely, Romano. I just want to be with someone. Is that too much to ask for?"

"Call your friends. I'm sure you have some boy-toy you can call."

"I don't want to be with boys, Romano. I want to

be with a man."

"We can't do this, Bianca."

"Why? Because your cousin tells you when to eat and breathe? Does he tell you who you can fuck too?" Bianca let her coat drop to the floor and stood there, looking like every man's wet dream.

***

Romano was a light sleeper. The short tone of a text arriving on his phone woke him up. He reached for his phone on the nightstand and realized that he was tangled in long arms and legs. Looking at the warm and soft body next to him reminded him of how phenomenally he'd fucked up. *Ah fuck.* Looking at Bianca's naked body was enough to make him forget about the text. He'd fucked her for hours, taking everything she offered. For someone barely legal, she was experienced, but he knew that already.

Leo might kill him.

But only for being a dumbass. Bianca wanted something from him, or she wouldn't have been all over him all of a sudden. She was a cunning bitch, and Romano had a feeling that all of this was connected. Freya's attack and Bianca's missing mother. This had 'Royal Clusterfuck' written all over it.

His phone beeped again, reminding him why he'd woken up in the first place. He untangled himself and reached for the phone. *Ah, fuck*! Trouble comes in threes. He should have known that. *Fuck*!

Chapter Forty Three

Rain pelted them as the casket was lowered into the freshly dug ground. Leo pulled Freya closer to him to better protect her from the rain with the umbrella he held. Mariana Santos' death was ruled as an accidental overdose which could very well be true since she was a drug addict, but Leo couldn't afford not to think of it as another move in his enemy's game.

Leo worried about Freya's health, both physically and mentally. Her mother's death had been a shock to her, and in her current condition, Leo had warned everyone to keep a close eye on her. Her doctor had warned him about depression during pregnancy and adding that this has been a stressful two months for her – hell, the whole year has been stressful.

He looked around and was happy to see *La*

Famiglia. They were there to show their support and pay their respects, even if they didn't know Freya's mother. It was the bond of the family and mafia. Dante and Castle had traveled from New York and Florida, not only to attend the funeral but to join them for Thanksgiving. Since they had lived with the Costa family for years, it had become a tradition for them to come *home* for the holidays.

His men and extra security made sure that the funeral went off without a hitch. It was a high target for enemies anytime *La Famiglia* gathered together. But the bond of family and friends was stronger than threats. They did not scare easily, and they trusted their people's abilities. His men have proved their worth. Well planned attacks on his family, like the restaurant shooting, Freya's kidnapping, and the recent ambush have all failed because his men did their job, which was to serve and protect *La Famiglia.*

He found Romano near his parents and Bianca. Bianca was leaning on him, her head resting on his shoulder, as they listened to the priest give his blessing. His eyes narrowed on their locked arms. Leo trusted Romano with Freya's life, but he didn't trust Bianca. She was as manipulative and cunning as her father.

***

Freya had expected a small funeral since her

mother hadn't really had friends. She'd decided to have the funeral two days before Thanksgiving because there was no point in waiting. She didn't want to drag it out, and there was no need to have a viewing period when they had no family or friends to attend. Mariana and Freya had not been part of any religious congregation, but Leo and his family were. Valentina and Leo had been her anchor since the news of her mother's death. Valentina had taken over the arrangement for Mariana's funeral, and Leo had handled the work that needed to be done for claiming her mother's body as well as dealing with her possessions.

She, on the other hand, couldn't understand her own emotions. At first, she'd been in shock of the news. It was followed by regret – regret that they did not have a good relationship and that the last time they'd seen each other, they'd had a fight – and guilt, but not for the right reasons. She felt guilty because her mother's death felt like a relief. She had always worried her mother would die from addiction, and when time passed when she and her mother had not talked, Freya would drive herself crazy with guilt from her thoughts of 'What if.' She felt guilty that she felt relieved of those thoughts. She knew that she would drive herself crazy with the guilt she felt, so she'd asked Leo to help her.

Leo had told her that he was there for her for anything she needed and wanted but that he thought that he wasn't the best person to speak to about it because he was biased in his opinion. In an unexpected move, he suggested that she should meet with a psychologist who was better trained and equipped for her needs. She'd thought about it and decided that maybe someone who had no history with Freya and her mother would be better at explaining her jumbled thoughts and emotions to her. She had her first session the day before the funeral, it was awkward but, in some ways, she felt better. She believed that it helped her face this funeral.

Though Valentina had felt that it was a bad omen for her, being pregnant, to see her mother's body, Freya had wanted to see her mother one last time. Leo had arranged for her to have a moment alone at the funeral home so that she could say her goodbyes in private. Her mother actually looked the best Freya had seen her in a long time. She was clean, dressed in a beautiful dress Valentina had chosen, and her makeup reminded Freya of their younger days. It brought back good memories. Though they were few, they were still good. Like the times when her mother was happy and would treat Freya to ice cream, even if it was her last dollar.

Freya quietly talked to her mother about those memories, and then talked about her regrets, before saying a final goodbye and joining the others.

At most, Freya had expected Leo's immediate

family and a few of her friends to be at the cemetery. She was surprised to see so many familiar and unfamiliar faces. Dante, his siblings, and Castle were among the people gathered. She was even more surprised to see Irene and her minions. It was somber, yet it made her feel like a part of them. She might not like some of them, might not agree with many of their activities, have no idea who many were, but they were there to help her honor a woman they had never known.

***

The reception was smaller than their other parties, and Freya hadn't wanted to bring a funeral home, so she agreed to have it at one of the Costa hotels. As usual, Valentina had made sure it was a beautiful event. It was a buffet arrangement so that the guests can come and go as they please. It was also cheerful.

Most of the people had never met or heard about Mariana and her problems, so they talked among themselves about others who have passed, told stories of their own parents, and treated the gathering as a way to connect with each other. Back in Mariana's early days, before the years of addiction, she would have liked this. Mariana would have liked people celebrating life rather than mourning the dead. Freya had spent almost an hour greeting and thanking their guests before finally being able to head to her friends' table.

Lena brought her children, her sixteen-year-old daughter, Dana who Lena had when she was just sixteen, and her four-year-old son, Danny. Freya had known Dana since she was a toddler and was Danny's godmother.

Alice was also there. Now that their wedding has been pushed up, Freya needed to formally ask her friend to be her wedding photographer. A few friends from college were there also. These were her closest friends, and even though a funeral was probably not the best place to talk about weddings, Freya had decided to ask them to be her bridesmaids.

She was so lost in her thoughts that she hadn't realized someone was calling her until she felt someone tap her shoulder from behind. She turned to find Irene, and Freya wondered if the woman was there to ruin the day. If she were, Freya might just grab the wine glass she was holding and throw it at her face.

"Freya, I just wanted to say I am sorry for your loss...and that I am sorry for being a bitch."

The confession surprised her, and she was left speechless for a moment.

"...I know I can be a real brat sometimes. I was just a jealous bitch, but I was wondering if maybe we could start over." She held out her hand to Freya. "Hi, my name is Irene. Nice to meet you."

Chapter Forty Four

Thanksgiving

Thanksgiving was a lively affair. Despite having her mother's funeral just days before, Freya was happy. The family was boisterous, the boys were together again, and it was exactly how Freya imagined a family should be. Recent events and her pregnancy have been making her emotional lately, and she had to swallow a lump in her throat before she started crying.

"What's wrong?" Leo asked her, always in tune to her needs.

"Nothing," Freya answered with a half-smile.

"You look like you're about to cry," he replied worriedly.

"I am," she said with a small laugh.

"What's wrong?"

"I'm just so happy."

Leo looked even more worried by her answer.

"It's alright, son," Giovanni came and put an arm around Freya's shoulder as he joined them. "Your mother cried about everything when she was pregnant with Luciano. Hell, she'd talk about what she was making for dinner and she'd cry."

"Talking about me again, dear?" Came Valentina's voice, before she joined the group.

"Never, dear."

"We should be talking about the wedding," Valentina insisted. Freya had chosen the weekend before her birthday to have her wedding, which would put her at almost five months. "We still need to pick a venue, and no, you cannot have your wedding reception at Mozzafiato."

"Why not?" both Freya and Giovanni said together. They looked at each other and shared a smile. It was Freya's favorite hotel...and Giovanni...well, he owned the hotel.

"We cannot have every party at the Mozzafiato."

"At least we have your flowers and colors picked out. Come, dear, we need to talk about your bridesmaid's dresses and food. We have to make sure there will be no artichokes..." Valentina led Freya away from them.

Freya looked like she'd rather be anywhere else, but Leo knew his mother wasn't one to be denied. He gave her hand a squeeze before she was pulled away from him.

"She'll be alright, son," his father told him.

"I know, I just worry."

"You always worry about everything. Let's worry in my office. The boys will join us soon." *They had to talk about enemies.*

"I will be there soon. I need to speak to Romano for a moment." He excused himself from his father and went to look for Romano. He was with the women, which wasn't unusual, but it was one particular woman that was the reason for this *talk*. He wasn't blind, he knew there was something going on between Romano and Bianca. If it was just them being intimate, he wouldn't have a problem with it, but he trusted Romano with Freya's life, he was the head of her security, and Bianca was a snake.

Romano saw him right away. He excused himself from the women and went to join Leo on the balcony. "Leo?" Romano asked hesitantly.

Leo didn't think there was a need to play word games and got straight to the point. "I need to know that you are prepared to do your job."

"You know I am."

"Bianca?"

"She's just a lay."

"You are family to me Romano, but I need to know that you'll be able to do this job. I need to know if this thing with Bianca will affect how you do your job because I am trusting you with Freya's life and the life of my child. They are my world."

"You know I am always loyal to *La Famiglia*. There is never a doubt about it." Leo could hear the anger in Romano's tone, and Leo understood. No one likes to be questioned, especially in *La Famiglia*.

"Good...Then it's time to go on the offensive and take our enemies out."

The two men shared a look before they made their way to Giovanni's office, where the others were waiting.

"I know you won't say who, but I would like to ask again who your contact is within the Bratva," Giovanni said to Castle.

"Giving his identity will do you no good. It will also create unnecessary danger to us and my contact," Castle patiently explained.

"You are telling me that danger is coming, but you won't tell me who is saying this," Giovanni insisted.

"Does it matter who it is? We know that they plan to hit the wedding. The hit on Freya was through her mother, and I can almost guarantee that her death was not an accident. Fedor has plans for your wedding, and it is bound to be bloody."

A red fucking wedding. It was a term used to describe a bloodbath during a wedding. It has happened in the past, at Leo's parents' wedding. Weddings have been known to be targets for planned attacks due to the large, important crowd. In those events, there was usually someone who betrays *La Famiglia*. He looked at the men around him. Each one of them were Made Men of *La Famiglia*. None of them would betray *La Famiglia*. He believed that down to his soul.

Chapter Forty Five

Christmas Eve

Giovanni and Valentina held a Christmas Eve party in their home. As prominent members of society, they often held balls and parties for the community. They had their annual Christmas Eve Lunch where they gave away presents to the less fortunate children of the community and hosted a lunch party to help celebrate the holiday. For some, it may be the only celebration they are able to have. Freya had fallen in love with the tradition and had helped Valentina put the event together. In between planning her wedding, adjusting to being pregnant, and helping Valentina plan community events, Freya was even more busy than when she worked.

As she became more involved with the Costa

family commitments, Freya realized that they were not just wealthy people who partied – or the other things that *La Famiglia* did that Freya preferred to not know about – the Costa family was involved in several charities throughout the Bay Area.

While the men handled businesses, the women in *La Famiglia* did a lot of work with the community, and it had helped Freya bond with them better. Even Irene and her friends had a changed of heart towards her. Irene had meant it when she said she wanted to start over. Freya would even say they were friends now, which was definitely far from their first meeting.

After the lunch event, Freya and Valentina headed back to Valentina's house to prepare for the Christmas Eve party that they were hosting Everyone seemed busier than ever. Freya had barely spent time with Leo that morning before he was off to work. She looked forward to the party because Freya...well, she didn't have anyone to celebrate the holidays with. In the past, she'd often spend the holidays with Alice and Claudia. Now that she had the Costa family, she wanted to make sure that Alice knew that they would always be family.

Freya knocked on Valentina's bedroom. Giovanni was out with Leo and Freya ended up getting ready at her in-laws' after prepping for the party. She needed help with the back of her dress.

"Come in," she heard Valentina call out.

Freya entered the room and found Valentina looking graceful as always in a formal gown.

"Hello, dear."

"Hi, could you help me with my dress?" She stepped forward and then turned to show Valentina the problem.

"This dress is perfect for you. Has Leo seen you in it?"

"Nope."

"Good, he'll be knocked to his ass when he sees you in it."

"You think?"

"Definitely." Valentina quickly zipped her dress, and then turned her, helping her arrange the dress and being the doting mother Freya never had.

"I have something to show you. Come," Valentina took her hand and led her deeper into their room. She led her into her walk-in closet, which was almost the size of Freya's old apartment. Valentina entered a code on a panel, and the shelves that held a line of designer purses and handbags slowly opened, revealing a safe.

"That's brilliant."

"I imagine Leo has something similar installed in your new home." Leo and Freya had moved into their new home after Thanksgiving. In fact, Leo and her were hosting Christmas dinner tomorrow night in their new home.

"Yes, in his closet." She watched Valentina open the vault and look through some things, before pulling out a heavy, old box. Freya moved next to her and was surprised to see a beautiful and delicate looking tiara.

"Wow," was all she could say. Valentina carefully lifted the tiara out of the box and placed it on Freya's head. They both turned to face the mirror behind them. "Wow...where...?"

"It is a family heirloom from my side. It has been worn by the women in my family for several generations on their wedding day. It was passed down to me by my father after my mother's death. If you would like to wear it on your wedding day, you can. It will eventually be passed down to Leo."

"Really?" Freya asked as she admired the tiara in the mirror. "I'd be honored to wear it."

"It can be your something borrowed," Valentina

suggested.

"Thank you." Freya turned to Valentina and carefully took the tiara off to give back to her. As soon as the tiara was back in its case, Freya gave her future mother-in-law a fierce hug. "Thank you, not just for the crown, but for making me feel welcomed from the very beginning. Thank you for making me feel like I belong."

"Oh dear, you do. I've known from the very beginning that you were the one for Leo. There was a look in his eyes when he looked at you that told me everything I needed to know...and you, you've made him happy. Even with everything that has happened, I can see that my son is the happiest he has ever been and it's because of you."

***

The Christmas Eve party was in full swing, and everyone was having a great time. She was worried that Alice and Claudia would feel uncomfortable since they were the only ones who were not part of *La Famiglia*, but she was happy to see that they seemed to be getting along fine. She'd have to remember to thank Vito and the guys for helping make them feel welcomed. Seeing that her friends were fine, Freya decided to head to the kitchen to see if Valentina needed her help. A hand grabbed her and pulled her into the dark hallway as she passed by, pulling a soft cry of surprise from her. She quickly recognized Leo as soon as she was in his arms.

"Leo!" she half-heartedly hit him for scaring her.

"I was about to resolve to throwing you over my shoulder and kidnapping you just to have a minute with you," Leo half-joked.

"I guess I've been pretty busy today," she conceded.

"Just today?" He half laughed. She'd been so busy helping his mother with her community projects and wedding planning that by the time Freya made it home, she was exhausted. Leo had worried that she was pushing herself, especially in her condition, but he knew his mother wouldn't allow that to happen. He trusted his mother to make sure Freya wouldn't exert herself. He felt that it was better for her to keep busy, it kept her from thinking about her mother. He also thought that seeing a counselor had really helped Freya settle into the family and her new situation better. Things have been happy between them.

"Okay, lately. I didn't know there were so many things involved with wedding planning, Leo. I thought you just had to pick a place, dresses, food, and that's it."

"That's why you have a wedding planner. That's all you need to do; their job is to get it done."

"It's not that simple."

"I'd marry you at City Hall if that was what you wanted."

"And face your mother's wrath?" she said with a small laugh, and the sound was something he could listen to for the rest of his life.

"We could move to another city, where she won't find us."

"She'd send your father to look for us."

"True...I guess we'll just have to have a real wedding then."

"We better, I've been working hard on it."

"I'm hard for you," he couldn't help but reply, making her laugh. To prove his point, he pulled her close to his body, letting her feel the starting bulge in his pants.

"We're having a party, Leo!"

"They'll be fine without us for a while," he gave her such a devilish grin that Freya almost melted on the spot. Leo took her hand and pulled her, leading her down the hallway, away from the party.

"Where are we going?"

"Somewhere no one will interrupt us."

"Luciano's room?"

"Yes, he'll be the last one to go to sleep if he even does, and no one would think to look for us here." He pulled her into the room and promptly closed and locked the door.

"You're serious."

"Dead serious," he answered as he started unbuttoning his shirt. "Get naked, babe. There's a party, remember? We're on limited time."

"I can't get the dress off. You need to unzip it."

"With pleasure," he answered as he threw his shirt off. She turned her back to him and felt him working on her zipper. "Be careful."

"I'll buy you another one."

"No, everyone will notice if I change dresses."

"Yes, this is a beautiful dress...but all I could think about since seeing you in it is getting you out of it." He let the dress drop to the floor. She stood in her lace thong, and nothing else since the dress wasn't meant to be worn with a bra.

"I've been thinking about how I'd slide my hand

between those beautiful thighs." His arm went around her, tugging her body against his, as his hand brushed the top of her underwear. "Thought about how I'd slide my fingers into this skimpy little underwear to see just how wet you were." His hands did exactly what he said. "While my other hand played with the most magnificent tits I've ever seen." His other hand cupped her breast, rolling her nipple between his fingers. Her head fell back against his shoulder. "Can't wait to fucking feel you wrapped around me."

His fingers worked her body until she felt her legs shaking.

"Leo," she could barely say his name.

"Fuck, I need you." Leo turned her around and kissed her hard. His tongue delved into her mouth without hesitation, brushing against her teeth and engaging with her tongue. She could feel him working on his pants, felt them drop to the ground, as he kissed his way down her neck, and then chest. He took a nipple into his mouth, and she cried out as he sucked.

His lips were hot, and his mouth on her breast sent fire through her body. He owned her. He positioned her on the bed, with him on top. He entered her in one long stroke. Her muscles spasmed around his cock, gripping him tight. She felt like she was burning from the inside out. Her legs went around his waist, wanting him locked inside her forever. He withdrew and then surged forward and kept going. Her breast swayed with every thrust, sending liquid fire through her veins. Her orgasm was swift, and his quickly followed; both of them moaned with their release. He emptied himself in her, before collapsing on top of her, pinning her to the bed. Her arms and legs were still wrapped around him, as they both fought for normalcy.

He was the first to recover, his lips brushed over her forehead, her eyelids, the tip of her nose and then her mouth. The kiss was gentle and perfect. They laid wrapped in each other's arms, his cock still in her, coming down from their high.

"I love you," Leo whispered as he slowly lifted up.

"I love you," she replied and meant it with every part of her being.

Chapter Forty Six

January

The new year brought the cold and wet air into the city. It was less than two weeks to her wedding, and she was doing her final dress fitting. She hadn't wanted something fancy, she wanted something comfortable. Finding the perfect dress had been the easiest part of planning her wedding. The stylist Valentina had insisted on had found the perfect dress almost right away. Freya had fallen in love with it at first sight. They'd kept her pregnancy in mind, and she was glad they did since her normal clothes were beginning to get tighter. She'd noticed that her stomach had started to take a rounder form though it wasn't noticeable, she just looked like she had a large lunch on most days.

"I brought something for you," Valentina told

her as they surveyed her reflection on the mirror. She turned and took something from her bag. Freya watched her lift a jewelry box. She opened the box revealing a ruby necklace with matching earrings. It was beautiful.

"It is a Costa family heirloom. Giovanni had wanted to give it to you, but can you believe the man actually got shy and asked me to do it?" Valentina explained. The thought of her father-in-law being shy was unthinkable. The man was a force to be reckoned with and imagining a man like him being shy was unheard of.

Freya realized it matched her wedding colors perfectly. The dark red would be perfect with her wedding dress.

"Why don't we put it on," Valentina said reading her mind. She held her hair up as Valentina clasped the necklace around her neck. "Perfect."

"It is," Freya replied in awe.

"It's been in the Costa family for nearly two hundred years."

"Oh my...really? He wants me to have this?"

"Yes. I suppose it could be your 'Something old'?"

***

Bianca made sure Romano was in a deep sleep before she slowly slid out of his bed. She admired his drool-worthy body. It was too bad he'll probably die when the time came. She'd made sure to listen to everything being said about the wedding. She knew the venue, had even gone with Valentina and Freya to see it. She'd told her father everything she'd found out about the wedding – down to who was catering – and offered to help with the invitations so she could see who would be there.

Payback was going to be a real mother fucker. The Costa family deserved to be eliminated. They've ruled over *La Famiglia* for too long. She quietly slipped into his office. She was a little sad about Romano being a casualty of the war since she actually liked him. He was one of the few men she could tolerate. He listened well, and he was neat. He wasn't a slob like most men she knew. *And he fucked really well.* He's the best fuck she's ever had. It didn't hurt that he looked gorgeous naked and had real muscles. Yes, she was definitely going to miss him. But he had a purpose.

She looked around his office and saw some rolled up papers on his desk. She'd seen him leaving their meetings with it, and when she casually asked what those super-secret meetings were, he'd told her they were wedding planning. She opened one roll and realized it was some sort of floor plan of a building. She couldn't really understand it, but she took a picture of it with her phone. She did the same with all of the others she found. She tried to get as many as she could without staying too long in case he woke. She quickly sent the photos to her father before deleting them from the phone. She loved doing spy work for her father, especially when it was all part of a revenge plan.

Sneaking around excited her, and she needed a drink to calm down. She supposed she could fuck it out with Romano. She headed to the kitchen and opened his fridge. Neat and clean, like the rest of his house. She pulled a water bottle from the door and closed the door only to drop the bottle and let out a yelp. Romano stood next to the refrigerator, watching her. She hadn't even heard him, and for a moment it scared her. *What if he'd seen her in his office?*

"Romano! You scared me!" she hit him on his bare chest. "What are you doing sneaking around like that?"

"I wasn't sneaking, just moving quietly. Woke up and didn't see you. Wondered where you were," he answered casually, making her believe he suspected nothing. She watched him make his way toward the cabinets where he pulled out a glass. He turned to the fridge, opened it, and took a pitcher of water out. Filling the glass with water, he put the pitcher back in the fridge before drinking. She watched his muscles as he did such a simple task. He was a walking wet dream in his sweats, riding low on his hips.

"You miss me, did you?" she asked seductively as she walked toward him. She placed her water bottle on the counter next to him, before wrapping her arms around his waist from behind. She licked the hot skin of his back knowing he liked it, while her hands went down to the waist of his pants. She slipped her hand in his sweats and stroked his hardening cock, gently raking it with her nails, knowing he liked it.

Rather than answer, he turned around to face her, removing her hands from his pants. He switched their positions, leaned her against the counter as he slipped his hand under his shirt, which she'd put on. She wore nothing under it. She moaned as his fingers worked their magic, quickly making her legs shake, and had her ready to cum in seconds. *God, he was so fucking good at it.* He pulled his fingers out of her and quickly disrobed her, all while keeping her leaning forward onto the counter. She heard a foil rip, where the condom came from, she had no idea and waited in anticipation for his cock. The wait was seconds but felt longer before she felt him entering her from behind.

She met his thrusts, loving the feel of him sliding in and out of her. His fingers flicked her clit and sent her over the edge in minutes, but he didn't stop.

He kept fucking her through her orgasm, until another orgasm ripped from her, leaving her crying with her release, legs shaking, and barely able to hold her up. He held her body, fucked her harder until his own release. Fuck, she was going to miss the best sex she'd ever had once he's gone.

Chapter Forty Seven

"They have the most recent floor plans, but these old wineries have been around long enough to go through several renovations. Sixty years ago, there was a tunnel, but it was closed off because of a mudslide. I sent some men to check it out, and the mud's been cleared out, but the old doorway is there and boarded up tight. We can chip away at it, test it out, and hide it well. We need to find out when they'll be doing security checks leading up to the day," Makar explained to the group of men who will be carrying out the attack.

Fedor tuned out Makar as he talked about the plans. The tunnel will bring them in without being seen, and Bartolo's daughter could get them through, or at the very least, cause distraction for when the time came. It won't be long before Bartolo will be killed, in fact, Fedor will probably have him be killed before going into the tunnel so the mother fucker didn't fuck shit up.

"This is a massacre, Fedor," Dimitri, his ever so pacifist brother said with disapproval.

"You do not belong in this kind of life brother. You should find a new purpose." Fedor has always found Dimitri to be weak.

"No, I just don't believe in senseless loss of lives, for an old war of pride."

"They killed our parents."

"We killed theirs. This attack does no good," Dimitri insisted.

"It is well deserved." Fedor was not going to change his mind. Eliminating them will not only give him control of the territory, it willgive him a step up on Czar. Czar was too much of a coward to take on the Italians, but Fedor will get rid of them.

***

Leo watched Romano enter quietly. They were in the middle of planning the final details for their protection strategy. He shared a look with his cousin, they knew they had to talk.

"Let me do it," Castle announced.

"This is my fight," Leo answered. Though they had an idea of what the plan was and could plan as best as they can against it, there were uncertainties, and he wasn't going to send his men—his people—without him leading the charge. A leader who stood back while his people went into battle wasn't a leader in his eyes.

"This is our fight. *La Famiglia* means you go against one, you go against all," Castle replied.

"I agree with Castle," Dante added.

"I will not send you all to do something I wouldn't."

"We all know you would do it, whether it was for Dante, Angelo, or Caterina, we know you would. There is no doubt about that. But this is your wedding. Your wedding should be a day of celebration. You have a wife that needs you and a child on the way," Castle explained passionately. "I owe your family mine and Angelo's life. We wouldn't be here if it wasn't for the Costa family-"

"You never have to thank us for that. We are family, period," Leo cut him off.

"This isn't just your war. This is a *La Famiglia* war. I want to do this. I need to." Leo knew that Castle wouldn't budge. It was hard for Leo to give this responsibility to another. This was his fight. He had confidence in his men, his family, but a part of him wanted to be with Freya and his child.

"I want to end this. I want the threat to my family...our family to end. I want you to burn them to the ground. End them all."

Chapter Forty Eight

January 11

"Something new and something blue," Lena said as she helped Freya into the royal blue heels. Stefanie handed her the bouquet which was a mix of crème roses, hydrangeas, and delphiniums in varying shades of blue. The shoes and her bouquet were part of her church ceremony colors. She couldn't decide on blue and red, so Valentina came up with the idea of having two themes. The church ceremony and decoration consisted of white, and different shades of blue colors, while the reception consisted of cream and dark red decorations.

"And something borrowed and old," Valentina added as she placed the tiara on Freya's head and arranged her veil. "Perfect."

"You're going to knock that man off his feet," Alice said and promptly snapped a photo. Alice had brought another photographer she'd worked with in the past to help her capture the day from both sides. Though most of the event will be captured by Alice, the second photographer will handle candid photos and video of the wedding, while Alice did the formal photos.

Freya stared at her reflection and caught her breath. Her hair had been arranged in a loose updo, and her make-up kept natural. But her dress, the tiara, and the overall image she saw made her look and feel like a princess.

***

Leo wasn't nervous, not about this. He'd felt like he'd been waiting for this moment his whole life. He stood behind the closed church doors, waiting for the time for him to take his place at the altar. He stood there with the men he'd grown up with, and the men who have helped and will help him in his journey to a new life, as a married man, a father, and the Don. These were the men who will stand by his side for life–made men.

He motioned for Luciano, his best man, and Vito and Dante, his groomsmen, to take their place. Romano stayed behind with Castle and stood guard.

Leo turned to Castle. "Thank you."

"There is nothing to thank me for. Go get married. You're family...our family will be safe."

"End it."

"I will," Castle promised. They gave each other hard pats on the shoulder before Leo turned to enter the church. He took his place next to Luciano. Both sides of the church were filled with *La Famiglia* and Freya's friends. His side outnumbered Freya's side, so they had spread out to fill the church.

The soft song played as the wedding procession began. Vito was paired with Stefanie, followed by Dante who was paired with Nicole. Then came Lena, Freya's maid of honor, followed by Lena's son, who was the ring bearer, and the flower girl, Leo's cousin. There was a pause, and then the wedding march song began. He watched the entryway; the bright light of the sun outside created a silhouette of Freya. Then the outside doors closed and all he could see was Freya.

They'd spent the night apart, her at his parents' home, and him in their home. It was a long night of staring at the ceiling, counting down the minutes to when he'd finally be with her. He'd thought about their unusual meeting and how it all led to this moment.

Though she had her veil down, he knew that she

was watching him as she made her slow walk down the aisle. He had to stop himself from meeting her halfway. He held his hand out, and the moment she placed hers in his, there was no doubt in his mind—there was no turning back. She was the air he breathes.

***

Freya lived her life full of indecision and turmoil. She struggled to figure out who she was, and then struggled to be Leo's woman. But here at the altar, holding Leo's hand, she had never been more sure of anything in her life. This was what she wanted – what was meant to be from the moment they met.

She'd known he would change her life when their eyes had met when she'd found him dying on the mountain, and when she woke up the morning after he'd rescued her, she knew that there was no possible way her life would ever be the same. She tried fighting it, tried resisting the inevitable, but it was useless. Leo was part of her body and soul.

"I, Freya Santos, take you, Leonardo Costa, for my lawful husband. To have and to hold from this day forward. For better, for worse, for richer, for poorer, in sickness and health, until death do us part."

***

Makar knew he could very well be on a suicide mission, but at least bringing down the great Italian families was something worth talking about. His own father had been killed in the war that took place years ago, it was about time he avenged him. Getting to the tunnel went down without a hitch, just as planned. He hadn't expected trouble, not there. The real test of fate was when they get through the tunnel, which led to an old wine cellar. He sent a final confirmation text to Fedor. The four men with him knew the real plan, one that was slightly different than the one Bartolo was expecting.

"Bartolo," Makar said quietly as they reached the tunnel door. The rat turned to face him. "Fedor, sends his regards," Makar relayed the message as he held the Glock with the attached suppressor to his face. Bartolo's eyes bulged, and Makar pulled the trigger before he could say anything. One of his men caught Bartolo's body before it hit the ground to keep it from making a sound. They dragged his body into the tunnel before closing the door and made their way through the dark to the cellar.

The cellar door was partially stuck, but a little force opened it enough for them to fit through. There was no time for small celebrations; they needed to get moving. It was dark and unusually quiet, too quiet. The cellar was close to where the reception was being held. *There should be sound from the celebration,* not complete silence. It raised the hair on his whole body. *Something was wrong.*

Then Makar felt it – the barrel of a gun to the back of his head.

***

Bianca checked her phone again. She didn't know when the hit would happen exactly, she just knew she needed to stay out of the reception room. She'd decided that the safest place for her would be outside, so she lit a cigarette and smoked as she waited for the fireworks to happen. She hadn't heard from her father since this morning, but she expected that.

"Bianca," she heard Romano call her.

She turned to face him. *Such a handsome man.* "What are you doing out here?" she asked as she blew smoke.

"Looking for you."

"Oh, are you?" she flirted. "Now that you've found me?"

"I'd like to take you somewhere," he replied with that dimpled smile she'd started to fall for.

"Where?" she asked as she put out her cigarette.

"Somewhere dark, so I can show you how I really feel." He held out his hand.

Maybe if he lives tonight, they can be together.

He took her through the hallway leading to the reception hall, and toward the kitchen. They passed the catering staff and headed further down an isolated hallway.

"Where are we going?" she asked, beginning to feel nervous now that they were alone in an unfamiliar place.

"Almost there." She started to pull away, unsure, but his grip on her hand tightened.

"Romano, tell me where we are going." She tried to pull away. Instead, he grabbed her arm and pulled her closer, dragging her.

"Did you really think that a silly, spoiled, eighteen-year-old was going to take down the Costa family?" he asked the question with menace.

"Let me go. I don't know what you're talking about."

"You do. You could at least own up to it."

"I don't know what you're talking about. You're

crazy." She tried fruitlessly to get away from him, but he held on tight and dragged her until they were walking down toward an old door. He opened the door, and she was greeted by men with guns. Beyond them, she found four men on their knees. She recognized the men with guns as *La Famiglia* soldiers. She didn't recognize the men kneeling, but she had a pretty good idea who they were. *Russians.*

"Miss Lombardi, glad you could make it," Castle Moretti greeted her as though it was a social gathering.

Romano shoved her toward the kneeling men.

She'd realized that the plan had failed. "Romano, I have nothing to do with this," she begged her lover.

He looked at her with cold, hard eyes. "Just like your father. A traitor," Romano said with despise. He spit on the ground in her direction, before turning around to leave.

"Romano, please!" She tried to reach for him, but one of Castle's men stopped her and shoved her back toward the kneeling men. He didn't want to drag it out. The room had been prepared to keep the noise down, fitted with soundproof padding to minimize any sound from escaping. Romano left the old cellar without looking back.

Bianca stood, dressed in an expensive gown, and enough jewelry to feed a third world country for a week. The woman knew she'd lost but Castle admired the look of defiance in her face. She wasn't simpering like her father would have. Had she been a man and not a traitor like her father, she would have made *La Famiglia* proud.

"This one is mine," Castle pulled his own gun, walked closer to Bianca. He looked her dead in the eyes, the same way she was looking at him. When his time came, he'd meet his end the same way she was. Tall and proud. He pulled the trigger without hesitation, leaving a neat hole on her forehead. Her body fell to the ground in a thud, the sound muffled by the dirt covered ground. Even when she was dead, she looked beautiful. Her eyes stayed open, lifeless and staring straight ahead. It left a bitter taste in his mouth to kill a woman, especially one so young, but she deserved it. Any enemy of *La Famiglia* must be eliminated.

"Light 'em up," Castle ordered. His men pointed their weapons at the Russians and fired kill shots at the four men.

For Leo, this was the end. For Castle, this was the beginning of his revenge on the men responsible for killing his family.

***

Leo cradled his wife in his arms as they had their first dance. Freya hadn't told him what song she'd chosen, just that it was the perfect song, chosen just for him. He recognized the song as soon as it started playing. It was a 90's song, he couldn't tell you who the singer was, but he knew the title, *I Love You, Always, Forever.*

"I love you, always, forever," he whispered to her as he held her close.

Something made him look up, an instinct. His eyes immediately found Castle, quietly entering the room. His friend gave him a subtle nod, and Leo felt an instant relief go through him. Freya felt it too, the relaxing of his body, releasing the tension he hadn't realized he held.

"What's wrong?" Freya asked, looking up at him.

One day, he'll tell her. But not now, not for a very long time.

"Nothing, everything is perfect. Just perfect." He leaned down and kissed her. He pulled her tighter against him, feeling her stomach against his. His whole world was in his arms.

Chapter Forty Nine

There was no need to hide his arrival. Fedor would have known it failed. No one but the parties involved would know. His wedding went off without a hitch, and as much as he'd like to have stayed home with his wife the following morning, this had to be dealt with. Castle and his men protected his wedding. Now, he was here to end it. The mansion was set on the outskirts of Sacramento, away from would be witnesses.

Romano, positioned on a tree with a rifle, took out the guards at the gate. His men opened the gate, while Romano continued to clear any remaining guards in the yard. Bodies fell as the posse of cars drove in. Vito led the way, using a Glock to open the front door. There was no hesitation in his men's step. They walked in, killed everyone in their path. One by one, bodies dropped, the only sound being made was the sound of bodies hitting the ground. Leo knew where he was going. Castle's man was there with Fedor. Drago didn't bother knocking on the door, he simply shoved the door open, startling two of the three men in the room. Drago quickly killed the man closest to the door – the only one who attempted to draw his gun.

Fedor half raised from his seat, but Castle pointed a gun at him with a simple order of "Down."

"Mr. Costa, what is the meaning of this?" Fedor tried to act cool. "How did you get in?"

"Your men are inept, Fedor. We simply walked in," Castle explained as he casually sat in the chair in front of Fedor's desk. To add to the insult, he lifted his feet onto the desk.

The third man was younger than Fedor, but the resemblance was clear. He casually leaned against the wall, his arms crossed, confidence radiating off him, no hint of fear showing on his body. Dimitri, the youngest Ivanov.

"It's good to see you again, Dimitri," Castle casually greeted.

"You as well," he replied.

Ah, Castle's source.

"Dimitri, you betray your own family?!" Fedor raged.

"I warned you that it would be a massacre," Dimitri answered, sounding bored.

"Your own flesh and blood?"

"I told you, Fedor, I don't believe in senseless killing. People like you need to go."

"You will get nothing from this."

"I want nothing of yours, Fedor. Never have. May God have mercy on your soul." Dimitri turned to Leo, gave a slight nod, and exited.

"Well then, who will end this?" Fedor demanded.

Leo pulled his own gun, something he rarely does. He didn't bother with a suppressor; he simply pointed the gun at the bastard and pulled the trigger, emptying the magazine. Fedor's body slammed back against the shelves behind him. He handed his gun to Vito, before turning to leave. There was no need to talk about it. There was simply an ending.

He made his way out of the house, and into the now cleared yard. His men had already cleaned the mess and were now dousing the mansion with gasoline.

He headed straight to his car, where Drago waited. He rolled the window down and tossed his lighter to Castle.

"Burn it down," he ordered.

Epilogue

Alessandro Marius Costa made his displeasure known when his mother moved a little slower in getting him his lunch.

"It's all right...shhh...it's coming," Freya told her hungry three-month-old son. She sat on the extra plush chair next to the crib, lifted the inside slip of her nursing dress and positioned her son towards her nipple. He quickly latched on, making sounds that made her laugh. It reminded her of when Leo would growl when she didn't quiet follow his rules. *Like father, like son.* Both bossy and she absolutely loved them both with everything in her.

Though Giovanni and Valentina had wanted to have Alessandro baptized as soon as possible, Freya had held off because she wanted Alice to be there as

Alessandro's godmother. Alice was due any day now and Freya decided that it would be better to wait, and they can both baptize their babies together, since they were each other's godmothers.

Freya's son's coo brought her thoughts back to him. Even this young he already showed hints of Leo's looks. He's going to be just as handsome, bossy, and perfect as his father. She glanced at the clock on the wall. Leo won't be home for a couple of hours—plenty of time for her to get ready for their date. It would be their first date, just the two of them, since Alessandro's birth. She was already worrying about being away from him, but at the same time, she was looking forward to having some alone time with her husband.

***

Leo stepped into the nursery where he knew he'd find Freya and Alessandro. His wife had wanted to be hands-on with their son and only wanted help from a nighttime nurse. He found her resting in the rocking chair with their son on her chest. He couldn't believe such a tiny being put Freya through thirteen hours of labor. Leo had stayed with her through the whole ordeal, and it was the first time in his life he'd felt helpless. It was the one thing that he wasn't able to help Freya with.

Freya was exhausted most days, but he knew she

was happy, and he could not feel anymore blessed. He watched them for a moment. He'll eventually wake her, since he had planned a date night for them, but he wanted to continue admiring the sight in front of him. They were his life. He'd set the whole world on fire if he needed to in order to keep them safe.

Translations and Definitions

Tenemos quematara esehijo de puta ya – Spanish: basically says "Let's kill the mother fucker now."

Pendejo – Spanish: Motherfucker (noun)

Cabron – Spanish: Asshole

Mozzafiato – Italian: Breathtaking

Figurati – Italian: Imagine

Sì – Italian: Yes

Grazie – Italian: Thank you

Stronzo Una Merda – Italian: Basically, a really bad insult to someone you hate

Che cosabella – Italian: What a beauty.

Ella é molto bella Leo. Avete scelto bene – Italian: She is very beautiful Leo. You picked a good one.

Circondata da puttanefinte – Italian: Surrounded by whores.

La Famiglia – Italian: The Family

The City: San Francisco as referred by locals.

Bay Area: The surrounding area of the (San Francisco) bay as referred by locals.

Capo: Caporegime or Capodecina, a rank in the Italian mafia, under underboss, above soldiers.

Triad: A branch of Chinese transnational organized crime syndicates.

Sophia Peony

Writing about dangerous women, antiheroes, the biggest stars, and a little magic.

In 6th grade I wanted to be a singer. In high school I wanted to be a lawyer, an astronaut and then a housewife when I thought I was going to marry my high school sweetheart. Then I wanted to be a pilot but found out I was too short to fly. So, I decided to become a photographer. When that didn't work out, I decided to be a writer.

Made in the USA
Monee, IL
26 October 2022

16609857R00252